THIS BOOK BELONGS TO

The Good Muslim

ALSO BY TAHMIMA ANAM

A Golden Age

The Good Muslim

A NOVEL

Tahmima Anam

HARPER

An Imprint of HarperCollins*Publishers*
www.harpercollins.com

First published in Great Britain in 2011 by Canongate Books Ltd.

FIRST U.S. EDITION

Library of Congress Cataloging-in-Publication Data

Anam, Tahmima
  The good Muslim / Tahmima Anam.
    p. cm.
  Summary: "From prizewinning Bangladeshi novelist Tahmima Anam, her deeply moving second novel about the rise of Islamic radicalism in Bangladesh, seen through the intimate lens of a family"— Provided by publisher.
  ISBN 978-0-06-147876-5 (hardback)
  1. Muslims—Bangladesh—Fiction. 2. Islamic fundamentalism—Bangladesh—Fiction. 3. Bangladesh—Fiction. 4. Domestic fiction. I. Title.
  PR6101.N32G67 2011
  823'.92—dc22

                                                        2010051646

11 12 13 14 15   OFF/RRD   10 9 8 7 6 5 4 3 2 1

for Roland Lamb

Prologue

1971

December

Eight days after the end of the war, Sohail Haque stands in a field of dying mustard. The petals of the mustard flower, dried to dust, tickle his nose and remind him of the scent of meat, which he has not tasted in several months. Underfoot, the grasses spit and cry; overhead, the heavy-lidded eye of a midwinter sun. He has been walking for days, following the grey ribbon of road that leads south, towards the city. In one abandoned village after another, he has eaten banana leaves and drunk from ponds, kissing their surfaces, filtering moss through his teeth. On the third day, a farmer told him that the war was over.

Now, on his way home, he turns the name of the country around on his tongue. *Bangladesh.*

In the distance, he sees a smudge against the flat.

A barracks. He circles the perimeter, his hand tight and

moist around the handle of his rifle. No sound, no movement. He draws closer, walking low, his body at ease with the postures of soldiering, haunches ready to spring, eyes darting to the edges of the vista, the finger hooked, ready. But this building is abandoned.

The retreating army has left its traces. He smells tobacco on the furniture; he sees their uniforms hanging on the washing line. He finds their plates, stacked neatly in a corner, their shoes, pointing away from Mecca. He sees their prayer mats. He smells them, soap and chalk and shoe polish.

On the bathroom wall someone has written 'Punjab Meri Ma' – *Punjab, my mother*. How these soldiers must have hated Bengal, he thinks, hated the way their feet sank into the mud, the way the air closed around them like the hand of a criminal, the mosquitoes, the ceaseless pelt of rain, the food that left them weak, shitting, dehydrated.

Now Sohail wonders if he should have reserved a little pity for these men. He feels the tug of an earlier self, a still-soft self: geographer, not guerrilla. In this mood of clemency he decides to lie down on one of the bunks with a half-smoked cigarette. It is the softer self who leads him to explore the room behind the munitions store, who slides open the heavy metal door, who palms the wall, searching for a light switch – who is met with a sight that will continue to suck the breath out of him for a lifetime to come.

Book One

All that is in the Heavens and on Earth

1984

February

It would not have been possible to go home if Silvi hadn't died. Maya's thoughts rested for a moment on this fact as she settled herself on the wooden bench in the third-class carriage, balancing on her lap the sum of all her worldly possessions: a small rucksack containing two saris, a kameez, a pair of trainers, a doctor's case with a stetho and, for her mother, a young mango tree. The tree had been difficult to wrap; it was heavier than it looked and bulged awkwardly where the roots were packed in soil. 'Tree won't live,' the farmer who sold it to her said. 'Rajshahi tree, it belongs in Rajshahi.'

An old lady with a tiffin carrier slid into the space beside her. She stared for a moment at Maya, then clamped the tiffin carrier between her knees, pulled out a string of prayer beads and began to mutter the Kalma under her breath.

La Ilaha Illallah, Muhammad ur Rasul Allah.

Of course it would survive. There was an empty patch at the western edge of the garden, and if anyone could coax mangoes out of that tree it would be Ammoo. But seven long years had passed – she couldn't even be sure the patch was still empty.

A group of young men entered the compartment. Immediately they began to laugh and smoke, passing around a box of matches and a packet of Star cigarettes. Maya resisted the urge to scold them and instead pressed her face to the horizontal bars on the open window, gazing at the litter-strewn tracks, the station platform where boys were selling peanuts and cold drinks, and beyond to the scattered patches of green where the groves of mango stood. She would miss it. The two-room house she had rented now stood empty, its rough concrete floor swept and washed. And the verandah where she had seen her patients, that too had been cleared, the examination table, the small stand on which she kept her equipment, the wooden chair on which she draped her white jacket at the end of the day, ballpoint clicked shut in its pocket.

It had started with a few handfuls of mud. She told herself the wind must have tossed a coconut or a piece of wood against the walls of her house. For three days she ignored the sound.

On the fourth night, the laugh. Unmistakable, escaping between the fingers of someone holding a palm over his mouth. A young man's laugh, nervous and girlish.

She ran outside and peered into the darkness, but she couldn't see anything. There is nothing darker than a moonless night in Rajshahi.

It had ended, months later, with the glint of a knife. She remembered it now: a gentle motion like the lick of a cat, the bright line of it; and the flash of white that caught her eye, the hem of a long robe floating just shy of a man's ankles as he slipped out of the room and disappeared. Her hand went to her throat, to the scar that still stood there, black and angry, but he hadn't cut her, only laid his knife on her: it was a way of saying that they had unfinished business, and that he could reappear at any moment to end the story.

Yes, she would miss it. Nazia and the house and the mangoes and the path around the pond. But the cat's lick of that knife, and the scar on her neck, meant she might never return.

Just before the train pushed off, a couple with two small children occupied the bench opposite. The mother held one of the children on her lap, while the other, older, squeezed into the space between her parents. The mother smiled shyly; Maya guessed it was her first time on a train – nose pin gleaming, a pair of thin gold bangles on her wrists, her fortune.

Really, it was no tragedy her brother's wife had died. The prospect of facing Silvi – sanctimonious, her face packed tightly into the burkha she hadn't been seen without since the war – was largely what had kept Maya from her home. There was, of course, also her brother, Sohail. And Ammoo, who had abandoned her to her rage – her rage and the deep, driving smell of burning books, a scent that had never left her during the seven years she had gone missing. The train made its way through Rajshahi, and then into Natore, the landscape remaining flat and dry, the smells of the paddy mingling with the mustard plants that shone yellow, the burning cakes of dung.

The old woman opened her tiffin carrier, releasing the aroma of dal and fried cauliflower. The family opposite followed suit, unwrapping their bread and bhaji. Maya felt a tap of hunger; she had neglected to pack anything for the journey. The mother carefully tore her bread into tiny pieces and placed them in the baby's mouth. She passed the rest of the food to her husband, avoiding his eye as he took the newspaper-wrapped package from her.

The older girl was refusing to eat, tugging at her mother's elbow and shaking her head. Maya rooted around in her bag and emerged with two tamarind sweets. She offered one to the girl, who stood up, climbed into Maya's lap and took the sweet from her outstretched hand. The mother protested, but Maya waved her away. 'It's all right,' she said. The girl pulled her knees up against her chest and fell asleep. Maya must have slept too, because when she opened her eyes the girl was heavy in her arms and the train was just outside Bahadurabad Ghat. She felt a nudge on her shoulder. The old woman was pointing to her tiffin carrier, which held half a slice of bread and a smear of rice pudding.

'Eat,' she said, pinching Maya's cheek; 'you're too skinny. Who's going to marry you?'

At Bahadurabad, Maya boarded the ferry. It was afternoon now, and the sun danced on the wide expanse of river. She waved her ticket at the ferryman and pushed her way to the deck, where she was the only woman who chose to sit in the full glare of the sun. The Padma lapped at the ferry, gentle, hiding the force of its current. She munched on a packet of biscuits, trying to remember if this was the same boat that had brought her to Rajshahi. That one had a strange name. 'Hey,' she called out to a young boy in a uniform. 'What's the name of this boat?'

'*Padma.*'

It must have been a different boat. That journey, running away from home, seemed a lifetime ago. She had turned to her old friend Sultana. They had volunteered together at the refugee camps during the war, Sultana shocking everyone by driving the supply truck herself. Maya always remembered what Sultana had told her that long summer before independence: that she dreamed of going home after the war, not to the city, but back to her father's village. 'I want to feel the earth pulling at my feet,' she had said. After the book burning, when Maya had decided there was nothing to do but leave, she had telephoned, asking if she might come to stay. Sultana told Maya she had recently married a boy she had known since childhood, a doctor. Together they worked at a clinic in Tangail; she could come; they could use her help.

She had stayed for three months, but Tangail was too close to Dhaka. Every day Maya stared at the buses shuttling towards the city, daring herself to climb aboard one and go home. And Sultana and her husband were newly married. Maya caught them kissing in the kitchen, their mouths open, his hands in her hair.

She left, wandered around the country on trains, ferries and rickshaws, finally arriving at the medical college hospital in Rajshahi town. She volunteered again, and then applied to finish her internship. After two years at the hospital, she was given permission to start a clinic of her own. It was Nazia who had given her the idea, Nazia who had come all the way to town on the back of a rickshaw-van, her baby stuck in the breech position. Impossible, Maya argued, for the women to travel all the way to the hospital to give birth. Too many babies were dying.

Somewhere along the way she had decided to become a lady doctor instead of a surgeon. She had seen how the women's faces changed when she entered the chamber, relaxing their grip on the examining table. At the time she told herself it was a practical matter. Anyone could become a surgeon, but a doctor for women, a doctor who could deliver their babies and stitch their wounds afterwards and teach them about birth control—that is what they needed. She didn't think of the debt she was repaying, that each of the babies she brought into the world might someday be counted against the babies that had died, by her hand, after the war.

They had never had a clinic in the village. Nazia spread the word, describing how Maya had saved her and her baby from certain death, how she had ordered the nurses about at the hospital, how expertly she had inserted the needle into her arm.

That year, before the monsoon, Maya taught everyone in the village how to make oral-rehydration fluid: a handful of molasses, a pinch of salt, a jug of boiled water. And they passed that season without a single dead child. By the following year, when she succeeded in petitioning the district to build them a tube well, she believed she had won their hearts.

Nazia and Masud had another child. They named her Maya.

It was dark by the time the ferry reached the dock at Jaggannathganj. Maya checked her watch, wondering if it was too late to catch the last train. The tree was heavy in her arms, the branches pricking her shoulder. She decided to try; it would be difficult to find a hotel here, and they would ask her questions: why she was travelling alone, why she didn't have a man with her, a husband, a father.

At the station she saw the old woman from the train, her tiffin carrier open. Maya went over and waved, strangely elated at the sight of her. The woman beckoned her closer.

'Eat, eat,' she said.

'Grandmother,' Maya said, 'how is it your tiffin carrier is always full?'

The woman smiled, revealing a set of tiny, betel-stained teeth. Maya dipped a piece of bread into the curry she offered, suddenly famished.

Hours later, in the molten dark of night, the overnight train pulled into the station, and Maya helped the old woman on board. Five hours to Dhaka, she whispered to herself, reciting the names of the stations: Sirajganj, Mymensingh, Gafargaon. Only five more hours.

*

Maya thought she might be overcome at the sight of Dhaka. She imagined the waves of nostalgia that would coast over her, forcing her to remind herself of the necessity of the last seven years away. She imagined emerging into the cool February afternoon, clouds moving fast overhead, and remembering everything about her old life – all the days she had spent at the university, the rickshaw rides to Ramna Park, Modhumita Cinema and the Racecourse, regretting the spare years in the country. But, as she stepped out of Kamalapur Station, she saw that everything was loud and crude, as though someone had reached over and raised the volume. It smelled of people and garbage and soot. She saw how tall everything had grown – some buildings reached five or six storeys – and how her rickshaw-puller struggled to weave through the thicket of cars on Mirpur Road, horns blaring impatiently; and she saw signs of the Dictator everywhere, graffiti on the walls declaring him the 'General of Our Hearts' and the 'Saviour of Bangladesh', posters of him ten, twenty feet tall, with his high forehead, his thin, satisfied moustache.

An hour later Maya was standing in front of the house of her childhood, Number 25, clutching her rucksack and wondering what she would find within.

Her eyes adjusted to the new contours of the building. The decline was far worse than she had imagined. Here, grey streaks across its back, where the drainpipe had leaked; there, the slow sinking of its foundations, as if the house were being returned to the earth; and, above, the collection of shacks that made up the first floor, built by her brother out of a mixture of brick and tin and jute, making it appear as though an entire village had fallen from the sky and landed on the rooftop.

She had loved this house once. It was the only place where she could conjure up the memory of her father – his elbows on the dining table, his footsteps on the verandah. Sliding off his chappals and raising his feet on to the bed. The smell of his tweed suit on a humid day. And lodged into the bone of this house was every thought and hope and bewildered fantasy she had ever harboured about her life, about the war she had fought and won, about the woman and man she had imagined she and her brother would become; but after it was all over, the killing and the truce and the redrawing of the border, he had gone one way, and she another. And she had foreseen none of it.

There is no time to linger, she told herself. Pull up your socks and go inside.

Everything was quiet and shining. The wooden arms on the sofa gleamed. The tiny brass chandelier was polished, the lace runner on the table starched and fixed perfectly in its place. Cushions with pointy edges. It came back to her, the way her mother always kept the house, as though a guest might arrive at any moment and run her finger along the windowsill, checking for dust.

The house was modest: three rooms set out in a row, connected by a verandah that faced the garden. At the far end, a kitchen with its own small porch. This was where she headed now, sure she would find her mother bent over the stove or washing the breakfast plates.

Instead, she found the kitchen packed with women. They wore long black burkhas and squatted over the grinding stone, the sink, the stove. Maya hovered at the entrance, wondering for a moment if she had strayed into the wrong house. She stood the tree up against a wall and set down her bag.

'Hello?'

One of the women rose to greet her. Maya couldn't make out her features beneath the loose black cloth. 'As-Salaam Alaikum,' she said.

'Walaikum As-Salaam.'

The woman reached over and held Maya's hand. 'We mourn our sister,' she said, then turned around and returned to her task, peeling cucumbers over a bowl of water. Maya stood and watched her for what felt like a long time. No one else spoke

14

or addressed her. She picked up her things and left the kitchen. Where was Ammoo? The urge to see her became acute. Maya bent over the sink in the bathroom and splashed a few handfuls of water on her face. She retied her hair, practising the moment she would set eyes on her mother. When she emerged, someone was waiting for her in the corridor. 'It's time,' she said, and led Maya to the living room.

The burkha-clad women were busy rearranging the room. They pushed the sofa against the wall, lifted up the dining table and leaned it on its side. A photograph of her father was turned upside down. The watercolour painting Sohail had done of Maya when she was seven, her ribbons red and yellow, was covered with a pillowcase. As the muezzin began the call to prayer, they sped up, spreading white cloths on the carpet, lighting incense and filling a long silver container with rosewater. Finally, they pinned a sheet across the room, dividing it in half.

Someone pushed Maya through the sheet and into the back of the room. 'Please cover yourself,' she said.

Maya grabbed the woman's elbow. 'Where is my mother, do you know?'

The woman shook her head.

'Rehana Haque. This is her house.'

The woman pulled Maya close, her grip tight. 'Doa koro, apa,' she said. *Pray, sister.*

She could go out and look for her mother. Maybe she was at the Ladies' Club, or visiting a friend. She might be at the graveyard, putting flowers on Abboo's grave. But the room was too crowded now for Maya to leave. The women seemed to have multiplied, taking every inch of space on the carpet. They leaned against each other and held hands. Maya packed herself tightly against the wall. She heard the men shuffle in, shadow puppets on the sheet, their capped heads crowding the tableau. A man separated from the group and positioned himself in the centre of the room. He cleared his throat and began in a high, nasal voice: Alhamdulilla hi rabbil al-ameen. *Praise be to God, cherisher and sustainer of all worlds.* As he uttered this sentence, Maya saw her mother slip through the curtain. The breath stopped in her throat. She wanted to call out. She waved her arms. 'Ma!' she shout-whispered. Rehana looked this way and that. The Huzoor raised his voice. Ammoo fixed her gaze on Maya and stood still for a moment, her hands moving to her face. Maya felt a burning in her eyes and at the back of her throat. Another seven years passed. Then, a whisper of a smile. Ammoo stepped through the crowd, her arms outstretched, and before she knew it Maya was in the cloud of her, the coconuts in her hair, the ginger in her fingertips. 'When did you come?' she whispered. All the years between them, trapped in the amber of her voice.

'Just now. What's going on?'

'Milaad for Silvi.'

Of course. Silvi would have been buried within hours of her death, but this was her Qul-khani, the prayer to mark the third day of her passing.

Seven months into her exile, Maya had written to her mother. *I am not angry,* she had begun. *But I cannot come home.*

For almost a year Ammoo had not replied. Those months had felt endless, as she rehearsed in her mind the furious words her mother might say, wondering if the silence would go on forever, willing her own letter back. But when it arrived, Ammoo's letter was packed with news, updates about the house, the neighbours, the garden. She showed no anger, but she didn't ask Maya to return. And that was how they corresponded, exchanging elaborate pleasantries, long passages about the weather, telling each other everything and nothing.

*   *   *

The Huzoor continued his sermon. Now the women were moving back and forth to the rhythm of his words. It occurred to Maya that when her father died there would have been a similar scene, men in white caps, the air scented with rose-water. She stole a glance at her mother. Ammoo was wiping tears with the back of her hand. She looked the same, exactly the same.

The Huzoor began to talk about Silvi. How pious she was, how good. How devoted to her faith. Sitting among these mourners, none of whom were crying because as Muslims they were instructed to mourn with modesty, Maya wondered how she could have kept away for so long – from this house, and this city, and this mother and this brother. Even though she had been the one to choose her exile, it was as though a thick skin had formed over it, and it appeared to her now as a mystery. On the other side of this curtain was her brother, newly widowed, and his son, Zaid. She thought of meeting him, of the beard that must be thick on his chin, and she remembered how much she had loved him, how fiercely she had needed him to be like her, how she had turned away when he had leaned towards God, taken it personally, as though he had done it to offend her.

When Ammoo closed her eyes and began to recite the final prayer, Maya looked closer at her. Maybe she looked a little older. Dark bruise shapes under her eyes, a line on her fore-head. But it was only when her mother turned around after everyone had said Ameen, when she turned around with wet cheeks and smiled again, that Maya noticed one of her teeth missing at the back of her mouth. Then the years opened up and took shape – the shape of that molar, craggy and smooth, big and small, a chasm.

Maya had told Nazia about the mud, about the laugh. Nazia was indignant. 'Those thugs,' she said, fanning herself. 'If this one turns out to be a boy I'm going to lock him up and only let him out for school.'

It had never been hotter. No one could remember a sari drying so fast on the washing line, the chillies thinning to husks in the field. The pond had begun to shrink back, and there was talk of a threat to the mangoes. 'I know,' Maya said. 'Let's go swimming. It's hot enough to drive anyone mad.'

'Really? We can do that?'

A beat. There were rules about pregnant women, about where they could bathe, but Maya brushed them aside; no one believed those things any more. She had been lecturing them for years now, about science and superstition and their rights. 'Why not?' she said to Nazia. She would remember it later, the moment of pause before she said yes, but on that day all she could think about was the water, its green coolness easing the lash of that summer.

They sat on the steps leading down to the pond, their feet submerged. Nazia lowered herself in and dipped her head under water. 'Subhan Allah,' she cried, 'thanks be to God for such a thing!'

'If my wife wants to cool her feet,' Masud declared, 'no one can stop her.'

The men of the village had appeared in front of his house, shaking their heads. A pregnant woman in the pond? It was too much.

They huddled around the cooking fire that night, Maya and Nazia, fanning the bits of wood until they flared high over the pot.

'What a fuss,' Nazia said. 'I hear they're having a meeting.'

'Ignore them,' Maya said. 'Main thing is Masud is a good man. They'll tire themselves out eventually.' She didn't tell her friend that she had heard the boys at her window again, that she had slept the night before with the windows shut, the heat-clotted air stopping her breath.

*　　*　　*

After the Milaad the women passed around dishes of food and Ammoo began playing the hostess, encouraging everyone to eat. Someone offered Maya a plate but she refused, her tongue heavy in her mouth. She was suddenly overcome with weariness, and she considered slipping into Sohail's old room and putting her head down for a few minutes. No one would notice. She closed her eyes. She heard people shuffle around her. Her head kept slipping sideways and when she opened her eyes the room was empty.

She found Ammoo in the kitchen.

'Ma?'

'Oh, you're up. I didn't want to wake you.'

Her lids were heavy. She took a few steps, faltered. Ammoo led her to the sofa. She wanted to talk to Ammoo, tell her about Nazia and the mud they threw at her window. And the lashes. She wanted to tell her about the lashes. But it was one thing for Ammoo to smile at her, to greet her tenderly, and another for the years to fall behind them. She collapsed on the sofa, struggling to keep her eyes open. 'I have to tell you something.'

'How did you come?'

'The train, the ferry, the train.'

'You must be tired. Lie down for a bit.'

She felt herself nodding off again. 'I brought you a tree.'

'I'll wake you up; it's only three now.'

She pulled her eyes open. There was a brown box against the wall. She hadn't seen it before – the upstairs women had covered it with a tablecloth. 'When did you get that?' she asked, stumbling to her feet and examining it.

Ammoo's face brightened. 'A little gift to myself.'

'Seriously?'

'I saved and saved. Took me two years of leftover rent. There's a German man living in the big house now, always pays the rent on time. You haven't seen *Magnum, P.I.*?'

'There's no television in Rajshahi.'

Ammoo's eyes widened in mock horror. 'That's very sad.'

They laughed. Ammoo sounded so cheerful she almost erased the loneliness of it, waiting with a plate on her lap for the BTV news at eight.

Maya lay her head on the cool pillow. Just for a moment, she thought, then I'll give Ammoo the mango tree and explain everything. She slept. Through the shutters she glimpsed the tiger stripes of sunset, and later Ammoo came in to cover her with a blanket. She heard the muezzin marking the end of the day. A whisper in her ear: did she want something to eat? She curled her hand around her mother's knee. No. Later, a cat slipped into the room and lay across her feet. She felt the quick heartbeat, the warmth radiating out of the little body.

She dreamed of Rajshahi.

In her dream it is the pineapple field that marks the end of everything. There is one day when she is as fierce and impenetrable as winter fog, walking around the village with the stetho wrapped proudly around her neck. No chains of gold; she is a doctor. Early that morning she saved a mother and a pair of twin boys, performing the emergency C-section herself, the cutting and stitching in perfect rhythm, her hands sinking deep into the shared womb. And, although she reminded the family they should have loved the babies just as well had they been girls, she enjoyed the tight embraces of the women, the relief; she munched on the triangle of wrapped betel leaf they offered her. Now she is striding through the village and on to the dirt path that leads to the road that leads into town. Her arms are swinging, January wind pinching at her face, and she is passing the pond, where she waves to the boy who lost a brother to snakebite last year (too late, that day), and she ducks under a pair of mango trees and decides to take a shortcut through the pineapple patch. A few steps in, and the sun is high, the field looks wider now than she had thought, but she is not the sort of person to turn around, so she lifts her sari above her ankles and treads delicately, avoiding the sharp thorns of the pineapple plants. She is tempted to peel back the leaves and check for a ripe joldugi, but she knows it is not the season. Still, the air is sweet and bee-heavy, and when she has reached the end of the field she lowers the hem of her sari and continues, humming a nursery rhyme she was taught by little Maya the night before. And then she sees the meeting. A dozen men in a circle. Masud stands in the middle. 'It's the doctor,' he says; 'she's the cause of all the trouble.'

Maya woke up to darkness. She was dressed in one of Ammoo's salwaar-kameezes, worn through at the elbows and smelling strongly of soap. By habit, she fingered the scab on her neck. A hard pellet, it refused to budge as she picked at its edges. She wrapped the blanket around her shoulders and went to find her mother. Ammoo was in bed, running a plastic comb through her hair.

'I thought you might sleep all night.'

Maya ducked under the mosquito net and climbed in beside her. 'I didn't realise how tired I was.'

Rehana parted her hair down the middle, creating a perfectly straight seam, and began to braid one side. The ritual brought Maya back to all those mornings before school, getting up ten minutes before Sohail so that her hair could be oiled, plaited and ribboned. She thought of her brother now, holding her hand as they walked through the school gates.

'Tell me about Sohail.' In all the letters they had exchanged, Ammoo had said so little about him – only that he had moved upstairs, that his wife had delivered a son, that she saw hardly anything of them, so busy were they with their religion.

Ammoo picked up the comb again and began to tell her. They called themselves Tablighi Jamaat. *The Congregation of Islam.*

Silvi had held meetings upstairs, preaching to the women about everything there was to know about being a Muslim. God, men, morality. Purdah and sex. The life of the Prophet. His wives, Ayesha and Khadija and Zaynab. The raising of children. How to be one of the faithful. And Sohail had his own group of followers at the mosque; many men had been led to the way of deen – the way of submission – under his direction. They brought their friends, their errant sons, and Sohail told them what to believe and how to live. He was considered a holy man.

'They have twenty, thirty people living there. And almost a hundred during the day. I lost count.' They had moved upstairs soon after Maya left. Started out with the brick room in front, then added the outside staircase so they could come and go without disturbing her. Then the tin rooms, the toilet, the kitchen.

'How did she die?'

'She had jaundice. They didn't notice until it was too late.'

She thought of Silvi's skin turning yellow, her eyes the colour of yolks. 'And Bhaiya?'

'For him, it is the afterlife that matters.'

'Things will change now', Maya said, 'without Silvi.'

'Maybe,' Ammoo replied, sounding uncertain. 'Come, let me comb your hair.'

Maya moved closer to her mother, but instead of sitting in front of her she put her head down on Ammoo's lap. Ammoo smoothed her hand across her forehead. 'I can hardly believe it,' she said.

Maya's eyes began to burn. The words rose up in her throat. Ammoo was running her fingers through her hair now, gently massaging her scalp.

'What's this?' She peered down, brushing the hair from Maya's neck.

'It's nothing, just a cut.'

'On your throat?'

The house was changed, but it had survived. And she had made it, two train rides and a ferry across the country, and she was laying her head on her mother's lap, and there was nothing to do now but remember all the times they had returned to this house, she and her brother, to find everything was the same and not the same, to find their mother waiting, waiting.

1972

February

The war ended and all the ugly and beautiful things were uglier and more beautiful. The Great Leader Mujib returned from exile and began printing the new currency and renaming all the buildings. Those who had sided with the enemy hid out, afraid of the back-from-war boys who had surrendered their guns but couldn't stop thinking about revenge. The women wore marigolds in their hair and smelled of coconut oil, and the refugees drifting back from India clutched the cindered husks of their village homes and raised stakes on empty graves.

It was a winter of return, mothers waiting at home, preparing elaborate meals with the leftover war rations, straining their eyes to the road, jumping at the slightest sound. Inevitably, the moment of homecoming did not happen in the way they imagined, with the young boy returning to a fragrant

26

house, rice on the table, everyone washed and smiling. No, it usually happened when she was at the market for a leg of mutton or looking for the lost pair of clothes pegs in the grass, and the boy would appear, dishevelled and with new depths in his eyes, new sorrows etched into him, and when she saw him it would be like birthing him all over again, checking he had all his fingers and toes, wondering if he would survive this new world. And the boy-soldier, quiet, his thoughts turning to ordinary pleasures, the feel of his mother's cotton sari worn down to its threads, and the shape of her hand on his forehead, and the smell of her, like lemons, puncturing every other sensation.

But Sohail did not return. December ended, then January. Rehana and Maya told stories of his return, of the light and pleasant things they would do. Ice cream and spring chicken. Maybe they would take a trip to the tea gardens, or to Cox's Bazaar. He had always wanted to see the brown tides of the Bay of Bengal.

When the moment arrived, Maya and Ammoo were at the Women's Rehabilitation Centre, where they had both signed up as volunteers. That day they returned to find him already home, sitting comfortably in the living room with a newspaper, as if he had been there all along.

He wore a red shirt and a dirty lungi. His face was obscured by the dark grey grizzle of a beard. 'I'm sorry,' he said, looking back and forth at them both. 'I meant to shave.' They smiled at one another and then Maya embraced him and held on for as long as she could, surprised by the fragrance of earth in his hair.

That night they took the lamp and settled themselves in the garden. Rehana slipped a mosquito coil under Sohail's chair, and the three of them pushed close to one another, huddling against the February chill.

'What took you so long?' she asked. 'The other boys have been coming in for weeks now.'

Sohail didn't explain. Smoke from the mosquito coil reached up and caressed them, pungent. He made a gesture with his left hand, which told them he was tired. Maya and Ammoo had been staring at him the whole evening; perhaps he was weary of being looked at.

They fell into silence. All the words seemed too small. The crickets raised their voices, the frogs. Maya thought about the other times they'd sat there. In winter they sometimes put their plates on their laps and ate breakfast and watched the fog curl back. Her father had wanted this garden, this porch that protruded into it. Two months before he died, he had planted a row of tomatoes, bending over the ground himself, sprinkling seeds, folding earth over the cleft. He died before they sprouted, and in the spring, when the plants released their buds of green, it was Ammoo who watered them, shooed away the crows. Years later, when the garden was shortened to make space for the big house, she rescued one or two tomato plants, migrating them to the smaller vegetable patch she had staked out in front of the bungalow, but they didn't survive the move; their stalks crisped and turned to dust. Maya had found her among them once, holding the bones of the plant, disbelieving.

'What will we do now, I wonder?' Sohail asked.

'Hasn't she told you?' Ammoo said. 'Maya's going to be a doctor. Look after me in my old age.'

Maya blushed, secretly proud of herself for choosing medicine. A noble way to serve the new country. 'The university will open soon,' she said.

'Back to school for us.' Sohail appeared unhappy at the prospect of returning to university, of answering yes sir, present sir, in the roll call. 'What kind of doctor will you be?' He pointed to himself. 'Arms and legs? Eyes and ears? Heart?'

He laughed, as though she couldn't possibly be trusted with anyone's heart.

'Surgery,' she said.

He clapped his hands together. 'Vah. Perfect, brilliant. Dr Sheherezade Haque Maya, sewer of wounds, extractor of tumours.'

'How long does it take?' Ammoo asked.

'Stitcher of arteries.'

'Six years.'

'Maybe you'll be married then.'

Maya bristled. 'So? I can't be a doctor if I'm married?'

'I was just saying, a lot can change.'

'Where will you be, Ammoo,' Sohail said, 'in six years?'

She turned her face upwards, to where the moon would be if there were a moon. Blanketed in darkness, they couldn't see her expression when she said, 'Only God knows. All this time I was just wanting your safe return, that's all.'

'Bhaiya?' Maya asked Sohail.

'Six years? No way. I don't know.'

'Married?'

'Can't say. It seems like a rather optimistic thing to do.'

'You've always been an optimist.'

He sighed, sank back into his chair. 'I'm not sure any more.' They knew what he was thinking. Ever since they could remember, Sohail had been in love with the girl who lived in the house across the road. Her name was Silvi. When the war broke out, her mother had married her off to an army officer. The officer had been killed, and now Silvi was a widow; she was still next door, perhaps waiting for the day Sohail would return and knock on her door.

Nobody said anything for a long time.

'She's probably still in mourning,' Ammoo said.

And they left it at that.

* * *

That night on the porch, with her brother back from war, Maya believed their waiting days were over. She watched her mother spread her prayer mat, face west and thank God for his return, imagining the future rolling out in front of them, as flat and endless and predictable as the Delta. How wrong she had been.

1984

February

Maya couldn't sleep. She waited until the first breath of morning, pulled on her trainers, wrapped a shawl around her head and headed into the fog. In Rajshahi she had devised an early-morning route: around the pond, cutting across her neighbour's sesame field, circumventing the mosque, past the road that led into town, and back again at her door before the end of the dawn prayer. Now she decided to make for Dhanmondi Lake via the back roads. Shrouded in mist, asleep, the city resembled the one she remembered, the whitewashed houses, laundry dancing on balconies, the wide, hushed streets.

She circled Dhanmondi Lake, noting that the trees had aged and the path around the lake had narrowed. A clutch of boats were tied together, with a sign that said TEN TAKA ONE HOUR. She stopped, leaned against a tree, her breath whistling in her throat. She'd been running hard, harder than she had realised. She squatted by the tree for a few moments. The dark lake was the colour of limes. She pushed off again, aware now of the sounds that began the day, people leaning out of their windows and clearing their throats into the grass, the tinkle of rickshaws, shops winding open their shutters. She ran across Mirpur Road, now studded with a trickle of cars. Then she turned a corner, and found herself in front of the graveyard where her father was buried.

She looked around. The caretaker was absent, the gate unlocked. She slipped inside. The graveyard looked smaller, with buildings crowded around on all sides. What would it be like, she wondered, to have your window opening on to those small rectangles of death, watching flowers placed and prayers said and people crying, telling your children every night there were no such things as ghosts. Maybe they didn't care. The city was running out of space, she had read in the newspaper that arrived in Rajshahi a day late; it was growing fast and soon they would have to build further and further away. Perhaps this is why the Dictator had decreed that no more than five people could assemble together at once. Because the city was too crowded, it was important to spread out.

Visiting the graveyard was a family ritual. Her mother had kept her father's plot tidy all these years, a hedge around its perimeter, the stone polished. Maya didn't know what to do; she had never come on her own before. She remembered the speeches her mother had made in the presence of this grave, the questions she had asked, the apologies, the regrets. She squatted next to the gravestone and placed her palm on its surface. *Hello, absent father.*

When she returned to the bungalow, Maya found a group of women at the foot of the stairs. At first glance, they appeared to be the women from the night before, but when she approached she noticed their faces were uncovered, and they were speaking rapidly to one another in a foreign language. Maya asked in

English if she could assist them. Without introducing themselves, they embraced her one by one and kissed her on both cheeks. In broken English, they explained that they were French missionaries. The Forashi Jamaat. Maya examined them closely. They wore soft leather shoes under their robes, light traces of varnish on their fingernails, and they had about them the air of tourists – hesitant, their fingers twisted around the handles of their suitcases and rucksacks. One of them was waving a tiny paper flag wrapped around a toothpick.

After a brief discussion, the women began to climb the narrow staircase one by one, ducking into the room at the top. Maya followed them up. Inside was a rectangular room that was crammed tight with people, the air spiced and heavy. A large woman at the front was speaking, her face exposed but circled in a black headscarf. She nodded at the new arrivals and continued her speech. 'Our Sister Rehnuma', she said, referring to Silvi by her Islamic name, 'has recently passed away. May her soul rest in peace.'

'Ameen,' the women agreed.

'But her work must continue. The Wednesday taleem will go on. And the jamaat missions from our sisters and brothers in foreign lands will also continue. Remember, this life is but a drop in the ocean of time; the hereafter is eternal, every moment is an age, infinite.'

Nods and murmurs of assent travelled through the room.

'We welcome our sisters from France.' Now the others turned to the French women and greeted them enthusiastically, touching their faces and fingering the material of their burkhas. The French women mingled, opening their bags and distributing gifts. A box of chocolates was passed around. The woman giving the speech began to circulate, embracing the visitors, speaking to them in a mixture of Bengali, Arabic and sign language. Then she sat down again and began to recite a passage in Arabic, gesturing with plump, graceful hands.

I should slip out before anyone notices, Maya thought. She left the scene reluctantly, her curiosity unquenched. On her way down the stairs she crashed into a boy carrying a bucket. Water splashed her sandals and doused the bottom of her salwaar. 'Watch out, kid,' she said, brushing past him.

'Hello!' he called out. 'Howareyoumadam?'

'Hello,' she said, turning around.

The boy looked her up and down and laughed out loud, revealing a mouth of misshapen teeth. He had unusually light eyes, almost grey, and a fine, delicate nose. But everything else about him suggested poverty: his too-short pyjamas, and the way he treated his lips, rubbing them roughly with the back of his hand.

'Why are you laughing?' Maya asked.

He pointed to her clothes, her trainers. 'You look funny.'

She was about to wave goodbye when it occurred to her that he might know where Sohail was. What had they called him? Huzoor.

'Hey, you know where the Huzoor is?'

He shrugged. Then he opened his mouth and laughed again. 'But you can't see him. Pordah, don't you know?'

'Never mind about that. Is he here?'

The boy released the handle of his bucket. 'No, he's gone. Did you see the French ladies?' he said.

'Yes, I did.'

'Last month we had the Russian jamaat. I can talk in Russian.'

'What can you say?'

He fired off a few foreign - sounding words.

'What does it mean?'

'Peace,' he said, bending his knees and jumping high, 'peace shanti peace. I know it in Spanish too.' And he uttered another string of gibberish.

'Do you have a book?'

He landed on his heels, rocked back and forth. 'No books. Only my head,' he said, pointing a finger at his temple.

'I have to go now,' Maya said.

'Goodbye. Khoda Hafez. Au revoir!' he called out. The French women must have been here before. He reached into his pocket and pulled out a flattened samosa. 'For you,' he said.

'No, you have it. I'm not hungry.'

He bit off one end of the triangle. 'Okay, ta-ta-bye-bye.'

Ammoo was in the kitchen. The servant Rehana had hired a few years ago was standing over the sink, washing the pots from last night's dinner.

'Maya, this is Sufia.' Taller than Maya by at least six inches, the woman came close, smiled and placed a large hand on her shoulder.

'I know all about you,' Sufia said. She looked her up and down. Maya saw her thinking, so this is the daughter who won't come home. Looks like a peasant. Cheap salwaar-kameez, not even starched. Long hair, yes, but what skin, burned all dark by the sun. She kept smiling and patting her heavily.

'I was running,' Maya said. 'I went to the graveyard.'

Ammoo nodded. Then she came close and put her hand on Maya's cheek. 'I am so happy.'

Maya was happy too. The warmth of it spread through her. She wanted to say it, to tell her mother she was home now, that she was staying put, but she couldn't. It wouldn't be true. When Ammoo took the samosas out of the frying pan, she remembered Nazia's children, how they would save up their Eid money and buy samosas in town, sharing one, arguing over who had been given the bigger half.

'Where is Sohail?'

'He came to see me this morning,' Ammoo said. 'He asked me to tell you he sends his love.'

Love? Was that the word he had used? 'Did he say when he's coming back?'

'Not for a few weeks.'

35

Sufia began to grind turmeric with a giant stone shaped like a rolling pin. She passed the stone back and forth over the turmeric bulb, smashing it into a rough paste, and then went over it again and again until it turned smooth, darkening to the colour of crushed marigolds. 'Always coming and going,' she said, scooping the turmeric on to a plate and starting the whole process again with a handful of garlic. 'Coming and going.'

'It's like the United Nations up there. They weren't even speaking Bangla.'

'They come from all over the world,' Ammoo said, pouring more oil into her pan.

'Because of Sohail and Silvi?'

'That's what they do – they go from country to country, like missionaries.'

As a boy Sohail had attended a Jesuit school called St Gregory's. Maya had visited him once on Games Day. The priests were dressed in long linen gowns with strings tied around their waists. An egg-and-spoon race. These were the images that came to mind when Ammoo said missionaries, not the cinnamon-scented women upstairs.

Ammoo lifted something out of the frying pan. 'You want a samosa?'

The thought came rushing into Maya's mind. Grey eyes. About the right age. 'Was that Sohail's son I just saw upstairs?'

'If he was carrying a bucket, that's the one,' Sufia said, turning now to a pile of lavender-skinned onions.

'But he looks . . . Ammoo, did you see him?'

Ammoo put down her spatula and gathered the samosas on to a plate. 'Yes, beta, I know. I was going to talk to you about it this morning.'

'And?'

'And', Sufia interjected, 'there's nothing to be done. Boy runs around like a ruffian; that's how they want it.'

'Doesn't he go to school?'

'Sometimes they read the Book with him,' Ammoo said.

'And you just let them?'

Rehana passed the plate of samosas to Maya. Maya saw a great weariness in her mother's gesture. She saw that, whatever was happening upstairs, Ammoo had decided to ignore it. She was no longer the protective, panicky mother she had once been. If Sohail wanted to burn his books, if he wanted to throw away his furniture and unscrew the light sockets and piss into a hole in the ground, so be it. Once she had given everything for her children. Now she was in retreat from them, passively accepting whatever it was they chose to do: turning to God, running away, refusing to send their children to school. There was nothing of the struggle left in her any more.

It was then Maya realised the years had been far, far longer for her mother.

'He's not my son,' Ammoo said simply. 'And he's not yours. We do what we can, but you have to remember that.'

Maya remembered something else. The tree. She fetched it from Sohail's room and presented it to her mother. 'From Rajshahi,' she said simply, knowing Ammoo would realise at once it was a prized mango tree, and that, if it survived the winter, it would yield the tart, complicated fruit that could be found nowhere else.

His name was Muhammad Zaid bin Haque. A long name for a small boy. The next day Maya kept her eye on the staircase, and as soon as she caught the shape of him she rushed outside and stood in his way. 'Zaid, remember me?'

He shook his head, then, seeing her face fall, he said, 'Ha ha, I fooled you!'

'So you're a joker and a linguist?'

'What's a linguist?'

'Someone who knows a lot of languages. I know some languages too. How about I teach you a few things?'

He held up the bucket, empty. 'I have to go,' he said, running to the tap.

Later, he knocked on the door. 'Do you want to play Ludo?' he said, slipping off his sandals and stepping into her room.

'Okay. You have a board?'

He unfolded a sheet of paper. On it, someone had attempted a crude reproduction of a Ludo board, the square boxes criss-crossing each other and filled in with a blue pencil.

Zaid produced a handful of stones. 'White ones are yours,' he said. 'Black are mine.'

'Where did you get this?'

'My ammoo made it for me.'

'Really?' Maya said, wondering if he wanted to talk about his mother, dead less than a week now. 'You played Ludo with her?'

He nodded vigorously. 'Every day.'

He produced a single die. 'You roll first,' Maya said.

Six. 'Chokka!' he announced, moving his stone across the sheet.

'Zaid,' Maya said, rolling a three, 'do you go to school?'

'No,' he said, blowing on the dice. 'But I'm going.'

'When?'

'Next year. Ammoo promised.'

'Do you know you have to wear a uniform to school?'

'Pant-shirt?'

'Yes, pant-shirt.'

He grinned. 'I know.'

'Your father might not allow it.'

He rolled a four. 'I ate you!'

'I think you skipped one.'

'No, it was a four.' He moved the stone back. 'One-two-three-four. See?'

She was quite sure he had been five places behind. She let it go, losing to him quickly, and as soon as the game was over he folded the paper, tucked it under his arm, like a surveyor carrying his plans, and disappeared.

Zaid came and went. Maya sometimes found him squatting in the flowerbeds, picking insects out of the weeds. His Bangla was coarse, his consonants slurred. And his body was a mess. A rash that peppered his skin caused him to scratch and bleed. There was a line of small indentations on his forearm, dirt in every crease and ripple of him. He was six but looked about four, his wrists and ankles narrow, brittle. He wore identical, pale blue kurtas that were too small or too big, and a cap on his head, pushed back so that it circled his head like a crown.

* * *

Maya was reluctant to leave the house. In the morning she jogged around the lake, and sometimes, when Ammoo asked, she walked over to the shop at the top of the road and bought a few things. She had written three letters to Nazia, pleading with her to stay in touch, offering to send money if she needed anything. She had tried to ring once, at the post office in town, leaving a message, saying she would ring back three days later at exactly the same hour. Three days later the man at the post office said he had spread the word, but no one had come to receive her telephone call.

She rang again the following week. The man was polite. He didn't know if Nazia had returned from the hospital. Maya remembered him: he was the one who had delivered her telegram.

'Are you well?' she asked him.

'Yes, apa, but my daughter is ill.'

Why did this give her pleasure? Was it that the villagers would get sick, now that she was not there to look after them? 'Will you tell her I rang?' she said, skipping over the catch in her voice.

'I will tell her, apa.'

'Thank you.'

'The joldugi will be sweet this year, apa.'

She would miss the pineapples, he was saying, and perhaps they would miss her.

*

'Zaid, I'm going to the vegetable man. Do you want to come?'

'Wait,' he said, holding up his hand. He bounded up the stairs, returning a few minutes later with a crumpled piece of paper.

Maya took it from him. 'Let me see that.'

A shopping list from upstairs.

Okra, it said. Potatoes. One gourd.

They set off down the road. 'Where are your shoes?'

He shrugged. 'Dunno.' Skipping lightly over the hot road. She steered him towards the shade. Turning a corner, they came upon a large building with open windows.

Two twos are four, three twos are six, four twos are eight.

Zaid, holding the shopping note, stood frozen.

The name on the gate said AHSANULLAH MEMORIAL BOYS' SCHOOL.

'You've seen it before?' she said, turning to ask him, but he had disappeared. A moment later he was the other side of the gate, peering into the window. He pulled the cap from his head.

'Someone will see you,' she called out as he worked his way around the building. 'Come back.'

He ducked out of sight. She waited five, ten minutes. She heard a whistle and followed it, turned a corner and found him waiting for her. He had scaled the high wall at the back of the school building and dropped into the street; his kurta was streaked with orange-brown dust. He pulled the cap from under his arm, planted it back on his head. 'Come on,' he said, 'we'll be late.'

The vegetable man measured out the okra and potatoes, then fetched the gourd. He didn't request any money; the upstairs people paid on account. 'Ask the Huzoor to pray for me,' he said.

1984
March

On Independence Day, Maya switched on the television and saw the Dictator laying wreaths at Shaheed Minar, the Martyrs' Memorial. He had a small dark head and wide shoulders fringed by military decorations. Last month he had tried to change the name of the country to the Islamic Republic of Bangladesh. And before that, he had bought a pair of matching Rolls-Royces, one for himself, another for his mistress.

Now, on the anniversary of the day the Pakistan Army ran its tanks over Dhaka, he was making a speech about the war. Eager to befriend the old enemy, he said nothing about the killings. He praised the importance of regional unity. All Muslims are Brothers, he repeated. She couldn't bear to listen. She switched off the television and found her mother in the kitchen, frying parathas. Sufia was lifting up discs of dough and patting them tenderly between butter-lined hands.

At dusk, Maya walked from Elephant Road to Shaheed Minar in her bare feet. She stepped on newspapers and plastic bags, feeling the rough grit of sand moving pleasantly between her toes, the warmth of the tarmac slowing her down until she was barely moving, tiptoeing her way forward. A light breeze caught her under the chin, and she held the straps of her shoes between her fingers and nodded, smiling, to the small groups of people on the road beside her.

All through the movement, they had walked barefoot from Elephant Road to Shaheed Minar in red-and-white saris, greeting one another with the national salutation, Joy Bangla. *Victory to Bengal.*

There were only a handful of people on the road today, making their slow way through the traffic. Horns blared impatiently behind them. On the corner of Zia Sarani, Maya sidestepped a broken bottle and considered putting on her sandals. The thought irritated her. They should have closed the roads and cleaned the pavements, and there should have been a bigger crowd, thousands of people carrying children on their backs, grasping at the retreating feeling of having once, many years ago, done something of significance.

She caught the eye of a long-haired man in a woollen shawl. The man shook his head, as though he knew what she was thinking, telling her not to mind so much.

She wouldn't be consoled. She cradled her anger, tightening her hands around the clutch of flowers she had plucked from the garden. Why hadn't Ammoo come, and Sohail? Why, when they had lived every moment of that time together, was she here alone, between the dark blue sky and a street full of rubbish?

The memorial was illuminated by candles. The wide steps

led up to three narrow concrete structures, each rising up, then bending forward, as if to provide shelter for the visitors. An enormous paper sun, painted red, was suspended from behind. The wind picked up, bending the tiny candle flames, pushing the willow tree until its leaves shook and fell forward.

Shaheed Minar was the first thing the Pakistan Army destroyed in the war. It was also the first thing to be rebuilt, taller and wider, but Maya wished they had left it broken, because now, shiny and freshly painted, it bore no signs of the struggle.

She sat down on the top step, the flowers in her lap, and watched while people made their offerings. Kneeling in front of the pillars, heads bowed. No one spoke. She saw a man weeping quietly in a corner of the arch. He brought his hand to his cheek, wiping roughly. Then he turned and looked directly at her. He stood for a moment, leaning his head forward as if to make her out in the dying light. She rose, the flowers dropping from her lap. He was beside her in an instant.

'Maya.'

'Joy – is that you?'

He picked up the flowers and held them out to her, and she was jolted by the memory of him, now almost a decade old. Joy. Younger brother of Sohail's best friend. He had spent most of the war at the bungalow, an errand boy for the guerrillas, ferrying supplies back and forth from the border. He had lost a brother, a father and a piece of his right hand to the war. And he had given her a nickname once; she tried to remember it now.

They looked at each other for a long time. He was taller than she remembered. He moved towards her and, without knowing it, she took a step back. 'I thought you were in America,' she said, recalling the last time they had met, when he told her he was moving to New York. She had taken it personally, his abandoning the country so soon after its birth.

'I was.'

'But now you're here.'

'I'm back. Almost a year now. And you? The grapevine told me you were somewhere in the north.'

'I'm back too.' She didn't know how else to explain the long way she had come.

'And how is Sohail?' His face was dark in the half-light of the candles, red in the shadow of the red sun behind Shaheed Minar, but she could see his broad forehead, the angle of his jaw.

'His wife died,' Maya said.

'Yes, I heard. I – I thought of calling him, but—'

'He doesn't have a phone.' They began to walk towards the university. Maya resisted the urge to make Joy recall what her brother had been like, in the battlefield, at war, as a student revolutionary, to share the tragedy of his transformation. 'Tell me about New York. How tall are the buildings, really?'

'Taller than in the films.'

'Taller than that? You must have felt very small.'

'It isn't the buildings that make you feel small.'

'What did you do?'

'I was a taxi-driver,' he said. He looked at her and she gave him a small smile, as if to say it was all right his driving a taxi, there was no shame in it. 'And I got married.'

'Married!' She stopped in her tracks. 'Unforgiveable. You get married and you don't tell anyone?'

They had reached the giant banyan tree in front of the Art College, under which they had passed so many afternoons before the war. He pressed a palm against it and leaned back. 'It wasn't that kind of marriage.'

'What, then?' She thought about it for a moment, the answer came to her, and before she knew it she had blurted out, 'Pregnant?'

He laughed. 'Maya-bee. Stings like a bee. Like Muhammad Ali.'

That was the nickname. Maya-bee.

He went on. 'I married her so I could stay in the country. My student visa ran out and I didn't want to come back.'

'So attached to foreign,' she said.

'I know how you feel about it – you made it very clear the last time we saw each other.' He pulled a box out of his pocket and held it up to her.

'A cigarette from New York? I can't refuse.'

He put two cigarettes in his mouth, lit both and passed one to her.

'I saw that in a movie once,' she said.

'Me too.'

'I thought you didn't like the cinema.' She was reminding him of the soldier he had been, the one who was worried about appearing soft.

'I'm not the same man any more.'

'I don't believe it.'

He changed the subject. 'But they tell me *you* haven't changed a bit. Still the same fighting spirit.'

She blushed, suddenly shy. She told him about Rajshahi, about becoming a village doctor, omitting the cause of her sudden departure. And she pictured him crying, the way he had lifted his hand to his face. She wanted to say something to him about his brother. Aref had been Sohail's best friend at university, the two inseparable once Sohail discovered that Aref's father, like Ammoo, was Urdu-speaking, that they both had relatives in Pakistan. It had set them apart from the others, having to square their politics with their family history.

She was still holding her shoes. When she bent down to slip them on she saw that he too was barefoot, his trousers rolled up. 'Where are your shoes?'

'I left them at home.'

'In New York?'

They both laughed. He hailed a rickshaw, holding out his

46

hand to help her to her seat, and just as she was about to wave goodbye he slipped in beside her. 'I'd like to see Sohail,' he said.

She wondered how much he knew – and if she should tell him about the upstairs, and all the visitors, and the sight of their clothes, hanging thick and black on the washing line, and how years ago they had thrown away all their light bulbs, their darkness now interrupted only occasionally by the tiny yellow presence of oil lamps.

'Now's not a good time,' she said. 'He's out of town.'

He lowered himself out of the rickshaw. 'Another day,' he said, nodding his head to her as if he were wearing a cap. Then he said: 'There's a party next Friday at Chottu and Saima's. Why don't you come?'

She had heard of Chottu and Saima's wealth, their big house in Gulshan. She was a little curious. And, she thought, she wouldn't mind knowing when she would see Joy again. 'Maybe. I'll phone you, okay?'

On her way home, Maya recalled the last time she had seen Joy. Sheikh Mujib had been released from jail in Pakistan and was arriving in Dhaka that morning. People were lining up along the streets all the way from the airport to Road 32 in Dhanmondi, where he lived. Maya met Chottu and Saima on Mirpur Road. Chottu had painted a green-and-red flag on his cheek. She told him he looked like a clown. 'I don't care,' he said. 'Joy Bangla!' By then the crowds were streaming in from all sides, pouring out of houses, shops, abandoning their cars, jumping out of rickshaws. Children were pulled up on shoulders. When she looked back, the road had disappeared behind her, replaced by a swell of bodies. Finally they came to the street where Mujib would be passing and staked out a place on the footpath. The singing grew louder. 'He's coming,' Chottu said, standing on his toes. 'I can see him.'

A roar travelled up the road. Mujib was standing in the open top of a very ordinary cab, one of those trucks that are used to carry bricks or crates of fruit. Tajuddin stood on one side, Sheikh Moni on the other. The cab was strewn with flowers. As it went by, Mujib was looking the other way, and she could see only the back of him, his coat, his white kurta. The convoy must have been moving rather slowly, but to Maya it sailed past, and she fell into its wake, swimming into the crowd. She locked arms with Saima and they inched ahead. By now they could see the backs of all those men who had finally returned from war, the people who would make their victory into a country, who would write the constitution and give them passports and anthems.

Maya felt someone tugging at her sari; she tried to speed up and pressed into the person in front. Saima's arm slipped out of hers as she pushed ahead. Then there was a tap on her shoulder. She turned around, irritated, and saw a man reaching through the crowd, a laugh in his eyes. She stopped. He stopped. They stood still and looked at each other, people flowing around and between them, like stones in a river. She reached for his hand, the one nearest to her, but he offered her the other, and it turned into a handshake. 'Hello, Joy,' she said stupidly.

'Maya-bee.' Stings like a bee, he used to say. It was impossible to stay in this position, against the tide, so she turned around and continued to walk. She felt him following. Occasionally they were jostled, and she could feel him crashing lightly into her. She began to hum a revolutionary song, and she heard him pick up the tune. Moved, she reached again for his hand.

Then she found it, the gap where his finger should have been. Hand swaddled by a thick bandage. Slowly, she moved the tip of her finger over what was now the tip of his finger, the bandage stretched tight and smooth. She turned around again, releasing his hand, and stared into his face. 'Where is your finger?' she asked.

'Army took it.'

She reached for it again, the crowd impatient at her back, and brought the interrupted finger to her lips. 'Goodbye, finger,' she said.

'Goodbye, Maya,' Joy replied, 'I'm going away.'

'Misunderstanding,' she said, We'll have to give your finger a proper burial.'

'I'm going to America.'

Impossible. She jerked herself away. 'Now, you're going now?'

'Day-after-tomorrow.'

It came back to her, the crudeness of his character. How he had bullied and cursed his way through the war. Looted a cinema hall for the projector, still rotting in her mother's garden shed. She clung to this evidence of his criminality. 'Goodbye, then,' she said. 'Good luck.' And she reached out to shake his hand,' the uncut one, as if to say, go on, you broken thing, I have no need of you.

Now, Maya counted Joy's losses and stacked them up against her own. He had lost his brother in the fighting, and then, after being captured by the army, he had come home to find his father gone. She was comforted by the nearness of this man, this man who had survived far worse than she.

*

There was a pile of boxes in the tin-topped garden shed, sheeted with dust and cobwebs. Rifling through it, Maya found her school report from Class VI. Mediocre marks, and a note from the teacher complaining that she talked too much and frequently interrupted the lesson.

A short shadow in the open doorway: Zaid.

'Well, there you are. I called for you yesterday – where were you?'

'At school.'

'Really, you went to school? What did they teach you?'

'French.'

'French? What a very nice school. Are you sure it wasn't one of the women upstairs?'

'No,' he shook his head; 'it was a proper school.'

'And you wore pant-shirt?'

He was holding something behind his back, and he produced it now, a package wrapped in brown paper. 'For you,' he said.

Maya tore it open. It was a brand-new Ludo board, with coloured pieces and a pair of dice. 'For me?' she asked. 'Where did you get this?'

'Mare-see,' Zaid said. 'That's thank you in French.'

Maya repeated the word. 'Thank you.' She passed the board back to Zaid. 'Why don't you hold on to it, and when you want to play you can bring it downstairs?'

'Now we can play with Dadu,' he said, smiling, and slipped out of the doorway, the Ludo board balanced on his head, returning the light to the shed. Maya continued her reconnaissance, sifting through old newspapers, cans of paint, a bag of leftover cement, until she found what she was looking for: a stolen cinema projector, still packed in its case, the hinges crimson with rust.

*

On Friday, Joy came to collect Maya for the party. He knocked on the door, smiling and smelling of soap. Ammoo greeted him warmly as he bent down to touch her feet, interrupting *Dallas* to inquire after his mother. His car smelled of leather and aftershave. He rolled down the window and stuck his elbow out, his other hand light on the steering wheel. 'So why did you move to the village anyway?' he said, as they made their way across town to Gulshan.

Maya shifted in her seat. She had decided to wear a simple cotton sari, and now, with the warm air whipping around Joy's car, her pleats already creased, she began to regret it. She should have listened to her mother and dressed up a little, maybe worn a silk or a chiffon. 'Things were changing too quickly,' she said. 'I couldn't stand it any more.' It sounded so harsh when she put it that way.

'And you gave up your training, everything?'

'I was a year away from finishing. I completed the internship at Rajshahi Medical. Then I just became a simple country doctor. But that's what people need out there, someone to help them deliver babies.' She felt the urge to tell him more, to explain about the abortions she had done after the war, and that she hadn't realised until later, much later, that she had racked up a debt she was still struggling to repay. How could he know – he was just a soldier, he had killed as a matter of principle, but the war babies, the children of rape, had been left to junior doctors, the volunteers in ragged tents on the outskirts of town.

They were on Road 27 now, passing Abahani Field. Maya remembered playing cricket with Sohail on that field, running between the wickets in her salwaar-kameez.

'Seven years, you've been in Rajshahi?'

'I went to Tangail first, but it wasn't far enough.' They sped through a wide road with a fountain at one end, an abstract sculpture at the other. She wanted to change the subject. 'So, what's new in Dhaka?'

'I haven't been here that long myself. Looks different, doesn't it?'

'Hmm.'

'They changed the road numbers – you must already know that.'

She did. Dhanmondi had been renumbered. No one knew whether to refer to their street by the old number or the new. Old 13, they said, new 6A. It was like a half-swallowed pill, stuck in the throat. Perhaps they were hoping the old places would not be what they had once been to people, the streets where they had marched and the streets to which they had taken to cast their votes. Road 27 was no longer the artery through which the army had driven its tanks. And Road 32 was no longer where Mujib had been killed, falling upside down on the staircase of his house, his pipe clattering to the chequered ground, the flower of blood pooling and colouring his hair. No, you could no longer say, it happened at Bottrish Nombor; you would have to say it was Road 26A, a new road on which no man had been killed, no man and his wife, sons, daughters-in-law, brother, nephew, bodyguards, drivers, gatekeepers. And 26A was not the kind of number you could assign to those deaths, attached, as it was, to an English letter. Yes, she knew they had changed the numbers.

They spent the rest of the journey in silence, Maya's eyes following the road as they passed the old airport, the cantonment, Mohakhali with its new office buildings and factories. Finally they turned into Gulshan, where the plots of land were twice as large and the cars were thick on the streets, where even the Dictator had a light touch.

Chottu's cheeks were shiny and pink. 'Yalla, I'm seeing a ghost!' He clapped an arm around Joy. 'Where did you find her?'

'Shaheed Minar,' Joy said. 'We were lighting candles.'

Chottu erupted into a growling, used-car laugh. 'Always looking for trouble, dost. Come, Maya, come inside. Saima will crucify me if I keep you to myself.' He led them through the house, through the garden, which had been decorated with fairy lights, and into a large yellow marquee.

A woman in a blue chiffon sari handed Chottu a drink. 'People, this is Maya, my old muktijuddo friend.' He gestured to the crowd with his glass. A few people turned around and waved. 'What will you have, Maya? Coke? A little veeno?'

He lowered his voice. '*Whisky?* Paul will get you anything you like.' A man appeared beside Chottu. He wore a suit and a pair of white gloves.

'Juice?' Maya said.

Chottu shook his head, disappointed, and motioned to Joy. Joy looked at Maya, cleared his throat. 'Juice for me too, thanks.'

'Bastard,' Chottu said. 'Making me look bad.'

'Pineapple, Mango, Tomato, Tang,' the waiter said. Maya heard a screech and turned around to find Saima careening towards her, a fat toddler in her arms.

'I'll kill you, I'll kill you right now, you're back in town, you didn't call me? Ei, Joy, you didn't tell me you were bringing her, thought you'd make it a surprise, you bad boy, OHMYGOD, I don't believe it.' She passed the child to the waiter and cupped Maya's face in her hands. 'Let me see you properly. Alhamdulillah, you haven't aged a day, you cruel, cruel woman. Look at me, I'm a shrivelled old hag next to you.'

Maya shook her head and returned the compliment, taking in the shiny sari Saima was wearing, and the carefully orchestrated strands of hair that fringed her face. People were staring now. Saima took Maya's hand and began to introduce her to the other guests. The Blue Chiffon woman was called Lovely. Her husband, Pintu, was a tiny, sweating man in a white T-shirt. 'This is Khaled and Minny, they live opposite, and Khaled's brother, Sobhan, and his wife, Dora. Dora bakes the most delicious cakes, chocolate, vanilla, lemon – the lemon is divine.' Dora threaded her arm through her husband's and gave Maya a watery smile. Maya wondered what had happened to their old friends, the slightly shabbier-looking ones with whom they had gone to school and run away to war. Pot calling the kettle, she told herself; you haven't kept up the old ties either. Saima's hand was soft and damp as she led Maya from guest to guest. She smiled and smiled, smearing a bit of lipstick on her front tooth. 'I want to hear everything,' she said, 'and

I mean ev-ree-thing. Let me check on the food first, I'll be back. They'll make a mess of it if I don't supervise.'

Maya perched on the edge of a tightly upholstered chair. Saima's Alhamdulillah was bothering her; once upon a time they would have laughed at people referring to God between every other sentence. But now everyone had caught it; just this morning she had been to the vegetable man, and after she had paid him and taken her leave, he had said Allah Hafez. 'What's wrong with the old greeting?' she had replied sharply. 'Khoda Hafez not religious enough for you?' And the man had scraped the feeling out of his face and returned her money. 'Please buy your vegetables somewhere else,' he said quietly.

The memory of it brought a flash of heat to Maya's cheeks. Now she would have to walk all the way to Mirpur Road if she wanted something. She looked around the room. Lovely caught her eye and waved. Maya waved back. Where was Joy? Her sari was now more than a little crinkled, and it puffed unattractively around her hips. Maybe she could find the bathroom and smooth herself out a little. She stepped back into the house and into a wide hallway lined with paintings. Little lights built into the ceiling shone on each one. She found herself in front of an oil painting of a rural landscape: bright yellow stalks of rice, and farmers, their ankles deep in the earth, their muscles bulging and round, working the fields. The painting looked nothing like the people she had lived among these past years; out there, the men who walked the paddy were more lean than round, the flesh carved out of them by work and hunger.

She spotted a woman in a pair of jeans and a brightly coloured kurta staring at another of Chottu's paintings. 'Hello,' she said, attempting to sound friendly.

The woman looked her up and down, taking in Maya's plain sari, her hands knitting nervously together. 'I take it you're not enjoying the jollity.'

'Jolly doesn't really suit me.'

'Nor me. My husband insisted we come.'

'I'm an old friend of Saima. Maya Haque.'

'I'm Aditi. Oh, yes, they told me about you. The crusading doctor.'

Maya smiled, enjoying that. 'Is this how it is, everyone jolly?'

'Mostly. You've been away?'

'Something like that.'

'You can't blame them, really. There's fun to be had. Who wants to remember the old days?'

They drifted back to the party together.

The music had come on, and a few people began to dance, tilting their hips this way and that, drinks rocking in their hands. They jostled one another, fingertips lightly touching. Maya found Joy and Chottu in a corner of the garden, talking about a business venture. 'So, what do you think, dosto, you want to come in with us?'

'I haven't decided yet.'

'Don't worry.' Chottu leaned close, tapped Joy on the chest. 'All kinds of nonsense people making money in this country, no reason we can't join the bonanza. Eh, Maya, you don't agree?'

'Yes, why not.' She caught a glimpse of Joy, who was looking over at her. She remembered now that his father had owned the jute mills in Khulna. 'Make money all you want. But you won't fix anything.'

'We leave that to the doctors. And the politicians.'

'Leave it to others and let the country go to hell?'

'Ah, Maya,' Chottu said, shaking his head, 'you're always taking things too seriously. We're all getting old, na, let's enjoy ourselves before we die, that's what I say.' He raised his glass, empty except for a few ice cubes. Maya shot Joy a look of horror, waiting for him to roll his eyes back at her, collude, but he just stared impassively ahead. One of Saima's friends – Molly or Dolly or something – nudged Maya's arm. 'Hello!' she said.

The woman, packed tightly into a sleeveless blouse, resembled a stack of bicycle tyres. 'Hello,' Maya said, trying not to stare at the dough of her neck.

'So you're a friend of Saima?'

'Yes, school friend.'

The woman stared intently into Maya's face. Maya stared back.

'You're not married?'

'No.'

'You don't want to get married?'

'I don't think so. I mean, I don't know, I hadn't thought about it.'

The woman's eyes bored into Maya. 'Come with me,' she said, taking Maya's arm. 'Meet my brother. Saadiq. He's a chartered accountant.'

Maya pulled away. 'Oh, no, thank you.'

The woman held fast. 'He's very, very eligible. All the girls like him. But I want someone plain and simple, not too – you know what I mean? The girls these days. Come, come, what can it hurt?'

Saima approached and put her arm around Maya's shoulders. 'So you've met my friend. She's one of a kind, you know. Not only is she a doctor, but she sings – sweeter than a nightingale, she does. In fact, Maya, won't you sing something for us, just a little something?'

The fat woman beamed. Maya shook her head. 'I'm out of practice,' she said.

Saima caught her eye. 'Please don't mind, I'm going to steal my friend away.' She laughed and led Maya towards the food. 'Don't worry about her, she's harmless.' A long table had been laid out across the back wall of the garden. Men in white jackets were serving freshly rolled rootis and kebabs. At the other end of the table, biryani, mutton curry, fish cutlets and salad completed the meal.

There had been a day, not long after the war, when Maya was in a rickshaw passing through one of the new roads in Dhanmondi. The lake was calm, the day cloudless, the sun biting hard. In '72 the houses in the neighbourhood were sparse; big lawns and open spaces separated each plot of land. The rickshaw was about to turn into Road 13, when Maya saw a woman crouching on a front lawn. She watched as the woman grabbed a fistful of grass and stuffed it quickly into her mouth, her eyes darting here and there. Although by then Maya had witnessed all manner of misery, all through the war and the summer after, when the rice died in the fields and people flooded the city with salt crusted around their mouths, it was that woman, caught under the glare of high summer, her sari falling about her like the sheltering wings of a long-extinct creature, who had always remained with her, and she had never been able to shake the feeling that they were all never more than a few steps from crouching on their lawns to be suckled by the very earth itself.

'You should come and visit Rajshahi,' she said to Saima; 'you can see more of the country.'

She sighed. 'Oh, I would love to. What a life you must have over there. My life is hectic, too hectic. There's so much to do here. The house isn't finished yet – upstairs still needs to be painted. And the toilets are a mess. The mistris, you have to watch them so closely.'

Maya nodded, distracted by how Saima pushed the food around her plate but didn't seem to eat anything. 'I can't even find good help any more, the children can't stand the bua, but at least she isn't a thief, like the last one. But enough about me. Tell me, what is it like, coming home after all this time?'

'It passed so quickly,' Maya said. 'Sohail's wife died, you know.'

'No, I didn't know. Innalillah. We haven't seen him in a long time. You both seemed to disappear together.'

Maya didn't like the comparison. 'He's living upstairs, he has a son.'

'What happened to him?'

She searched for the right words, but she couldn't find them. She never knew how to tell the story of Sohail's conversion, how he had morphed from an ordinary man into a Holy one. She wished she could be more honest with this woman who had been her friend. Long ago she could have told Saima that all this disgusted her – the painting of peasants, the weight of the food on her table, the way Blue Chiffon rested her hand on Chottu's arm. But not any more.

Joy approached them, wiping his hands on a cloth napkin. 'Delicious dinner, Saima. You're as talented as you are beautiful.'

'Flirting with my wife?' Chottu said, slapping Joy hard on his back. 'Someone should, I don't have time for flirting-shirting – too busy making enough money to keep the woman in saris and earrings.'

Saima smiled, her face broad and tight.

'Better be careful,' Joy said. 'Your wife is beautiful and your stomach is getting bigger by the day.'

'Wife will come and go, my friend, but my tongue serves no woman.'

Over dessert – fruit trifle, made of tinned pineapples and peaches – the woman called Aditi approached Maya again. 'Eaten?'

'Yes, it was delicious.'

'Saima always cooks enough to feed an army.' Aditi lowered her voice. 'To be honest I prefer dal-bhaat to this biryani stuff any day.'

'Me too,' Maya said.

'Perhaps you'd like to meet other dal-bhaat people.'

'Other dinosaurs, stuck in the past?'

'Journalists.'

Maya was sceptical. 'You mean the people telling us the Dictator is a great leader?'

'We're not all the same.' She wrote an address on a piece of paper. 'Come in for a visit.'

She folded the note into her palm – something to set against Saima's biryani, her Alhamdulillah.

'Call me,' Saima said, hugging her tightly. 'What am I saying, you're playing hard to get. I'll call you. I'll call you tomorrow. We'll have lunch. Oh, and tell your mother I send my love. Tomorrow, okay? Don't forget.'

Maya hoped Joy wouldn't speak on the ride home. Her sari had collapsed, and she had given up on it, putting her foot on the seat and allowing the pleats to unfold on her lap. The night was making her queasy. She thought about how excited Saima had been to see her – and how eager those villagers in Rajshahi had been to get rid of her. She was hovering in limbo. She felt too old and too young. Ugly. Ugly spinster in an ugly sari. Even so, it would be easy to slip back in. They would all forget about this awkward encounter and there would be afternoons with Chottu and Saima, swinging her legs over an armchair. She might persuade them to talk about the past, but mostly they would talk about each other and the people they knew, gossiping and complaining about the heat. A part of her wanted to do it, but she knew she wouldn't. Was Joy thinking this, driving her home in silence? She didn't care. He hadn't exactly jumped to her defence. It was a mistake, this party – a mistake to think she could come home and everything would be as it was before.

*

Maya tried to forget about the party. She occupied herself with observing the comings and goings of the upstairs. The plump woman was called Khadija and she was the daughter of a wealthy farmer in Sylhet. She took over Silvi's sermons; twice

59

a day the crowds of women arrived and packed themselves into the upstairs rooms. There were rumours of groups from as far away as Italy and Cuba.

The bungalow telephone rang at four every afternoon, and a young woman from upstairs sat waiting for it. She came a few minutes early and hovered in the doorway, removing her shoes and nervously curling her socked toes.

By the time the phone rang she was ready to spring, but she would wait for someone to come out of the kitchen and answer, and when Maya or Rehana extended the receiver, she grabbed it with both hands. Then she squatted on the floor and whispered. The conversation lasted only a few minutes before she hung up and scampered back upstairs.

Maya collected these titbits. A girl who whispered into the telephone, a boy who carried water in a bucket.

They prepared the empty patch at the western edge of the garden. It was the perfect location, catching the south-facing wind, sheltered from the sun by the coconut tree that towered over it. Ammoo leaned over the hole Maya had dug and unwrapped the jute sackcloth, running her fingers along the delicate roots of the young tree. She whispered a prayer and, softly, blew the air out of her mouth and over the tree. Long may you bear fruit, she said. Maya helped her close the earth over its wound, and together they poured a few cupfuls of water on the mound.

'Ma,' Maya said, 'I think Sufia is stealing from me.'

Ammoo's head swivelled around. 'Where did you get that idea?'

'Some notes missing from my bag.'

Ammoo put a finger over her mouth. 'Quiet,' she said. 'She could come out of the kitchen and hear you.'

'If she's a thief I shouldn't have to whisper about it.'

'She's been with me for six years, she's never taken a pie.'

'Well, maybe she has something against me.'

'Don't be ridiculous. Why don't you check again? Maybe you miscounted.'

Ammoo seemed so sure. 'I suppose. Maybe.'

Maya discovered one of her old medical journals in the shed, an issue of the *Lancet* from 1960 – she remembered coming upon it at a second-hand bookstall in Nilkhet just after the war. 'Common Causes of Eye Injury in the Young', she read. Suddenly she heard a scuffle, and her mother saying 'This is not the first time, beta' in a low, serious voice. Maya closed the journal and tiptoed towards the kitchen. A heavy crash. Maya found Ammoo standing over Zaid, her hand in the air.

Ammoo turned around and saw her. 'Maya, please go.' Zaid was holding a plate in his hand; around his feet were the remnants of another. He refused to meet Maya's eye, his head down. 'Maya, I said please go, I will handle this.'

Maya slipped out, blinking into the sunshine. Later, Ammoo paced the verandah in a pair of rubber slippers, her footsteps mimicking the sound of slapping.

'It was him,' Ammoo said. 'He took the money.' She handed Maya a few notes. 'Here, take this.' Ammoo's hand was shaking. Tiny pearls of sweat along her hairline.

'Please, Ma, it's no big thing.'

'He steals, he lies. I don't know what to do.'

Maya remembered the Ludo board, suspiciously new. 'His mother has just died, he's trying to cope.'

Ammoo shook her head. 'It's not that.'

'Did you hit him?'

Ammoo shook her head. 'He has a temper. A few months ago he set the curtains on fire. I thought the whole house would burn down.'

The next week Rehana was rolling out rootis. Maya and Zaid squatted on a couple of low stools, waiting for her to fry the bread and pass it around. A crow shuffled sideways on the high wall outside the kitchen window.

'Why doesn't it have shoes?' Zaid said.

'The crow?' Rehana asked.

'Because it has claws,' Maya said. 'And anyway, birds don't need shoes, they have wings.' You'd like pair of wings, wouldn't you, she thought. Then she said, 'Do you know your alphabet?'

'Alif, ba, ta, sa,' he mumbled, chewing intently on his rooti.

'Not Arabic, Bangla. Do you know ko kho?'

He tore off another piece of bread. 'No,' he said.

'All these languages and you don't know your own alphabet. I'll teach you.'

'I have to go.' He darted from the kitchen, skipping over the rui fish that was laid out on the floor, gutted and glass-eyed.

Zaid filled his water bucket, and Maya helped him to heave it up the stairs. At the top she saw that the washing was out today, three sets of black burkhas and a white jellaba hanging between them like a flag of surrender. Rehana had told her the upstairs women dried their underthings at night and took them away before the Fajr prayer at daybreak. Fine for these hot spring nights, but probably not very effective in winter. A roomful of cold arses – the thought made her laugh out loud.

'Come tomorrow,' she said; 'we'll do ko kho.'

He looked unsure, his eyes pinched together.

The next day, when he was still unwilling to repeat the names of the letters, she said, 'You know, I used to live in a village, and I know a lot of boys who still haven't learned ko kho.'

'As big as me?'

'Bigger.'

He was constantly moving, scratching his ear, ramming his finger into one nostril, then another, smashing his palm into a line of red ants crossing the garden. 'I want to go to school,' he said.

'Try again,' she said, exasperated. 'Ko.'

He ignored her, pressing his thumb down, assassinating one ant at a time.

She tried another tack. 'You know that crow you saw yesterday?'

'Hmm.' Thumb, smash, thumb, smash. 'The one without shoes?' He found one filing across his arm, and crushed it between his fingers.

'The one without shoes. Don't you want to know how to spell "crow"? You could write him a letter, ask him about his shoes.'

'Crows don't read letters.'

She fell back on the grass, defeated. 'Okay, you're right.'

'I want to go to school,' he repeated.

His bucket was full. She let him carry it up the stairs on his own this time, pretending not to count the very long minutes it took him to negotiate the stairs, or the large splashes that fell overboard on the way, interrupting the dust of the driveway below.

They played Ludo almost every afternoon. 'I can tell you're cheating,' Maya said one day, holding up the red Ludo piece. 'Ammoo, did you see what he did there?'

'Yes,' Rehana said. 'Beta, you moved an extra square.'

'See, your dadu agrees.'

'Fine,' he said, folding his arms over his chest, 'put it back, then.'

'How about the alphabet?'

He shook his head. 'I have to go.' He lifted up the board, letting the Ludo pieces scatter to the floor.

'Ma,' Maya said after he had gone, gathering up the round discs, 'there's something I've been meaning to ask you.'

'Of course, beta.'

'I've been thinking about Zaid. You know, that day we walked to the vegetable man together and he was acting so strangely.

63

And the stealing. There's only one thing I can think of, and I think, if we can do it, it will really work. I want to enrol him in school.'

Ammoo nodded, as if she expected this. 'It's true, he talks about school.'

'I made an appointment with the headmistress at the school down the road. She said she would give him an exam, and if he passed, he could start next January.'

Ammoo folded up the Ludo board and passed it to Maya. 'I've had this conversation with your brother many times, Maya.'

'But he's never here; he won't know the difference.'

'You don't understand. You think Zaid does what he wants, but he is watched like a hawk. Every minute, from upstairs.'

'If Sohail finds out, I'll say it was all my idea.'

'He'll take it out on the boy.'

Maya waved her away. 'I'm telling you, I won't take no from him, I won't.' She was determined to find a way to do it.

At the end of March, just as the cool evenings were replaced by dust-coated heat, she caught him wrist-deep in her handbag. An expression of surprise came over him, but he just stood there and stared at his own hand, as though it might tell him what to say.

She ran over to him and snatched the bag away. Now he was on his knees, his hair was brushing her feet as he uttered the words, sniffling as he did so. 'I'm sorry, I didn't mean to.'

She crouched down and raised him by the armpits, until they were eye to eye.

'I am not a thief,' he said, shaking his head.

She believed him. 'Then don't steal from me as though you were.' A fresh wave of tears overcame him as she set him down on the sofa. 'Do you need money?' she asked.

'No,' he said. Then, 'Yes.'

She tried to give him some money, but he couldn't take it from her, his body trembling. 'Please don't tell Abboo,' he said, 'please please please.'

She thought of what his father might say. About lying, and cheating at games, and stealing money from his aunt. She wanted to tell him these things, lessons that one taught a small child about the difference between right and wrong. But where would he be, this kid, without pretending he could speak French? God sees everything, his father would tell him, but that wouldn't bring back his mother.

After that day, whenever she noticed a few notes missing from her bag, she assumed Zaid had taken the money. She didn't care; in fact, she took a sort of pride in it. She imagined him with a piece of fruit or a boiled egg in his hands, then filling his stomach, having an ounce of pleasure because of her, because she had looked the other way.

1972
March

The change in Sohail began as soon as he returned from the war. Maya and Ammoo remarked on how thin he'd become, trying to scale the distance between them by talking about his appearance. It didn't take them long to see that he had fallen into himself – become a man of few and exact words, fastidious. Bathing twice, sometimes three times a day. Ironing his shirts, one in particular, a red-and-blue check, which he wore in the morning, removed in time for lunch and wore again at dusk. Those first weeks Maya waited every evening for him to tell her about the war, hoping he would begin his story as soon as Ammoo had said goodnight and taken the lamp away, telling them both not to stay up too late.

'So . . .' she began one night, turning to him.

He reached into his shirt pocket. 'Do you mind?' he said, waving a packet of cigarettes.

'No, of course not. Since when do you ask my permission?'

'I don't know. Won't you tell me I'm picking up bad habits?'

'Revolutionaries are exempt from all social conventions. Haven't you heard?'

'I've dodged so many bullets that now I'm immune?'

'Exactly. No one can touch you.'

'Good,' he said, inhaling sharply. 'I've had enough of following orders.'

Once again, she hoped he might unravel himself now, tell her the whole thing from start to finish, war to peace, so that, by the end of it, it would be as if she'd been there, the distance between them traversed, forgotten. It wasn't as if her own return had been uncomplicated. There were things she wanted to tell him too, and the telling would mean that it was over, that there was somewhere to lodge those nine months, somewhere comfortable and remote.

Instead, he smoked so intently she could hear the tip of his cigarette as it burned towards him.

'I'm tired,' he said, though he made no move to get up.

'Was it a long journey?' she asked, realising she didn't even know how far he'd travelled to get home.

'Yes.'

'You walked?'

'Mostly.'

He crushed the cigarette under his heel, then picked up the butt and tossed it away. They watched it disappear into the black of the garden.

'I'm tired,' he said again, and she understood, in that moment, that he had no intention of telling her anything, that he was going to keep it all to himself and parse it out over the years, and in the meantime it would lie between them, silent and angry.

And then Piya arrived, and everything changed.

*   *   *

By the time Maya found her in front of the gate she had been standing there all morning, afraid to ring the bell. Maya was about to leave for her afternoon shift at the Rehabilitation Centre; she was dressed smartly in a churidaar and kurta. She had even allowed herself a tiny smear of lipstick.

'Are you looking for someone?' she asked, taking in the girl's worn sandals, the limp, old sari she had wound tightly around her head. The woman said nothing, just handed Maya a note. In Sohail's handwriting was their address, and the words 'Inshallah, we shall meet again.'

Sohail was smoking a cigarette in the garden. He flicked it aside when he saw her.

'Someone is looking for you.'

'Who?'

'I don't know. Some girl. She won't tell me anything.'

He rushed to the gate. 'Piya?'

The woman appeared to straighten at the sight of him, and a moment later they were hugging and she was wiping her face with the end of her sari. 'They threw me out,' she cried. 'I have no place with them.'

'You did the right thing,' he said.

Maya stood there awkwardly, her hand on the latch, guilty for the stab of jealousy she felt at the sight of their embrace. Then the woman shifted, and the covering fell from her head. Maya inhaled sharply. Her hair was short, obviously shorn just a few weeks ago. Sohail led Piya inside, casting only the briefest glance at Maya, a look that seemed to say, please don't ask me; for once, please don't ask.

When Maya returned from the Rehabilitation Centre in the evening, Piya was sitting in the living room. Rehana was patting her on the back. 'Piya is going to stay with us.'

Piya nodded at Maya, who nodded back. No one said anything about why she was there. They guessed that Sohail had met this woman during the war, that she was in trouble and that her family had sent her away – and there was only one kind of trouble, Maya knew, that would have led to her appearance on their doorstep.

Maya saw women like Piya every day at the Rehabilitation Centre; they had been pouring into the city for weeks. Some had been raped in their villages, in front of their husbands and fathers, others kidnapped and held in the army barracks for the duration of the war. Maya was tasked with telling these women that their lives would soon return to normal, that they would go home and their families would embrace them as heroes of the war. She said this to their faces every day knowing it was a lie, and they listened silently, staring into their laps and willing it to be true.

Some recognised the lie for what it was. The new government had allowed a few of the enemy soldiers to return home to Pakistan, as a gesture of generosity in the face of victory, and a number of the women decided to go with them. Maya was woken one morning by a phone call from the Centre. *They're at the airport, they're trying to leave.*

The airport was a mess, people trying to get in or out of the new country, pushing themselves to the head of any queue that formed as soon as a desk was manned. But dressed as brides, the women were unmistakable, nose pins strobing in the sunlight, bangles weighing down their wrists, making each motion heavy and musical. Some wore flowers in their hair, and one or two had even gone to the trouble of painting henna on their hands.

Nearby, the soldiers were being unshackled, one by one. They clustered around each other and whispered casually among themselves. Occasionally, one of them smiled.

A volunteer from the centre, dressed plainly and with her hair loose, appealed to the departing women.

'It's not right,' she said; 'you haven't even told your families.'

One stepped forward. 'They said they don't want us. Where are we supposed to go? What do we eat?'

'The Women's Rehabilitation Board will make provisions for you.'

'What provisions? Will you give us our families? Will you take us into your homes?'

'We will rehabilitate you. Back into society. Didn't you hear what Sheikh Mujib said? He said you were heroines, war heroines.'

Another woman spoke up. 'We don't want to be heroines. We are ashamed. We want to leave our shame behind, start again.'

Maya joined in. 'Please don't abandon us now.'

The soldiers filed on to the aeroplane. How tall they were, how straight they stood.

The brides picked up their tiffin carriers, their small cloth bags. They lifted their saris so they could make their way up the stairs and into the aeroplane. And then it swallowed them; the hatch was closed, the engine roused, leaving the volunteers on the black and blue tarmac.

It was time, they were told, to forgive. Forgive and forget. Absolve and misremember. Erase and move on. The country had to become a country. Just as it had needed them, once, to send their brothers into the fighting, to melt their pots and surrender their jewellery, so it now needed them to forget.

It was the least they could do.

The prisoners of war were released, put back into their uniforms and sent home to Pakistan. No sorrys were exchanged. Anointed by the hand of forgiveness, they would grow old without shame.

Maya knew exactly what had happened to Piya. No explanation was necessary.

Piya slept all day, oblivious as they worked around her, ate their meals, tied and untied the mosquito nets, swept the floor by her feet. Maya sometimes woke in the middle of the night and found her gone, but she was only in the garden, or out on the verandah, squatting and staring into the distance. She did not attempt to take Maya into her confidence, and Maya did not try to appeal to her. If she needed something, she addressed herself to Rehana – Maya saw them whispering to each other in the kitchen a few times. Piya began to help Ammoo in the kitchen, grinding spices with the rough-edged stone, rolling the rootis for breakfast. Other than that, she was a half-presence, a person both with and without them. Maya sometimes forgot she was there – she was busy too, feeling her way around the strangeness of peace, of having her brother at home again, of being encouraged, now that it was all over, to make a display of enjoying the country.

Two weeks after Piya arrived, Maya saw her in the garden with Sohail. It was early evening, the shutter of darkness about to close. She watched them from the verandah. If they had looked up they would have seen her, but both pairs of eyes were lowered, staring at the same thing in front of them. Piya rubbed her hands across her arms, and Sohail offered her his shawl, wrapping it loosely around her shoulders. Their hair was of a similar length, and from a distance they seemed like brothers, two men sharing men's secrets. The light began to fade; Piya looked up and saw Maya staring and nudged Sohail. They waved.

She walked over gingerly, knowing she had interrupted something.

'Come,' Sohail said, 'sit.'

She squatted down on the jute mat next to them. They edged over to make space for her but the pati was too small, and Piya ended up on the grass. 'Let me get another one,' Sohail said, quick to his feet.

They were alone. Piya plucked at the grass while Maya looked uncomfortably up and down the garden, wondering if they should talk about Sohail, or the war, or why Piya was here.

Finally Piya said, 'You're very good, letting me stay.' She pulled out a blade of grass, twisted it between her hands.

'Where were you,' Maya asked, 'before?'

Piya concentrated on the long blade of grass, tying knots across its length. 'In an army camp,' she said. 'He found me there, in the barracks.'

'Where is your family?'

'Not far. In Trishal. You think I should go home?'

She hadn't meant it that way. 'No, of course, you can stay here.' She wanted to tell Piya how glad she was that she had come, that she had brought a flash of life back to her brother. She made an awkward attempt at friendliness. 'Stay as long as you like.'

Sohail returned with the pati; they stood up, rearranged themselves.

Piya didn't sit down. 'I'm just coming,' she said, and darted into the kitchen.

'She's better,' Sohail said. 'Doesn't she look better, already?'

'Yes, she does.' Maya wanted to ask him if he was better, but there seemed no reason to ask him this. For once he looked relaxed, his white cotton kurta gleaming in the fading light. He appeared in perfect health, in perfect cheer, rather than like a man who had yet to shake off the war, a man who had brought home a strange woman. An ordinary man. She decided to treat him as one.

'When I found her, she looked as though she might slip away, at any moment.'

Before Maya could reply, Piya stepped back into the garden, holding a kerosene lamp in one hand, and a large bowl in another. 'Jhal muri,' she announced, placing the spicy puffed rice in front of them. As she scooped a handful into her mouth, Maya noticed a bracelet-shaped scar on Piya's wrist. She looked closer at Piya's arms: the other wrist was similarly marked. Piya set down the kerosene lamp, and suddenly Maya was filled with wonder that she should be here, among them, bearing the scars of her captivity, making snacks and sitting with them in the garden. What other wounds still marked her?

It was getting darker. They could barely see one another now; there was just a faint, oval-shaped pool of light cast by the kerosene lamp.

Piya and Sohail hatched a plan. Piya had never been to the cinema, and Sohail was trying to explain it to her. People on a wide, flat surface. Not real people – well, real, but not present. Acting – she knew acting, she had seen the jatra when it came to her village.

'When it reopens,' Sohail said, 'we'll take you. Won't we, Maya?'

She nodded. 'Did you know,' she said, 'Joy brought a film projector to our house during the war?'

'From where?'

'I don't know. An abandoned theatre, I think.'

'What is a projector?'

'It's the machine that shows the film.'

'You have the machine?'

'Do you want to see it?' Joy had brought the projector for Ammoo. Now it was lying somewhere in the garden shed. 'I think it's still here.'

Sohail hesitated. She could tell he was thinking about whether it would cause him pain, or happiness, to see an object brought to this house by his friend.

'Yes,' said Piya, 'I do, I want to see.' She stood up and clapped her hands together.

'All right,' Sohail said, 'let's see it.'

The shed was a crude little building beside the lemon tree. Maya went inside first, holding the lamp high. They stepped over a few trunks and boxes, off-cuts of wood, a half-open bag of cement that had hardened over the years.

The projector was exactly where she had left it, wedged into a corner of the room, covered in dried banana leaves. 'There it is.'

She remembered now, carrying it from the big house and tenderly placing the leaves on top, as though she were burying it.

Sohail heaved the box on to his shoulder and Maya helped him manoeuvre it into the house. They decided to set the box down in the corridor and examine it without turning on the lights. Maya held the lamp as Sohail unfastened the hinges.

All the pieces were there – the two round cases, one on top of the other, the protruding lens, the smaller pieces, the clips that held the film in place, the metal fasteners that opened and closed over the reel.

Piya reached forward, passing her hand delicately over the metal plates. Sohail pulled the projector out of the case and stood it upright on its sturdy metal legs.

'This is where the film goes in, I suppose,' he said, pointing. 'It goes up here, and through this part, and the light catches it and makes it big, very big. The film itself is only the width of two fingers. It's the light that makes it bigger.'

'How big?' Piya asked.

'Bigger than a person,' Sohail said.

Piya fixed her eyes on him.

'Sometimes when they show just the face, you can see every-thing, you can see inside them,' he continued.

'You can see inside?'

Maya thought the girl might weep from the wonder of it.

'Shall we see if it works?' she said. 'I think there are a few films in there.'

Piya lifted her hands from the machine and turned to face her. Her tiny eyes disappeared behind a pool of tears. 'Yes, oh, yes.'

'No,' Sohail said, his voice suddenly distant. 'We can't do that.'

'Why not?' she asked, surprised by this change of heart.

'It doesn't belong to us, we have to give it back.'

'But it's here now.' Maya couldn't understand it. One minute he was gaping at the machine, the next he was acting as though the whole thing was done without his consent.

Sohail moved to replace the projector. 'Let's not do something we'll regret.'

'I won't regret it,' Maya said. 'And neither will Piya. Will you, Piya?'

Piya had sensed the shift in Sohail too. She shuffled away from the projector and leaned against the verandah wall, squatting in the village way, with her elbows on her knees. 'I don't know.'

Maya pursued her and crouched down beside her. 'Haven't you ever done anything you might regret later?'

'Maya, please, don't be childish.' Sohail was packing up the projector, tucking it back into its felt grooves. 'Look, here's the stamp. Modhumita Cinema. How many times have you and I gone to that cinema? And who knows how Joy got the thing here anyway.'

'What are you saying, that your friend is a thief?'

'I'm saying a lot of things happened during the war, but now it's not wartime any more, and we have to behave like citizens, rather than rebels.'

'I don't think Piya cares about that,' she said. 'I think we should let her see a film. Isn't that why we fought this war anyway, so we could be free?'

'That's a completely bogus argument, you know that. Freedom comes with responsibilities, with limits.' He snapped the lid shut, as though there could be no further debate.

'I have done something,' Piya whispered from the darkness. The lamp was burning low, and didn't reach her any more. Sohail lifted the projector box into his arms and was about to stand up. He paused.

'What?' he asked.

'Something very bad.'

Sohail squatted down in front of Piya. He came very close to her, but he was careful not to touch her. She was shrinking from him anyway, pressing her back into the wall. 'It doesn't matter,' he said. 'Forget it. You should try to forget it.'

She grew silent, but they could hear her breathing, as though the words were struggling to get out of her and she was struggling to keep them in. Maya didn't want Piya to forget what had happened to her, she wanted her to remember. She wanted her to remember and she wanted to know. But she did not press Piya. Everyone else was determined to forget, to move on and leave behind whatever dirty things had happened in the past; it would be cruel to deny Piya this, a chance to begin again.

'It doesn't matter,' Sohail said. 'Whatever it was, it wasn't your fault.'

'He's right,' Maya said. 'Don't blame yourself.'

Certainly they had only meant to comfort her. But Piya was different after that night. Something had rippled within her, demanded to get out, and they had silenced it.

A few weeks later, she was gone.

1984
April

The queue snaked out of the tent, wrapped around the corner and doubled back on itself. In some places people had taken to crouching on the ground, holding their hands up against the fierce heat, quieting their babies. They shared stories and bits of food while they waited. Maya heard the call of the muezzin, and saw great swathes of pilgrims making their way to the prayer ground. But the people in the queue did not budge: they were here for the free medicine.

They had all the usual ailments – dysentery, dehydration, broken legs that hadn't healed properly, wounds that should have been stitched up but never made it to hospital. Jaundice, malaria, typhoid. It had taken her the better part of that morning to organise the clinic. The other doctors – young interns and trainees who had probably never left their city hospitals – were relieved to be told what to do. She barked out orders, telling them to run down the line and divide the patients into groups. Put the young children first. Check for infectious diseases. Separate queues for men and women. By noon she was seeing a patient every seven minutes, and a pregnant girl with gestational diabetes had hugged her and cried. She felt the murmur of a thrill. She was right to have come.

Her brother was here, somewhere among the worshippers. Zaid had given her the idea. 'Abboo will be at the Ijtema,' he said. The upstairs had emptied out, no more footsteps on the ceiling or groups of jamaatis pooling in front of the gate.

'Maybe you can meet him,' Zaid said. Someone had shaved his head that morning, there were two neat crimson scars at the nape of his neck. She considered the idea. Perhaps it was time to face Sohail.

The Ijtema provided free medical clinics to all pilgrims. It was easy to offer her services, set up a curtained area for women. And here she was. Millions of people. Somehow it was easier to meet him in this context, his foreignness multiplied, but made plainer, by the replication of people like him, clusters of men in beards and white robes. Since her return he had been away, travelling from one jamaat to another, and she had been relieved to accustom herself to the house, the city, without the prospect of seeing him. But now she was ready.

Though he was a relative newcomer to the Tabligui movement, Sohail was already known for his bayaan, his sermons. Maya could bet none of the people who listened to him now had any idea where he learned to speak like that. If they had asked her, she could have told them about the time when at sixteen he beat the debating champion in college, the very handsome Iftekar Khan. *Speak for or against: does the arms race decrease the possibility of another world war?*

Sohail had studied Iftekar Khan and decided he was, in fact, a very fragile man. Twice the All-Pakistan Debating Champion, he had risen too high; he was full of the fear of disappointing his fans. So Sohail paused, longer than was necessary, before beginning his two-minute opening. And he spoke very slowly. By then Iftekar was already jamming his finger between his neck and his shirt collar, trying to create a bit of space for his swelling throat, his itch to fill the silence. And Sohail continued to draw out his words, so that, after he had won, the college newspaper dubbed him the Tortoise that Beat the Khan. It was on that day that he learned his trick of manipulating the moment, of deciding the beat and tempo of a conversation, and it was that day that led him to become president of his university hall, and the object of much speculation among the girls, and eventually a protester on the streets, shouting through a megaphone against the army. It was the day that led him, finally, to the war.

But none of these pilgrims would know that. They probably believed it was a gift from God.

Zaid was flitting in and out of the medical tent, translating the day. 'There's an American tent,' he said, gasping. 'They gave me this.' It was a red-and-green-striped sweet in the shape of a walking stick.

'You can eat it after lunch.' It would be a very late lunch; already the afternoon prayer was under way. Along the banks of the Turag River, thousands upon thousands of men bent their heads and faced west. They pointed themselves towards Mecca, but they were also bowing to the afternoon sun, which cast sharp beams into their eyes as they raised their hands. Together they stood, turned their heads from side to side. They folded their hands, kneeled and performed the Sejda, putting their foreheads to the ground. It was at this moment, Maya thought, recalling something her mother had told her, that the heart rose higher than the head.

Zaid led her to a tent and found them a small square of carpet. A woman walked past, willowy in her chador, and handed them a bowl of spicy chickpeas. 'As-Salaam Alaikum,' she said, pinching Zaid's cheek and wandering away.

Maya unwrapped their lunch, a box of chicken and rice. 'I saw Abboo,' Zaid said.

The chicken dried up in her mouth. 'Where?'

'Over there.' He pointed in the direction of the praying men on the river bank.

Here was her chance. At the prospect of seeing him again, she allowed herself a sliver of hope. A reunion. She would approach him, ask about Zaid. Toe in the water. See if there was somewhere they could meet, she and her brother. She had travelled to his home turf, he might like that. She looked at the boy, allowing herself, for a moment, to wonder what it would be like to take charge of him. School, first of all. He would go to school. She would have to teach him not to wander off in the middle of a sentence, and how to sit behind a desk all day. He would have to wear a uniform and carry his tiffin to the playground.

They finished their chicken and rice, washed their hands by the side of the tent. 'All right,' she said, 'let's go and find your father.'

They pushed through the stream of pilgrims and made their way to the river, passing row after row of tents, each one housing tribes of men, their lungis hanging on strings to divide the space between them. They would eat, sleep and pray here for a whole week. The larger tents were set up with speakers and microphones and makeshift stages where famous orators from India, imams from Jerusalem or Shanghai or Mozambique, would stand and spread the word. Maya had heard on the news that it was the biggest gathering of Muslims after the pilgrimage to Mecca. Even the Dictator would be attending the final recitation, to seek blessings from the spiritual leaders of the jamaat.

The prayer ended; men shuffled away, putting their shoes back on and wiping the sun from their eyes. Zaid was holding her hand and dragging her forward. They pushed against the tide of men leaving the prayer ground, inching slowly towards the

lip of the river. Large boats packed with pilgrims were floating
on the river, waiting for a space to drop anchor. Impatient, some
jumped into the water and waded, their capped heads bobbing
as they swam. Zaid wriggled his way through the crowd, tugging
on Maya's arm, and finally they came to a stretch of sand.

'There,' Zaid said, pointing. A clutch of men stood talking.
Sohail was smiling, gesturing with his hands. He embraced each
person in turn, and then the group dispersed. Zaid hesitated
for a moment, looking up at her as if she were about to tell
him what to do, and then he released her hand and scurried
away, disappearing into the crowd.

Sohail was standing with his back to her, gazing into the
water, his hands folded behind him. She watched him quietly
for a moment. She had practised this meeting countless times.
His back was broad, his hips. The white that draped his body
ended above his ankles, which were black, his thick heels in a
pair of cheap rubber sandals.

He turned. They regarded one another for a moment, and
then he held out his arms to her, and she dived straight into
them until she was wrapped in his pillowy chest, his fragrance
of rosewater and attar.

He kissed her forehead. 'As-Salaam Alaikum,' he said. She
clung to him, and slowly, gently, he shifted away.

'Walaikum As-Salaam,' she heard herself reply. 'How are
you?'

'I am well, by the grace of Allah.'

Maya shifted her weight from one foot to the other. The things
she wanted to say, dense, historical words, sat at the bottom of
her. 'I'm so sorry, about Silvi.'

There was a time when she would know, from the way he
glanced at her, or the shape of his lips when he spoke, exactly
what he was thinking. But he had learned to disappear within
himself, and his face told her nothing. 'It was her time.'

She wanted to touch him. He was fragile and he was remote.

She watched the Adam's apple moving up and down in his throat. She steadied herself. 'You know I've come back,' she began.

'Yes, I know.'

He knew. He hadn't come down to see her; she hadn't gone up to see him. Brother and sister, once inseparable. Tell me, she thought, tell me you've missed me, that you wished for my return. That you want to make up. He stepped closer to the water, and she followed. 'I – I'd like your permission to enrol Zaid in school. There's a new one on Road 4, I went to see the headmistress and she agreed to take him at the start of the next term.' She was so nervous. Every word was a struggle.

He stopped. 'He's lonely, I know.'

Because you left him alone, only days after his mother died. 'He's a sweet child.' She had said the wrong thing, revealed how little she knew the boy.

Sohail shook his head. 'His education is continuing in the hands of Sister Khadija.'

Maya swallowed the lump of anger rising in her throat. 'Do you remember what it was like, when Abboo died?'

He turned, smiled, his lips criss-crossed by the beard. 'Of course I remember.'

'How hard it was.'

'Yes.'

She guessed that he was not unaware of suffering, but had decided he would no longer be in thrall to it. That he would embrace it. The death of his father, his wife. There was a grand design, and it left no room for self-pity. But she ploughed on. 'He's only six. His mother has just passed, he needs us, me and Ammoo. We're his family.'

He said nothing, turning his face away and peering into the water. Perhaps he was about to tell her about all the ways he had reconstructed the word 'family', and that she was nothing more than a girl he once knew.

She looked towards the camp, where Zaid was no doubt waiting, swinging his arms and pacing through the alleys. She was about to renew her appeal, repeat the arguments, but Sohail reached out and clutched her arm, pulling her towards him. He peered straight into her, awakening all the parts of her that he had once known.

This was it. This was her moment. She had thought of it so often, it was a dream, a dream worn out from constant dreaming. He would see himself reflected through her eyes – see the absurdity of what he had become. He would see the ugliness of turning his family away, the cruelty of his own fathering. Cracks would appear in his belief, his faith would be shaken – not in the Almighty, she would not wish to take that away from him (or perhaps she did, but she was not willing to admit to it), but in whatever force had taken him from her and delivered up a stranger.

He would remember himself, awaken and resume the life she had imagined for him. And he would forgive her for wishing him different.

A man is not born once, she would say, a man can come into the world again.

The years disappeared.

She was ready to forget everything.

Brother, I will be yours again. I don't care about the people upstairs, and it doesn't matter if you've forgotten about our war, or our youth, no matter if this life is no longer your concern, that you have given up Ghalib and dear, dear Shakespeare, and no matter that I have ached in my bones because you appeared to forget me. If you want to put it aside, I say, yes, I accept, I forgive you, I ask you the same, let us return to it.

'School is out of the question,' he said.

Out of the question. *Out.* The burning sensation started in her gut and rose to her throat. She felt herself struggling to breathe. How foolish she had been to imagine she could come here and get her brother back; the dream was just that, a mirage. Her limbs were restless, angry. Yet she fought the urge to run from him. She had done enough running. Think of the boy, she said to herself. Forget your disappointment and think of the boy.

She swallowed her anger, ready to negotiate. 'All right, then. Can I teach him a few things – sums, the alphabet? When he's not busy upstairs, of course.' For the moment, she would settle for this. One agreement at a time.

'All right,' Sohail said finally. 'I will consider it.' He bent to embrace her again, and she knew the meeting was over. She darted away, tucking a few strands of hair behind her ear, clinging to her small scrap of victory. She would be Zaid's tutor, and when Sohail saw how quickly he learned, she would persuade him to send the boy to school. She would mourn her little dream later, at night when the sight of him came back to her, his serious, closed face. But for now she told herself to be satisfied, and so she slipped into the crowd, eager to share the good news with her little charge.

Zaid came down for a few hours every day, at lunchtime. He ate undisturbed while Maya taught him the alphabet. Then, as a treat, she showed him a few card games. He cheated, hiding cards under the table or in the sleeve of his kurta. Sometimes her purse was lighter than it should have been, but she didn't tell Ammoo. She didn't mind. It was only a few coins, only Gin Rummy and 21. Sohail departed again, on a mission to Nepal, and she didn't see him after that day by the river. She tried to call Rajshahi again but the line was constantly engaged. She wrote another letter to Nazia, pleading for a reply. She spent another day in the garden shed, looking for newspaper cuttings from the war, and she stumbled across a typed page dated September 1971. It was one of her old articles from the war – no one had agreed to publish it, she remembered, and she smiled now as she read the title: 'The World Looks on as Bangladesh Bleeds: A Cry for Help' by Miss Sheherezade Maya Haque.

1984
May

It took her awhile to find the shabby building in Old Dhaka. It was at the back of an alley that led down to the river, flanked by a leather factory. The stench of the tannery was overpowering. She held her nose and knocked. Aditi came to the door.

'Ah, the doctor!' she said. She was dressed as she had been at Saima's party, in a pair of jeans and a short kurta, but she looked different. Her fingertips were stained with ink, and she wore a green bandana around her hair. 'I'm so glad you decided to come. I won't hug you, I'm filthy.' She waved Maya inside.

'It smells like death,' Maya said.

Aditi laughed. 'It's horrible, isn't it? We're all used to it, don't even notice any more.'

Inside was a windowless room, piled high to the ceiling with stacks of newsprint. There was a large table on one side, scattered with pens, books, empty cups of tea. A man sat with his back to them, huddled over a typewriter, his knees bouncing up and down.

'Aditi, is that you? Bring me some tea, please, my nimble fingers are about to produce a miracle of a sentence.'

Aditi cleared her throat. 'We have a guest, Shafaat, please behave.'

The man swung around. 'I am so sorry, how rude. Hello, I'm Shafaat. Shafaat Rahman.'

'Shafaat is the editor.'

'Editor, reporter, manager, tea-boy.'

'Well, not the tea-boy, it seems,' Maya said.

'Yes, you've spotted my weakness. What can I say, I like to give orders. But don't worry, no one ever listens to me.' He lit a cigarette and dangled it on the edge of his mouth. 'The next issue comes out in a week. Here's a mock-up.' He handed her a leaflet printed on cheap paper. She began to flip through the articles. There was one about the Dictator's wealth, another exposing corruption in the army. It ended with a tirade on the changes that were being made to the constitution.

'You can print this?'

The man smiled through dark, tobacco-stained lips. 'No, but we do.'

'Won't you get arrested?'

'Arre, who's afraid of a little time with uncle?'

As she turned the pages, the ink bled on to her fingers. She looked around, took in the typewriters, the empty glasses of tea, the floor littered with bits of paper, and for the first time since returning to the city she felt a ripple of belonging.

'Aditi tells me you've been away.'

'I lived in Rajshahi for a few years.'

'Really? Do you have people there?'

'No, my people are here.' She could count all her people on the fingers of one hand.

'So you went all the way to the middle of the country, for what?'

She looked at Aditi. 'I was a "crusading" doctor.'

'Aditi tells me you want to write.'

That's what she had told Aditi, when she had called and asked if she could visit the newspaper office. But suddenly she wasn't sure any more – it had been years since she'd picked up a pen. 'Well, I thought – I did some writing during the war.'

'You have something you want to say?' Shafaat lit another cigarette, threw the match on the ground. A young boy in a tattered vest and lungi entered with a broomstick and pan and began to shift the dust to the corners of the room.

'Something about village life, I guess.'

'You mean all that bucolic I-love-the-countryside crap?'

'No, nothing like that. About what's really going on out there, sort of like a memoir. I was there for seven years, I saw a lot.'

'All right, 500 words by next week. Let's see what you come up with. But please, don't write any sentimental drivel about the green valleys of Rajshahi, eh?'

She smiled. 'All right.'

'You sure your husband won't mind?'

'Does Aditi's husband mind?'

Aditi looked up from her desk. 'He's too busy playing golf. I just ignore him.'

'So, yours will?'

'Stop harassing her, Shafaat, she's not married.'

He raised his eyebrows. She imagined what he was thinking – poor girl, still without a husband. But he surprised her by giving her a thumbs-up. 'I have a daughter, and I tell her, marriage only if she meets a prince. Otherwise men are bastards.'

'My,' she said, 'I could sign you up right now – first male feminist of Bangladesh.'

'Do it!' he said, slamming his fist on to the table. 'We'll make an official announcement in the next issue.'

'You'll be a celebrity,' Aditi said drily. 'Now come with me, Maya, I'll show you the rest of our humble establishment.' They went down a corridor and into a smaller room. There was a desk at the back with a large rectangular box on top. 'You'd better look out for Shafaat, he's a flirt.'

'He reminds me of my brother.' There was something about the way he thumped his hand on that desk that brought back a flash of Sohail.

'Really, I thought your brother had gone the religious way.'

'He was different before.' No one seemed to remember the old Sohail. They heard he had become a mawlana and forgot how he had been before. Only Maya had archived his image – hands wedged into his jeans, the cap he wore with a red star in the middle.

Aditi showed her the typesetting machine. She had to take every letter of every word and slot it neatly into a groove. The words were then dipped into the ink and pressed on to the paper. 'Try it,' Aditi said. Maya pulled out a few letters, arranged them on a tray. Dipped into black ink. *MynameisMayaHaque*.

'You have to remember the spaces between the words, Doctor.'

*

The typewriter's keys were tight. Probably angry with her for all the years it had spent under Ammoo's bed. There was a time you couldn't take it from her; she would bring it to the table and tap away while eating her dinner. And when she wasn't banging on the keys, she was scribbling on anything she could find, an old newspaper, a piece of brown paper that the vegetables had been wrapped in. Now she struggled to find the words. *Chronicles of a Crusading Doctor*? That sounded pompous. There was nothing so lofty about what she had done. She began to write about the Dictator, the sight of him tossing flowers on the Martyrs' Memorial. She tore the paper out of the typewriter. No one wanted to read about that. Five hundred words on the true story of the countryside. The true story. She remembered all the children she had brought into the world, all the mothers she hadn't been able to save. She thought of Nazia – Nazia who had been punished because it was the hottest day of the year and she wanted to cool her feet. She started at the beginning. *I once knew a girl called Nazia.* What was she thinking – she couldn't use real names. Nazia. Zania. Inaaz. Aizan. *I once knew a girl called Aizan.*

1972

April

Sohail's friends couldn't understand his conversion, because they hadn't really grasped what had come before. They had thought his life was full of happiness; they used words like jolly and cheerful to describe him. Happy-go-lucky. Happy and lucky, jolly and laughing, bell-bottomed. Rock and rolled. Before he found God. They remembered how good-looking he was, and that he showed his teeth when he smiled.

Had they known him better, they would have seen that the teeth, the smiling, the happy and the lucky had been taken by the war. By a girl whose captors had shaved her head so that she could not hang herself. Purdah, the preaching – all of this followed naturally, filling the hole left behind by his old mutinies.

And people misremember about the Book. They assume that Silvi gave him the Book and told him to read it, because by the end of the war Silvi had lost her husband and already found God, and she had defied everyone and been the first to cover her head, to turn her back on her country and face life after life.

But it was Rehana who had given Sohail the Book, a few months after he returned from the war. This was how it happened.

It is a Wednesday, Rehana's shopping day, and she is walking along New Market, wondering how high the prices have risen since last week, wondering if she can afford a chicken, a half-leg of mutton, when she sees, across the road, someone familiar. Her own son. She catches the barest glimpse, but she is sure it's him. He is getting down from a rickshaw, and she lifts her hand, is about to call out, but he looks beyond her, his face changing. He crosses the road, approaching her but not seeing her, and now he is both her son and not her son, as he walks directly past her. She turns to see what he sees: a man in another rickshaw. He approaches the man, says not a word, hauls him out of the rickshaw and punches him in the face. Three times, three punches. Then he turns and walks towards her, the muscles in his back rippling, telling her he knows this man, that this man has done terrible things, that he has seen these terrible things, and she knows now that these are the visions that have him pacing the hallway at night, the ones that leave his pillows wet and his mouth frozen stiffly, even as he tries to smile and act as if everything has gone back to normal.

And, not knowing what else to do, because he has asked her never to speak about it, she gives him the Holy Book. The book has helped her through so many difficult times, times she could not imagine surviving. But he shakes his head, because he has come to believe that the Book was part of the problem, before the war, before Bangladesh. Because people were attached to the Book, or their idea of the Book, more than to each other, or to their neighbours, or to their country. They had called themselves revolutionaries, and believed that faith was beneath them, a consolation for simpler, lower minds. Sohail turns his face from the Book and waves his mother away.

This wounds her, because she too has her memories, of her son, a boy who would not dismiss his mother, who would not punch a stranger in the street. That her son has seen, and committed, acts of violence, is not surprising to her – but she cannot account for the lingering of his passions so long after the end of the battle.

Sohail rejects the Book. He lets it gather dust on his desk, and then he shelves it away high, where its spine is not in his sight.

She decides to read to him. You don't have to listen, she says, just sit with me.

This was how it began. It hurt her to remember this, because everything that happened afterwards could be traced to Sohail's first steps towards God, beginning with the Book that she gave him, that gathered dust on his bookshelf, that she prised from between Neruda and Ghalib, that she read aloud while he ate his breakfast, that he was unable to resist, that he began to memorise, then understand, then love, that finally fell into his hands as he learned to read, that wove itself into his heart – that led to revelation and his conversion, the alchemy of which none of his loved ones could trace to a single moment, a single gesture.

1984

June

Several months after Chottu and Saima's party, Joy telephoned with another invitation. 'The party wasn't really your cup of tea, was it?'

'Was it yours?' She was glad to hear his voice. 'Why haven't you rung?'

He laughed. 'I was waiting for the right opportunity and it has just come up.'

'Oh? What's that? Not another evening of whisky and dancing?'

'Maya-bee, your heart is as hard as sugar. No, this is something totally different – I thought you might like to see the other side.'

'The other side of what?'

'People who care about the same things you do.'

'No, thanks. I already did. You remember Aditi – I met her

at the party? She took me to her newspaper office. The editor is giving me a column.'

'Shafaat?'

'You know him?'

'Everyone knows him.'

She didn't like the way he said *everyone*. She was about to tell him so when he said, 'I'm talking about real revolutionaries. Look, you won't regret it – I'll pick you up at three.' Before she could reply, he hung up. Real revolutionaries. He knew she wouldn't be able to resist that, even if it was only a joke. Everyone knew there weren't any real revolutionaries left, not in Dhaka, not in the world. It was 1984 after all.

They drove to Kolabagan. The woman who answered the door introduced herself as Mohona. 'Come with me,' she said, leading them down an unlit corridor that smelled of old books and damp. The corridor opened into a drawing room with large windows on one side. Money plants climbed up the grilles and fingered the ceiling. There were a handful of people there already, seated in a loose circle. It was a long time since Maya had been to a meeting, but the scene was familiar: the women in plain cotton saris, the sparse jute furniture, the smell of paper and incense. She drifted away from Joy and sat down beside a man in a uniform.

'Hello, I'm Sheherezade,' she said, using her formal name.

'Lieutenant Sarkar,' he replied, nodding. 'You have been to the meeting before?'

'No, my first time.'

'Jahanara Imam is coming today.'

Maya's eyes widened. 'Really?' Jahanara Imam had written a book about losing her son in the war. Everyone had read it; they called her Shaheed Janani, *Mother of Martyrs*. Joy was right about bringing her here. Maybe she could even write about it for the newspaper. She settled into her seat and pulled out her notebook. Soon the room filled up; when the chairs ran out, people leaned against the wall or crouched on the floor. 'That's her,' the army man said, pointing to an elderly woman who had just taken her seat.

The meeting was called to order by Mohona. She welcomed everyone, including, with a nod to Maya, people who were joining them for the first time. Joy found a seat in the row behind her, tapped her on the shoulder. 'What did I say?'

Jahanara Imam rose. Tiny, in a white cotton sari, she looked insubstantial, like a froth of smoke. Her voice, however, was firm, her words direct. 'It has been thirteen years,' she began, 'but I know that, like me, you have not forgotten. It has been thirteen years and our war is not over. Perhaps we gained our freedom, perhaps you can hold your head high and say you have a country, your country. But what sort of country allows the men who betrayed it, the men who committed murder, to run free, to live as the neighbours of the women they have widowed, the young girls they have raped?'

She told the story of Ghulam Azam, whose thugs had collaborated with the Pakistan Army, led them to guerrilla hideouts, helped them burn villages. Not only was he acquitted of any wrongdoing, but he was being considered for Bangladeshi citizenship.

Maya had always prided herself on remembering exactly who she had been before the war broke out. She remembered her politics, the promises she had made to herself about the country. She remembered the sight of dead men with their hands tied behind their backs, their faces lapped with blood, and she remembered every day she had worked in the camps, scooping bullets out of men with nothing but a spoon and a hunter's knife.

She remembered everything she had done and who she had been and who she had vowed to remain. But now, listening to this woman, she felt herself pulled and folded back into another body, one that hadn't been lonely all these months and years,

96

one that hadn't left home and trodden carelessly around the past decade, one that could shore up the memories of that time and get angry when the moment came for anger.

She clapped along with the others, between Jahanara Imam's sentences. The room was growing hot now, bright sunlight filtering through the thicket of money plants. Someone turned up the ceiling fan, and the women readjusted themselves as the folds of their saris flapped open. Maya held down the pages of her notebook.

When Jahanara Imam was finished, Mohona stood up again. 'How many of you have lost a loved one to the war?'

Hands went up. Maya's too.

'Madam,' said a man in a grey suit, 'I lost my father and mother. They went to the university and shot the professors.' From the back of the room, another voice added, 'My relatives lived in Old Dhaka. They killed my uncle, my grandfather.'

More people spoke up, announcing the date of their loss, the circumstances. Caught in the crossfire. Shot by the army on a raid in their village. Tortured to death at the cantonment.

The confessions made Maya grip the underside of her seat. Would they each have to get up and confess who they had lost, exactly what they had done, in the war? She found herself shivering under the whirr of the fan. A woman was talking about documenting all the atrocities of the war. 'We should make a list,' she was saying, 'and identify all the killers.'

Maya found herself raising her hand. Mohona pointed to her. 'I think – I believe – that the first thing we must do is admit our own faults, our own sins. So much happened during the war – we were not just victims.'

The room suddenly grew quiet.

Lieutenant Sarkar turned to her and said gently, 'You are speaking to a room full of wounded souls, my dear.'

She could hear people breathing quietly, waiting for the awkward moment to pass. Finally Mohona stood up. 'We all have our private grief. But we are here to talk about the collaborators. Let us focus on the task at hand. If we document the atrocities in a systematic manner, Ghulam Azam will surely be denied permission to stay in Bangladesh.'

The voices rose again, and Maya was left with a sharp pain under her ribs. She thought of her own casualties of war, the reason she had raised her hand. But there were also the things that she had done, which returned to her now, the memories clear and sharp. She turned to Joy. 'I have to go,' she whispered.

'Wait – it's almost finished. Another ten minutes.'

She couldn't wait. She stood up, stepping over Lieutenant Sarkar's knees. At the end of the row she overturned someone's teacup, and the clattering made the room quiet again. 'Excuse me,' she mumbled, and fled. She emerged into the fading afternoon, a busy road with a succession of trucks lumbering by. In the distance was a jumble of tin shacks, and when she grew near she saw that it stretched far beyond the horizon, row after row of frail-looking structures, pasted together with bits of paper, cinema posters and calendars and newspaper and jute and cow dung. She found an overturned crate and sat down to face it.

'I'm not getting it right.' It was Joy. He crouched beside her.

'You're not my tour guide.'

'But you're back after so long, I don't want you to get the wrong impression.'

'I could show you a few things too, you know.'

'Like what?'

'Look over there. You want to know the most painful thing about living in that slum? If you're a woman?'

'What?'

'Drinking water.'

'Why, because the water is dirty?'

'That too, but it's not just that. See, if you are a woman and you live in that slum, you wake up in the middle of the night while it's still dark, and you make your way to the edge of the shanties, and you lift up your sari and squat over the open drain. And then you tiptoe back into bed with your husband, and for the rest of the day, you wait, you wait and wait until it gets dark, your stomach feels like it's full of needles, your insides are burning, but you can't do anything, no, you can't, you have to wait until it gets dark and everyone else has gone to sleep so you can have your one solitary piss of the day.'

His head was bowed, and she saw his hand moving towards her hand and she moved her hand away, because she didn't want him to think that his gesture was a way of resolving this, the cruelty of the country, the collaborators that ran free and never went to jail for murder and rape – because there were things that could not be erased with the squeeze of a hand, memories and sins and conditions of humanity.

She turned to him. 'I'm not made to sit in meetings.'

'You shouldn't. You argue too much.'

She laughed. 'That's true.' She leaned against him. 'Find me a rickshaw.'

'Let me take you – make use of my skills as a taxi-driver.'

*

She had just taught Zaid the numbers in English, one through ten, and he was repeating them aloud, his voice high and proud, when the phone rang. Maya looked at her watch – four o'clock, must be for the girl upstairs, though she was nowhere in sight. She picked up. 'Hello?'

The line was sandy. 'Hello?' It was a woman. 'Maya?'

Nazia. 'Nazia?' Her heart flew to her throat.

'Maya Apa,' she said, addressing her formally. 'Are you well?'

'Yes, I am well.'

'And your mother?'

'She is well also. And how are your children?'

99

Maya heard the sound of Nazia clearing her throat. 'I got your letter – your letters. Both of them.'

She tried to remember what she had written. The long, meandering explanations, the apologies. 'There was much to say.'

Nazia blew into the receiver. 'I'm sorry you had to go, like that.'

'It was my fault. I should never have let you swim in the pond.'

A pause. 'I'm going home today, doctor says.'

All this time she had been at the hospital. 'The children will be so glad to see you.'

'I have to go now.'

'All right,' Maya said. For some reason she wanted to add, God Bless You, but before she could say anything the line went dead. She pressed several times on the receiver, but there was only the sandy sound, not even a dial tone.

*

'Zaid, what do you know about your grandfather?'

'He died.'

'That's right. Did you know he had your chin?'

She was making it up. 'Really?'

She placed her thumb in the dent of his chin. 'Yes, it was yours exactly.'

They took a rickshaw to the graveyard. He was wearing his sandals today, and a clean kurta that smelled of industrial soap. He could almost sound out the words on the gravestone: MUHAMMAD IQBAL HAQUE.

'Did you know', Maya said, 'I was the same age as you when my father died?'

'Did you cry?'

'No, I didn't cry. I didn't know how sad I should be.'

'Me too.'

She knew. She had watched him talking about his mother, putting all his optimism in his recollections of her – the Ludo board, the promises about going to school. 'She was very beautiful, your ammoo,' Maya said. 'She had grey eyes, like yours.'

He circled the grave, tapping his hand on the gravestone as he passed.

'Do you want to say something to your mother, Zaid?'

'This isn't her.'

'Yes, but she can hear you. What do you want to say to her?'

He stopped, crouched. 'Ammoo,' he said, 'I would like a cycle.' Then he cupped his hands, as he had been taught, and recited the Kalma.

That night, in her sleep, she stretched her feet to the edge of the bed and found herself in contact with something warm. Sitting upright, she reached with her fingers. A sleeping form, breathing in and out. She must be dreaming. She switched on the light. The boy, his hand fanned over his face, did not stir.

She draped the blanket over him and he shifted, pulling it up over his head. In the garden, the trees were licked by moonlight.

Later, as the room coloured, she pulled him into the mosquito net and curled around him, feeling his shoulders loosening, his feet drifting towards her.

*

On the last day of June, when the searing heat of spring was about to move aside for the monsoon, Rehana persuaded Maya out of the house and stood her in front of the newest, grandest building in the city.

'I hate it,' she said, shielding her eyes. 'It's hideous.'

'Come on, beta, don't be so harsh.'

'Hideous.' She swivelled her head around, trying to take in

the whole building, making sure she didn't miss any of it. 'Is that water?'

'Yes, it's built on a pool of water, like a shapla flower floating in the river.'

'Why is it so big?'

'Doesn't matter, it's our parliament now. That very nice American chap built it.'

'Well, I don't like it,' she said, moving forward nonetheless, climbing the wide steps that led up to the building. 'Where's the entrance?'

'I don't know. We're not supposed to go inside; just admire it from here.'

They turned their backs to the building and took in the view of the grounds. The lawn stretched out on either side, reaching Sher-e Bangla Nagar to the east, Mirpur Road to the west. It was impressive, there was no denying that. Already the trees ringing the compound looked ancient. Dotted around the gardens, she saw couples holding hands, trying to catch the shade of a tree. On a patch of grass near the main road, a phuchka-vendor had set up his cart. He waved, beckoning. 'Hungry, Ma?' Maya said.

They settled into the crude wooden chairs and ordered two plates. The sun was starting its rapid descent, sending horizontal ribbons of light across the wide carpet of green that led up to the building. Suddenly she wanted to be somewhere else; her eye ached for the groves of Rajshahi, for her little brick house. She wondered if Nazia would call her again, imagined the trouble it would be for her to pay the postman, get him to dial the number. 'That little village was like home,' she said suddenly, her eye lingering on the building, resisting its grey curves, the way it floated, solid yet delicate, on its American-made lake.

'It will be hard to leave behind,' her mother said. I can still go back, Maya thought. I can pack up again and march out the door and become a country doctor again.

The phuchkas arrived, a dozen shells, each filled with its chickpea and potato mixture. Maya poured in the tamarind water and popped one into her mouth. Immediately her eyes began to water. 'Mmm,' she said, smiling.

'Ay,' Rehana said, 'he's put too much chilli.' She waved at the phuchka-man.

'No, Ammoo, leave it, they're perfect,' Maya said, wiping her streaming eyes. 'Seriously. Perfect.' Her mother passed her a handkerchief. 'I'd forgotten how yummy they were.' A steady procession of cars drove past the wide avenue in front of the parliament compound. In between bites of phuchka, Maya heard car horns, and the tinkle of rickshaw-bells as they turned corners or changed lanes, and, every few minutes, the Dhanmondi–Gazipur bus, tilted to one side as the passengers hung, Tarzan-like, to the railings.

Now, with the pastry about to collapse in her mouth, and sunlight beaming sideways, pink and orange, against her mother's cheek, she suddenly remembered all the times she had been loved. It was like that with her mother – memory upon memory stacked together like the feathers in a wild bird, there to keep her warm, or when she needed to, fly. She was the wings of her, the very wings.

'The road is so busy,' Maya said, sipping the tea they had been brought by the phuchka-man.

Her mother nodded. 'Everything is speeding up. Only thirteen years since independence and you can't recognise anything.'

Thirteen. Her broken wishbone of a country was thirteen years old. Didn't sound like very long, but in that time the nation had rolled and unrolled tanks from its streets. It had had leaders elected and ordained. It had murdered two presidents. In its infancy, it had started cannibalising itself, killing the tribals in the south, drowning villages for dams, razing the ancient trees of Modhupur Forest. A fast-acting country: quick to anger, quick to self-destruct.

The phuchkas were finished, the tea cooling in their cups. Maya didn't want the day to end. 'I know,' she said, 'let's go to New Market. I want to buy you a sari.'

'Why?'

'Because I've missed seven of your birthdays, and seven Eid days – fourteen, if you count both Eids.' A sari, she realised as she said it, would never add up to that many missed days. But she liked the thought of returning to their favourite shops in New Market, haggling with the sari-vendors who would order cold drinks and model their wares on the hips of their young sons.

'Okay,' Rehana said, 'let's go.'

The rickshaw-puller turned on Mirpur Road, crossed its length, past Gawsia and Chandni Chawk. Just as he was about to make the turn into the market, a crowd emerged from Fuller Road, a wall of people marching towards them, holding up a large painted banner.

'It's the Chattro League,' Maya said, recognising their logo from her university days. The marchers advanced slowly, filling the area in front of the New Market gate. Their megaphones blared. She saw herself multiplied. 'What do they want?'

Their voices were drowned out by the chanting. Something about the vice-chancellor being sacked. And the Dictator's corruption.

A canvas-covered truck arrived, and uniformed men spilled out of the open flap at the back. The marchers took a step back, still holding the banner in an uneven line. A man behind the megaphone said, 'We are here in peace. We want to be heard.'

The uniformed men held up their shields and their lathis.

'Chattro League demands—'

As they charged, the policemen looked like angry house-wives. They smashed their rolling pins on the backs of the front line. The banner collapsed, falling to the ground and getting tangled in the legs of the protesters. The marchers scattered, but the police chased them down, beating hard on their backs, until they crumpled, one by one, and were dragged by their armpits into the waiting truck.

Maya saw a boy with his hands around his head, blood leaking from between his fingers. The rickshaw-wallah tried to turn around, but there were too many cars behind them, and the police vans were blocking the road ahead. 'Forgive me but you'll have to walk,' he said, refusing to take his fare. 'Hurry, if you don't go now you'll get stuck here for hours.'

They followed the footpath and headed west, away from New Market. Behind them, clouds of teargas billowed upwards. Maya grabbed her mother's elbow. 'Quickly, Ammoo.' They broke into a jog, turned off Mirpur Road and began to cross the bridge. They turned a corner and the side streets were suddenly quiet, no sign of the police. Maya turned around and hugged Ammoo, out of breath. Tears clogged her throat.

'You used to look like that,' Rehana said, reading her thoughts.

She laughed, wiping her eyes. 'Like what? Youthful and carefree?'

'Like you were only alive to be on the streets.'

They returned to the bungalow. At six o'clock Maya switched on the news. The newsreader, her sari pinned tightly to her shoulder, began narrating the day's events. The Dictator had announced he would build a strong Bangladesh. The finance minister announced they would not trade with India on unfavourable terms. There was no mention of the protests, the arrests or the beatings.

'What a bullshit newsreader. All that lipstick and she can't tell the truth. I don't know why you keep this stupid television here.' Maya slammed her palm against the dial.

'Leave that on,' Ammoo said. She was ironing a sari, leaning heavily on the crumpled border.

'I can't believe you're falling for this propaganda.'

Rehana stood the iron upright and straightened her back. 'Who do you think talked to me all day long? Before you came back? Nobody. Sometimes I used to ask Sufia to sing a village song while she was dusting, just so I knew there was someone else here. I bought the TV because otherwise it's so quiet I can hear the rats trying to get into the house. So don't you tell me to switch it off. I'll have it if I want to.' And she, in turn, slammed a palm on the dial, making the images jump on to the screen, then disappear. She fiddled with the antenna. 'Damn,' she said, while the picture flickered in and out. Finally she found the signal and, with the iron still plugged into its socket, leaned against the sofa and listened to the weather report.

'I don't want to go back,' Maya said. And there it was. Easy as one sentence. Maya felt herself warming with relief. She wouldn't stop sending letters to Rajshahi, and maybe, once the seasons turned and the memory of that day receded, she would go back for a visit. Check up on the postman's daughter, hand out a few packets of antibiotics. But she would stop imagining it was possible to return; she would stay here, begin some kind of life with what was left. She would not forget Nazia; Nazia's story, her daring to swim in the pond and the lashes with which she paid for such bravery, would be chronicled. It would be there in black and white; people would read it and they would know that their freedom was as thin as the skin around Nazia's ankles. But she would stay here, with her mother, the Dictator at their doorstep, the little boy under her wing.

There were tears in Ammoo's eyes. 'It's your house,' she said. 'Stay as long as you like.' They embraced again, and then the news programme ended, and it was time for *Dallas*. Maya promised to watch if Ammoo would fill her in on the plot. 'All right,' she said, 'but it's going to take a while, it's very complicated.'

As Ammoo put up her feet on the coffee table, Maya noticed a slight swelling around her midriff. 'What's this?' she said, patting her mother's stomach.

'It's nothing,' Rehana said, batting Maya's hand away.

'Let me see.'

'Leave it alone, beta. I'm just getting fat.' And she bent towards the television again, turning up the volume.

That night, Maya lay awake and thought of Sohail. When she was six and Sohail eight, they were sent away to live with their aunt and uncle in Lahore. Their father had died not long before, and everyone thought it would be better if they went away for a while to give their mother a chance to recover, build a new life for herself. There was talk of another marriage, more children. They would only be in the way.

Ammoo did not agree. There was a judge, and a court case, which she lost.

They lived in Lahore for two years with their father's brother, Faiz, and his wife, Parveen. An enormous house. She and Sohail had an ayah who slept on the verandah outside their room. If they needed something, they were told to ring the bell beside the light switch.

On some nights Parveen would slip into Maya's bed and put her hand gently on her forehead, believing she was asleep. Maya would hear her sigh deeply, her breath medicinal and light, and she would drift off to the sound of Parveen's gentle snoring.

Her memories of those two years were full of Sohail. Sohail holding her hand on the aeroplane. Sohail bending down and retying her shoelaces. Sohail's handkerchief against her lashes. Sohail instructing her to stay silent at school until she knew enough Urdu. Sohail breaking her rootis into small pieces and stacking them up, just the way she liked.

He was father and mother and bhaiya to her. Her closest human. Her only friend.

When they returned to Dhaka, a very large two-storey building stood where half of the garden had once been. Ammoo took them on a tour, their shoes clattering against the bare cement floors. From the upstairs verandah, which wrapped around the building like a vine, you could see the flat roof of their shabby little bungalow, rainwater gathering in mossy pools, whitewash greying.

They couldn't live in it. Ammoo was going to rent it out and buy them things with the money. It was her two-storeyed bit of insurance, that house. She whispered a prayer every time she stepped into it; she dusted and redusted the banisters; she stretched her hand up, touching the frame of the front door. And she made them call it Shona, as though it were built of solid gold.

Book Two

Every soul shall taste death

1984

July

'It's a good thing you're staying,' Ammoo said; 'you'll be here for the surgery.'

Maya was only half listening, her hands twisted into a mound of warm dough. Ammoo was teaching her to make parathas, the trick of which, she said, was that the water should be boiling hot when mixed with the flour. She thought her mother was telling her she would be here for so-and-so's wedding, or daughter's naming ceremony. Then she heard it. 'Surgery?'

'You were right. I went to see the doctor. I have a tumour.' She patted her stomach. 'In my uterus. They have to take it out.'

Maya could see it now, protruding lightly from her middle. And she hadn't been the one to diagnose it. Her hands moved in the dough, but Ammoo shook her head. 'Parathas first, then you can doctor me.'

'How long have you known?'

'Not long.'

Maya began to knead, hard and furious, reaching into the elastic warmth of flour, water. 'Enough, Maya,' Ammoo said; 'now divide it. Put some flour on your hands, like this.' She pulled off a section, rolled it between her palms, fingers extended like a dancer's, and passed her a perfect sphere.

'More flour,' she said, and handed Maya the rolling pin.

'You didn't tell me.' She rolled, pressed, turned the disc, rolled again.

Rehana wiped the flour from her hands. 'I was going to tell you, I just didn't want you to worry unnecessarily.'

'Why would you do that, why would you keep this a secret?'

She came up behind Maya, guiding her hands on the rolling pin. 'You're making it square,' she said. 'I told you, I didn't mean to. And they said it isn't anything serious.'

The dreams Maya had had in Rajshahi, the blade of premonition when the postman delivered the telegram, were coming true. She shrugged off the sensation that it had somehow been ordained, and that Ammoo would die now, just as she had dreamed, wrapped in a shroud of white and sent into the ground with prayers and fistfuls of mud. The air thickened in her chest. Stop, she told herself. You're a doctor, focus on what you can do. Tumours in the uterus were the best kind of tumour; they lay in the womb like a seed, and they grew within it, but the uterus could easily be disposed of. Ammoo didn't need it any more. That is what they would do. They would perform a hysterectomy, and the whole thing would be over. Finished.

She immediately called her old professor Dr Sattar, scratching at a loose bit of plaster on the wall as she waited for the medical college switchboard to connect her. He was the best surgeon at the hospital; people waited months for his steady hands to cut into them. He came on the line, irritated, and she introduced herself formally, reminding him of the year she had enrolled at the medical college ('Sir, it was just after the war, sir . . .'). There was no softening, no note of recognition, but he asked for details of Ammoo's tumour, its location and size. Maya read from the report Ammoo had given her. And then he agreed to see her, to do an X-ray and decide the next course of action. Yes, he said, a hysterectomy was probably called for. He didn't say anything about the risks, or the complications, or about her chances; he just treated it like any other thing, something to put in his diary. Call my secretary, he said, make an appointment. That's what she liked about surgeons, they didn't stand on ceremony.

*

The day before the surgery, Rehana's friend Mrs Rahman appeared with a plate of shemai, her five-year-old grandson trailing behind her.

'I've got Surjo for a week,' she said, clamping her hand around the wrist of the wriggling boy. 'Neleema and her husband have gone to Shillong.' She smiled broadly. The boy was sullen and immediately wanted to tear the heads off the lilies.

'Don't touch that,' Maya said, wondering what her mother would say if she returned from the hospital to find a shorn flowerbed.

Rehana appeared a few moments later wearing a sari that Maya had always liked, a moss-green cotton with a pink paisley border. She had joked once that she wanted Ammoo to bequeath the sari to her, and she remembered this now as she positioned her mother in a garden chair, with a cushion at her back.

'It's nothing,' Rehana said to her friend. The boy came charging towards them, complaining he had been bitten by a fire ant. 'Poor dear,' Mrs Rahman said, kissing the spot on his arm where a tiny red welt had appeared. He wandered off, wielding a stick against the insects, and Rehana continued, 'There's nothing to worry about, please don't make a fuss.'

Mrs Rahman nodded. 'It's up to Him. What's written on your forehead is already written.'

Maya hated, more than anything, the forehead explanation of life. She was about to say something but she remembered how just that morning, when a neighbour had sent a piece of paper that she claimed would shrink the tumour because the Saint of Eight Ropes had blown on it, her mother had pleaded with her to keep her opinions to herself.

'How are Neleema and her husband?' Rehana asked.

'Yes, they are well. She's expecting.'

'Oh, Alhamdulillah.'

Mrs Rahman paused, guilty at having imparted this piece of good news.

Maya had left Zaid in the kitchen, gnawing on a chicken leg. She found him still eating, the yellow gravy stuck to his palms and the corners of his mouth. 'Always hungry, poor child,' Sufia whispered.

'Berry, berry good,' he said, tilting his head from side to side, crunching on a piece of chicken bone.

'Come with me,' Maya said, pulling him to the outside tap. She scrubbed his hands with soap as he looked on. 'When was the last time you ate?' she said. She'd been neglecting him. Between the doctor's visits and the cold feeling that Ammoo's illness was her fault, she had hardly seen him. She moved up to his wrists, scrubbing now with a small washcloth, digging at the dirt that had ploughed into the creases of his hand. She rolled up his sleeve and stopped, looking at the small round scars that disappeared into his kurta. She had seen them somewhere before. Worms? She patted his stomach, taut from having just eaten, then drew him close. When he wrapped his arms around her, she caught the smell of sick.

'Did you vomit today?'

'No.'

She wasn't sure if he was telling the truth. 'Bring down your clothes,' she said. 'Sufia will wash them.'

He nodded.

'And what about ABC, do you remember any of it? A for?'

The blood rushed to his cheeks. 'Apple,' he said, unrolling his sleeves and shaking out his legs. 'I have to go.'

'Don't you want to say goodbye to Dadu? She's going to the hospital.'

His eyes widened. 'Is she going to be dead?'

'No, she's not. But she'll be gone for a few days, so come and say goodbye.'

In the garden, Sufia was serving tea to Mrs Rahman. Surjo was darting out from behind the mango tree, balling his hands together and pointing at his grandmother. 'Dishoom Dishoom!'

Mrs Rahman feigned mortal injury.

Zaid's palm grew damp in Maya's. 'Who's that?'

'Mrs Rahman's grandson. Do you want to play with him?'

'No.'

'Don't worry, he's much smaller than you.'

'I don't want to.' He made to turn around, but Mrs Rahman had already spotted him. 'Is that Sohail's boy?'

'Yes,' Rehana replied, quickly scanning Zaid. At least his clothes weren't torn.

'Come here,' Mrs Rahman called, and when she saw him hesitating, holding Maya's hand in front of his face, she said, 'I'll give you a Mimi – come here.'

Zaid stopped for a moment, then inched closer, releasing Maya's hand.

'Come here.' Rehana had given her friend a few sketchy details about Sohail, but Mrs Rahman couldn't stop the shock from passing briefly across her face. Zaid was holding out his hand now, and Mrs Rahman was stroking his capped head. She fumbled in her bag for the promised Mimi chocolate.

'That's mine!' The grandson crawled, commando-style, towards them.

'Hold on, darling boy, I think there's enough for both of you.' She brandished the small bar of chocolate with the photograph of an orange on its wrapper, breaking it in two and offering half to each.

'It's mine.' Surjo stood up and grabbed both halves, stuffing one aggressively into his mouth.

'Be a good boy now,' she said. 'Don't you want to share? No? I'll buy you another one on the way home. I'll buy you two. Now give the chocolate to the little boy. There's a jaanoo. Yes, what a little angel you are.'

Surjo passed the half-bar of chocolate to Zaid, smearing it against his palm. Zaid gazed at it for a moment as it softened against his hand. Then he turned around, holding the chocolate as far from his body as he could, and walked slowly, one foot in front of the other.

'Khoda Hafez,' Rehana called out. 'I shall see you again very soon.' Zaid turned his head towards her and nodded once, then continued his slow tread until he reached the edge of the lawn, where he stopped, raised his hand to his mouth and lapped delicately at the treasure on his palm.

*

The copy of *Rise Bangladesh!* came through the gate and landed on the porch. Shafaat had published her article on the third page, next to a long essay about the military–industrial complex, and opposite an advertisement celebrating the anniversary of the socialist revolution in Bulgaria. 'Confessions of a Country Doctor', by S. M. Haque. She had thought of choosing a more glamorous penname, but nothing had sprung to mind. Already the time before Ammoo's illness seemed a long way away. She had started with Nazia's story; now she wondered where to go next. Being here in

Dhaka, living in the bungalow, had breached levees she had carefully constructed of what she remembered about the past, about her brother, the war. She remembered the meeting with Jahanara Imam, the way she had stormed out. And why. And the projector in the garden shed. *I once knew a girl called Piya.*

*

Zaid had given her lice. In the hospital, Rehana parted Maya's hair into sections, seaming each one with kerosene, mining her scalp for the white lice eggs.

'Ammoo, stop now, I can get Sufia to do it later. You need to get ready for the surgery.'

Sufia was sobbing heavily in the corner. 'What will I do if you die?' she wailed in Rehana's direction. 'Who will look after me?'

Behind her back, Maya could feel her mother sighing. 'I won't be dead for a long time. You'll be dead before me, I'm sure.' Having oiled and thoroughly picked through Maya's hair, she began to run a thin-toothed comb through it.

'This one', Sufia said, pointing at Maya, 'doesn't even like me. She'd have me on the street in half a second.'

'She only looks mean,' Rehana said, combing Maya's hair into a towel. 'Inside she's as soft as rice pudding. Maya, you have an infestation. Look.'

Maya turned around and saw a smattering of little black insects nestled on the towel. Ammoo began squeezing each one between her thumbnails.

'Disgusting,' Maya said. 'I can't believe they grew so fast.'

'It's because you didn't take care of it straight away.'

'That kid. I'm going to thrash him.'

Rehana reached over, pulled Maya's face into her hands. 'Don't ever say that,' she said, 'don't say it. Ever.'

'I'm sorry, Ma, I just – sometimes I just don't know what to do with him.' That morning she had made him promise to practise his lessons, but he had insisted she take him to the graveyard, so he could ask his mother again about the bicycle. And he had irritated her on the way back, demanding to go to school, a proper school. But don't you like Maya-school? she teased, and he shook his head. It's no good, he said. No good.

'She hasn't said a word to me since she arrived,' Sufia said, blowing her nose.

Rehana had finished combing and braiding Maya's hair. 'It's a routine operation,' Maya said, standing up and straightening her kameez. 'She'll be fine.'

'Maya, I don't think she knows what a routine operation is.'

'Oh, for God's sake,' Maya said. She stepped out of the room and paced the corridor until she found what she was looking for: a medical student. 'Excuse me,' she said, 'may I borrow that?' And she pulled the stethoscope from around his neck before he could protest. 'I'll give it back,' she said, returning to Ammoo's bedside. 'Sufia, come over here.'

Sufia approached tentatively. Maya put the chestpiece of the stethoscope on Ammoo and let Sufia listen. 'You hear this? It's her heart.'

Sufia's eyes widened. 'Strong.'

'Strong as an ox,' Rehana said; 'they can't kill me.'

'The surgery will take two, three hours at the most,' Maya said, repeating the sentences she'd been telling herself over and over again. 'Dr Sattar is one of the best surgeons in the country.'

Rehana put her hand, IV-threaded, on her hand. 'Say Aytul Kursi with me.'

Maya turned away from her, facing the doorway of the cubicle; the thin curtains parted to reveal the scene in the corridor, the nurses walking purposefully, holding metal kidney dishes, bags of blood and saline. She was suddenly afraid for her mother, and the feeling she'd had under the jackfruit tree in Rajshahi came flooding back to her – all the things that could go wrong, and the nagging sense that it was all her fault, that the tumour had somehow grown out of her mother's loneliness. She wanted to ask Ammoo to cancel the surgery, postpone it to another day, perhaps till winter, when it was cooler and the electricity was less likely to go out; or perhaps until there was a better doctor, a younger man who had just returned from foreign with new techniques, advanced anaesthesiology. And Sufia was right: if her mother died, she could never be the one to replace her – the bougainvillea would die and the fruit would fall from the guava tree, unpicked. And Ammoo was the only person left in the world who still loved her.

All Ammoo wanted was a prayer. Surely she could give her that. She tried to unlock the words, but they were buried deep, and knotted among all the other things. The disappointments, the heartache, the state of the country and the Dictator who said Allah between every other word – all latched on to those words, that Book. Don't worry, she wanted to tell her mother, we don't need Aytul Kursi. We have science. But she couldn't help but remember that every death she had ever witnessed – on the battle-field, at the field hospital, in the wards – had been accompanied by the sound of prayer, the same words embroidering every parting of flesh and spirit.

Dr Sattar pulled the curtain aside and stepped in. A clutch of medical students followed, crowding into the space. 'Is my patient ready?' He picked up the chart at the foot of the bed.

Rehana waved at him, as if from a great distance. 'Dakhtar, you needn't have come yourself.'

Dr Sattar surprised Maya by smiling. 'Nonsense. We take good care of our own, don't we, Dr Haque?'

'Yes, sir,' she replied.

He ordered the students to check Rehana's blood pressure and adjust her IV. They shuffled nervously around him. 'Your brother is waiting outside,' one of them said.

'Brother?' Maya and Rehana spoke in unison. For a moment

Maya thought it might be a distant cousin of her mother's, here from Karachi after receiving the telegram she had sent their relatives about the surgery. Then she knew it must be Sohail.

'Ma,' she said, 'I'll just be back. The nurse will be here if you need anything.'

Sohail was leaning against the balcony railing, his eyes on the mosaic tiling below. The sky was darkening overhead, purple and grey, the air quiet, everything hovering in that moment before the afternoon rain.

'How is Ammoo?' he asked.

'She's fine. You should go in and see her.' Our mother might die and we might be orphans and I might be your last remaining kin. Was he thinking the same thing?

'The surgeon—'

'He's very experienced, don't worry. She'll be all right.' Or she won't. Was he persuaded by the tone she tried to bring to her voice, the doctor's certainty?

He nodded. 'Inshallah.'

'And you, are you well?' She looked him up and down, her eye lingering on the bruise that blossomed on his forehead, pearly and blue-black, from his daily submission to the prayer mat.

'I am well, by the Grace of Allah.' It started to rain, that slanted, sideways rain that reminded Maya of childhood, the smell of wet cement, the two of them rushing to close the windows before the mattresses were soaked. Sohail did not retreat from the edge of the railing, Maya too remained beside him, and now they were both being pelted with rain. His beard took on the sheen of water. He straightened, fixed his gaze on her. Was it tenderness she saw? She struggled to keep her eyes open against the torrent. *It would be too much*, she wanted him to say, *too much to lose our mother now*. But instead he said, 'Zaid tells me you're teaching him the English letters.'

'Yes. Soon he'll be reading *Middlemarch*.'

He laughed. She laughed. The rain stopped as suddenly as it began. She wanted to hug him, and she did, and he returned her embrace, squeezing his arms around her. Rain mixed with tears, salty and warm.

'Nothing bad will happen, Bhaiya,' she said.

'Sister Khadija told me you taught Zaid to play cards.'

'Yes,' she said, 'he's a shark.'

'Sister Khadija is dismayed. Gambling is not allowed.'

Maya stepped back, the shock of his words dipping slowly, painfully into her. 'But it's just a game. Ammoo plays too.'

'You know the difference between Halal and Haram. If you don't, then perhaps Sister Khadija should take over Zaid's education.'

That's not what she had meant. She felt desperation spreading through her. 'Please, no.'

He put his hand on her shoulder, as though she would have trouble understanding otherwise. 'The boy misses his mother, I know that. I should give him more time, but . . .'

She tried to keep the sarcasm out of her voice. 'Your duties?'

He looked wounded, his gaze pointing beyond her, to the small patches of sunshine now visible through the clouds. 'A boy needs to find his way in the world.'

She wasn't sure what he meant, but she wanted to agree with him, to tell him it was all right, that he was doing his best. It couldn't be easy, raising a son. He was laying down the law, she could see that, but he made it appear as if he had no choice, as though there were something natural about the rule he was imposing. She struggled with herself, knowing that if she pushed too hard he might abandon her entirely, that perhaps he was giving her this chance simply because his wife was not here to admonish him, dead before she could pour that last drop of venom into his ear and make him deaf to her for ever. Maya tried to be grateful for this.

'Go in and see Ammoo – she's expecting you.' And she turned around and made her way down the stairs and towards the operating theatre, drying her hair with the end of her sari, the rain still heavy on her cheek.

1972
May

Sohail finds, in the spring after he has returned from the war, that his hands will not stop shaking. He holds his hands to his chest. He wraps them around the teapot. He stands on the threshold of his mother's room. Ma, he wants to say, my hands will not stop shaking. Will you say a prayer and blow on them? Will you twine your fingers through mine and bind them to yours? But he stops. He isn't a child any more; he's a man, a soldier back from the war. He asks himself if he can be right again, if he can be good. After Piya, after the killing.

This is how the war made its way into their house. Sohail, spilling water from his glass, flicking dal over the side of his plate. A vanishing woman. A shake of the hand. A silence between siblings.

He had killed an innocent man. The man was not an enemy, not a soldier. Just someone who had let the wrong word come out of his mouth. There is only one way to be good now. The Book has told him he is good, that it is in his nature to be good. The words have been reclaimed and he swells up with love for the Book. Weeks after Piya has disappeared – leaving only the faint trace of her scent, which he tries to pick up in the kitchen where she had squatted, or the rectangle on the floor where she had spread her sleeping mat – he finds himself climbing the ladder up to the roof and sitting cross-legged under the open sun. It is May, a windless, rainless month, heat tearing through the sky. He sits and reads the words. His mother has given him the Book and he reads the words, refusing to see his friends or celebrate the victory. Dimly, he hears them: time to go back to the university; stop worrying your mother, na, and be happy, yaar, war is over. Time to sell-e-brate.

Most of all he is afraid to talk. Maya is always regarding him hungrily, eager for small scraps of detail. Yesterday he told her about the food at the guerrilla camp, how it had danced on his tongue though it was only a few spoonfuls of rice and dal. Freedom food. She devoured the story, begged him for more. How greedy she is. He wants her to be quiet so she can hear the roar in his head, thinking that if she could hear that roar, the roar of uncertainty and the roar of death, she might understand. But she refuses to be quiet for long enough. She searches his face and then she launches into her latest story, telling him who has returned from the war, who has lost a son, a brother. Worse things have happened to other people.

I have committed murder. If he were to tell his sister about the war, this is what he would have to tell her. She wants stories of heroism. She wants him to tell her that he planted bombs under country bridges and that he got away just before the flame hit the powder, and that the felled bridge cut off the army, and the people of north Tangail or Kushtia or Bogra were saved.

But he has no story of this kind. She grows angrier and

angrier at his silence, and even after his mother has given in to the mornings on the roof, Maya continues to follow him with her eyes, reproach him with a stony silence. Silence for silence. When he asks her about her work at the Women's Rehabilitation Centre, she snaps, what, you don't think women are victims of the war too?

He thinks of all the people who have died – the enemy combatants, and the people he didn't save, and his friend Aref, and all the boys who went to war and were killed. Every day he thinks of them. How very selfish of her to want a piece of that.

Ammoo is not greedy, but she has been worried about him, climbs halfway up the ladder and calls out, it's very hot, Sohail, won't you come down and have something to drink?

On the roof he has assembled a number of things. There is a comb that used to belong to Piya, a shirt that belonged to his friend Aref, killed last summer by the army. And a photograph of his father, taken in front of the Vauxhall. Not handsome – his father had not been handsome – but looking confidently ahead, living the life that was intended for him. And Ammoo's Book.

There has come to you from God a light and a Book most
   lucid.
With it, God guides him who conforms to his good pleasure
   to the paths of tranquillity;
He shall lead them from the fields of darkness to the light,
   by his leave,
And he shall guide them to a straight path.

The book believes he is good. He begins to read.

He comes to Maya one day and tries to tell her. He says it is the greatest thing that has ever happened to him. He has found something, something that explains everything. Does she want to know what it is? Isn't she curious? He is pale and the skin is stretched tight over his face, and she sees that death hovers inside him, the death to which he had come so close in the war, he and death in a tight corridor. Now it is like a bruise that won't heal, and he is pressing his face close to hers, and she sees that whatever it is that he is telling her about is what stops the bruise from spreading from his cheek to his bones and from his bones to his blood. It is a dam, like the one they are building in Rangamati that will hold its water like a giant cupped hand and power the fields; it holds him together, it lights him up.

At that moment Maya makes a decision, one that she will come to regret many times in the years that follow. She sees in his bright, water-lined eyes that he is telling the truth. She sees that he fell into the abyss and that this Book is what brought him to the surface and allowed him to breathe. She sees too, in herself, the need for such a rescue, such a buoy, such a truth. But because it has suddenly become clear to her that religion, its open fragrance and cloudless stretches of infinity, may in fact be what he is claiming it is, an essential human need, hers as much as his, and because she feels the twinge of his yearning, turning like a leaf in her heart, she decides, at that moment, that it cannot be. She will not become one of those people who buckle under the force of a great event and allow it to change the metre of who they are.

And neither will Sohail. She will not let him. She believes – oh, how foolish she is, how arrogant – she believes she has a say. She believes she can do something to prevent it. She believes her will is greater than the leaf in her heart and the leaf in her brother's heart.

He approaches her. 'I've been praying.'

'For what?' She is reading the *Observer*.

'Not for anything. Just praying.'

'Please, Bhaiya,' she says, 'don't start talking religious

mumbo-jumbo, we won't recognise you any more.' She turns her attention away, folding her newspaper to the classified ads.

'But that is what prayer is. It is the abandonment of all other thoughts, all other pursuits.'

She looks at him then, and he sees her searching for the joke.

'I'm serious,' he says, answering the question she is too stunned to ask. He pauses, levelling his thoughts before replying. Outside, a man is shouting on the street and banging on what sounds like a cooking pot. 'Allah, Allah, Allah. Give to the poor, give to the poor.'

'It doesn't matter what brings us to God; it only matters that it does.'

'Are you quoting from some mullah now?'

'No, Maya, I am telling the truth.'

'So this has nothing to do with Piya, with the war. Did something else happen? Did you do something?'

She is close, too close. 'I told you, it doesn't matter.'

'Of course it matters. How can you accept the cure without considering the disease?'

'Is it your opinion that I am ill?'

The beggar's voice grows louder. 'God forgives you,' he cries. 'God forgives you.'

The window behind Maya is illuminated with the gold tones of morning. The light spills across her back, and, overflowing, falls into his eyes. He can see little of her face, only the orb of her hair.

'I've been reading about it,' she says; 'it's called shell shock.'

A splinter of anger enters his voice when he replies. 'You're not listening to me. I'm not ill. Maybe, yes, after the war, it is always difficult.'

'So it has just come out of that, that's what I'm trying to tell you.'

'But even if one thing has led to another, I can only be grateful.'

Now it is her turn to be angry. 'You remember, don't you, what they did to us in the name of God?'

'Just because it was usurped for evil ends doesn't make it a bad thing. That is the mistake I made.'

'Mistake? You think it was all a mistake?'

He shifts his gaze away from her, unsure how to reply. It's not that he wishes there hadn't been a war, or that he hadn't joined the fighting. But his life wasn't for that, it was for something else. How can he explain this to her? That there was a reason for his living while so many others had died. He longs for her to know, to know something of what it was like, longs for her to have a heart as heavy as his, a heart that needs to wrap itself around a certainty, a path.

Maya is gulping down her tea, and making to leave the table. 'I can't believe it,' she says, 'after everything, you do this.'

Rehana comes upon them at this very moment, carrying a bowl of semolina halwa she has reheated on the stove. She sees Sohail pointing to the window behind Maya.

'There's someone there,' he says.

They look. The man is bare-chested and unadorned except for his long and elaborately knotted hair, which hangs down past his shoulders. He taps on the window. 'God forgives you,' he says. 'God is merciful.'

They all stare at each other for a moment, and then Maya says, 'What does your book tell you to do about this man, Bhaiya?'

Sohail fishes in his pockets and pulls out a folded note. The man cups his hands as the window is opened and the note slips through.

'That's it? That's all you're doing? Don't you want to know how that man came to be here?'

'Why don't you ask him yourself?'

'I'm not the one pretending to be holy.'

Sohail's fist comes down on the table. 'There's nothing holy about me – nothing. Only I have the humility to admit it. There is something greater.'

'But look what your greater being has brought us. War, and a beggar tapping at our window.'

'Maya,' Rehana says, raising her voice, 'that's enough.'

The man raises his hand to his forehead, then turns away, slipping through the opening in the gate. Sohail darts out of the room. They hear his door slamming shut.

Maya turns to her mother. 'He's going to turn your house into a mosque, didn't you hear?'

'Why, child, why do you have to be so intolerant?' She puts her face close to her daughter's and whispers, tender, 'He's going to pray, he's going to go to the mosque on Fridays. Don't be so frightened of it. It's only religion.'

Rehana was right – at first. Sohail was almost back to his old self, smiling at meals, whistling under his breath. He started to attend classes at the university, though he didn't linger on campus or go to any of the student-union meetings. He was occasionally seen with his friends, playing cricket at Abahani Field, and in that second summer after the war, when the constitution was written and the cyclone ebbing away, Rehana told Maya it was only a slight change in Sohail, that the mother had been right about her son. He didn't even grow a beard.

There were ripples of darker things. They heard that the Hussain boy, a few years younger than Sohail, had drowned himself. And the neighbour's son Shahabuddin had beaten his pregnant wife because he believed she was carrying a demon child.

But most of the boys and girls were as serious and obedient as they had ever been. They attended their classes; they married and bore children and warmed milk for their parents every evening. They put their memories away as best as they could, and they wiped the traces of blood from their hands and from the hems of their saris. And Rehana rested easy, sure that her son wouldn't take his interest too far. After all, she was the one who had given him the Book.

1984
August

Cancer. Every time Dr Sattar said the word his voice dipped, until he started calling it 'the disease' and then, occasionally, 'the C'. The operation was only the beginning. Rehana would need chemotherapy, powerful poisons that would kill the cancer. But they might kill her too. It was an uncertain science, the treatment often worse than the disease. Maya listened and the words went straight to her blood. She had never taken seriously the possibility that she might someday have to live without her mother. Death was something that had already happened to her; her father had died before she even knew that death was longer than sleep; later, death happened to the people she treated; she held her hand up against it every day, against dysentery and malaria and snakebites. Death had even skirted past Nazia, leaving scars on her legs but allowing her to live. She had never imagined, never seriously, that death would take something from her again.

That year the rain was everywhere. The gutters overflowed in Dhaka, and the rivers burst their banks, the Padma, the Jamuna, swallowing houses and farm animals and drowning the young rice. Maya brought Ammoo back from the hospital and paced the verandah. At night she cried into the crook of her arm. She found Sufia in her bedroom once, holding up the kerosene lamp and nodding, nodding.

The telephone girl brought Maya a message. Sister Khadija was going to hold a special Milaad for Ammoo. The upstairs women would recite, between them, the entire Qur'an and direct their blessings to Ammoo's recovery. Would she like to come? The picture in her mind was serene, the smell of bodies mingling with the cinder waft of attar. She found herself saying yes.

The women were casually laid out, in clumps of three or four. Their heads were covered, but their hands and feet, normally gloved and socked, were visible, and busy: they carried plates of food into the room, distributed cushions, stepped purposefully around each other. Khadija embraced her warmly.

'Sister,' she said. 'Please, sit down, sit here.' The floor was cleared, a fresh cloth placed under her feet. Maya looked around and saw many faces turned towards her. 'This is the Huzoor's sister, Maya.'

A chorus of salaams travelled through the room. 'Everyone knows who you are. Huzoor has spoken of you.'

A young woman approached, raven-haired, and smiled dazzlingly at Maya. The telephone girl. 'Maya, this is Rokeya.' Rokeya salaamed. 'You're a doctor?' she said.

'Yes, I trained in surgery.'

'Under Sattar sir?'

'Yes, he was my supervisor. You know him?'

'I trained at Dhaka Medical.'

'Really – what batch?'

''83.'

So she had finished her training only last year. What a waste, Maya thought; now she was waiting for her husband, probably some wrinkled old thing, to call every afternoon, laying out blankets for me and calling my brother Huzoor.

'Let me make you a cup of tea,' Rokeya offered, adjusting her scarf. 'How do you take it?'

She darted away and Khadija motioned again for Maya to sit down. Then she turned to the other women and said, 'Bismillah ir-Rahman ir-Raheem, it is time.'

Each of them pulled out a tasbi and began to recite the Kalma under her breath. The beads of stone and wood passed through their palms as they pulled the tasbi across with their thumbs. Empty bowls were passed around, and in the four corners of the room were small piles of dried beans. As soon as someone finished a cycle on her tasbi, she put a chickpea into the bowl in front of her.

Khadija sat down heavily and opened her Qur'an. She began to recite.

*

On the second day Rokeya told her that Sohail was going to make a rare appearance at the taleem. A personal sermon. Would she like to come?

When she arrived, it was already quiet, and the women were rearranging themselves around her, turning to the back of the room. They worked silently, clearing plates and lifting sheets from the floor, shaking them out, pointing, you sit there, let Sister Zayna have a cushion.

It was just like the funeral. A curtain was pulled across the room, dividing it in half. The women fitted themselves into what had become the back of the room. On the other side, footsteps, lowered voices, the sound of men filing in. Men, clearing their throats. On the women's side, the scarves were pulled tighter, as though the very sound of their brothers on the other side warranted an extra dose of vigilance.

From beyond the partition, her own brother began to speak.

'My brothers and sisters, Bismillah ir-Rahman ir-Raheem. I speak of the prophet Abraham, may peace and blessings be upon him. The story of Abraham is an old and sacred one. Our prophet and brother Abraham, peace be upon him, was a man of letters. He translated the ancient texts into Hebrew; he was fluent in the language of the Greeks and the Assyrians. In his great learning, he yearned also to know the secrets of human feeling, the joys and pleasures – not of the flesh, but of the heart and the mind. Thus, when he picked up his son Isaac, he felt the swell of love rise in his breast like the pull of the moon. He recorded it in himself; it was a matter of learning. And when the myths of the ancients caused Abraham to cry, with pity or fury at their folly, this too he recorded as a piece of sacred knowledge, for the ability to empathise is a purely human trait, given to us by the Almighty.

'All along, Abraham was a seeker of knowledge. But his knowledge was woven to the will of God. When his followers began to worship idols of clay, he told God and God struck them down. His quest for knowledge was second only to his deference to the will of God. So when God asked Abraham to sacrifice his son, Abraham could not rebuff God. Abraham was God's servant, and it was not in his nature or his will to say no; but he was motivated by more than his duty. He sought to know, in himself, the true nature of his faith, and whether this faith, which had become so beloved to him, could withstand the pull of his devotion to his son. He leaned over his son, the knife heavy in his hands. And God gave him a ram instead of Isaac.

'We come to know God by giving our will to him. By accepting that He knows better than we do, and that surrender is the only path to true faith. The very best of our humanness is in our ability to recognise the truth of the Almighty, the truth that is beyond us.'

She heard the pointed tone of his voice. He was telling her something. He was telling her that she had not learned to be humble; that she had put her will before that of God's. And was she being punished, was that it?

Maya was reminded of a story she had heard during the war. A man had been shot with a machine gun, three bullets entering his back. The field doctors had operated (no anaesthetic, only a rag between his teeth) and removed two bullets, missing the third entry wound. A fragment of the bullet had entered his bloodstream and circulated within him, travelling through arteries like a tourist, until it had finally lodged in his heart, killing him instantly.

Medically, she knew the story could not be true. But she allowed herself to imagine it was this way with her and Sohail. They had been injured, perhaps by the death of their father, or by the thin whisper of poverty that hung on their backs throughout their childhood. In Maya, the pointed black thing travelled freely, now touching her liver, now her limbs, now her stomach. She would awake to it, and unleash some of its poison on whoever happened to be nearest. Ammoo had received the worst of it; Sohail too.

But Sohail's shrapnel had lodged in his flesh, percolating through him ever so slowly, until, like the rest of them, he was dying on his feet, only faster, and the knowledge of this speed, that earthy scent of the grave, was what had made him, from that early age, a creature half-spirit, half-man. It was why he commanded an audience whenever he spoke, on the march or in the pulpit, why those in his orbit scrambled for a closer look, a touch. He had been born for prophesy, already, from those early moments, the master of himself. But what he was saying to her now was that the source of his power was not in command but in surrender. She too should now accept her smallness, her human limitations. And if she did not, the consequences would be unhappy.

Afterwards, the men cleared out, the curtain was drawn open, and the women began to make their preparations for the evening meal. Sohail's sermon nagged at Maya. She left the meeting room and found Khadija squatting over a small gas burner in the kitchen.

'Were you pleased by the bayaan?' she asked. Even without the cadence of recitation, Khadija's speech was formal.

Maya didn't know how to reply. Pleased was not how she would have put it.

'The boy,' she began, 'my nephew.'

'You are referring to Huzoor's son?'

'Yes, Zaid. I've been teaching him a few things, lessons, but with Ammoo's illness, I don't have as much time. I would like to enrol him in school.'

Khadija appeared to consider this for a moment. She stirred a handful of chillies into the pot of dal.

'He's troubled,' Maya continued.

'You are right,' she said, taking her by surprise. 'I will not deny it. Your brother agrees.'

'So you know.'

'We were discussing it yesterday, with Haji Mudasser.'

Maya knew who Haji Mudasser was. The people upstairs consulted him on every matter, no matter how small. They lowered their heads in front of him and took his blessing on their heads. They did everything he said.

'Haji Mudasser has told us that it is our duty to ensure the boy's proper upbringing. We understand that we have failed at this.'

Khadija stretched out her hand, thick and solid, and wrapped her fingers around Maya's wrist. 'We have resolved to do better. Amra neyot korechi.' They had made a promise, under the watchful eyes of the Almighty.

Khadija appeared unwilling to say more. Maya allowed herself a thin thread of hope.

'Will you join us? The Maghreb Azaan will begin in a few minutes.'

'I have to get back. Ammoo needs me.'

'We pray for her every day. The Huzoor is a devoted son.'

'Thank you,' Maya said, suddenly moved by this statement.

'Have faith, Sister Maya,' Khadija said. 'The boy will be looked after, and your mother will soon recover.' Khadija continued to grasp her hand. Maya had a flash, a presentiment, that Khadija would be her sister, the fellow spirit she had always searched for. Khadija put her hand on Maya's forehead, which she took as a sign that it was time for her to leave.

Maya walked back downstairs, her forehead hot from the imprint of Khadija's hand. Surprised at how reluctant she had been to leave her.

On the third day, Maya went upstairs without an invitation. She had just spooned a bit of broth into her mother, checked her stitches and watched as she fell asleep. The women were sitting in long rows along the wall, heads bent over plates. Rokeya passed along the rows, ladling rice. 'Maya Apa,' she said, 'please, eat with us.' Khadija nodded to her, smiling. Maya liked their lack of surprise at seeing her. A new jamaat had arrived from South Africa. Black and white women fingered tasbis and joined in the prayers. When the recitation began, her eyes filled with tears.

She found herself leaning into Khadija's arms. 'Ammoo, will she be all right?'

Khadija caressed the top of her head with a light, tender touch. 'Of course, God willing, she will remain with us.' She braced herself, worried Khadija was about to feed her some story about the importance of accepting death as God's will. But Khadija remained silent, moving her hand now to Maya's forehead, where she kept it like a poultice, until Maya closed her eyes and began to believe her.

1973

March

After Piya disappeared and Sohail was spending more and more time on the roof with his book, he was invited to meet Sheikh Mujib. The Father of the Nation was now the prime minister, and he wanted to see the faces of the boys who had delivered the country. Maya was thrilled. She had an idea that the sight of the great man, fatherly and expectant, would give Sohail a reason to snap back into his old life. When the invitation arrived, it included all of them – Sohail, Rehana and Maya.

On the morning of their appointment Sohail turned up at breakfast wearing a kurta-pyjama and a Mujib coat, sleeveless and with a high collar. It was a hot day, too hot for a coat, but he couldn't be persuaded to take it off, not even while they ate. He fanned himself with a copy of the *Bangladesh Observer*. Then he drank three glasses of milk. Maya had spent the entire morning trying to decide what to wear. She practised greeting Bangabandhu in front of the bathroom mirror, putting on her widest, most grateful smile.

Rehana was nervous too. She looked radiant, if a bit severe, in a white cotton sari and a pair of thin silver bangles. She served them burnt toast, which Sohail devoured without even scraping off the charred bits. Then she disappeared into the bedroom and locked the door. Maya knocked a few times – they were going to be late – then went around the back and through the kitchen. She found Ammoo using her dressing table as a writing surface, scribbling something with her head bent so close to the paper it was as if she were chasing the words with her eyes.

She ignored her when Maya announced the time. Maya leaned over and caught a snatch of writing.

Respected sir
Most gracious sir
Dear Father
Bangabandhu, I know you are a man of compassion

'I'm getting ready,' Ammoo said, putting her things into a small leather handbag.

'What's that you're writing?'

'He's a great man,' she said, opening a drawer and retrieving a tube of lipstick.

'Then what's this?'

'Nothing.' She twisted open the lipstick and touched the tip with her finger. 'I'm very honoured to be meeting him.'

Maya couldn't remember the last time she had seen her mother wearing lipstick. Ammoo appeared unsure of what to do with it, how to apply it now that she had daubed her finger. Her hand hovered above her face for a moment, then landed on her top lip. She stabbed at this lip for several moments, then scrutinised herself in the mirror.

'Are you ill?' Maya asked, wondering if, after all, she didn't look a bit pale.

Ammoo turned to examine her, as if noticing her for the first time. 'You need to comb your hair,' she said.

'Fine,' she said, grabbing her brush from the dressing table. 'You are the one who kept telling Sohail he should meet Bangabandhu.'

Ammoo was facing the mirror again, wiping away at her lipstick with a handkerchief. 'You never told me what you were doing for the Women's Rehabilitation Centre,' she began.

'As in?' Maya knew what she was getting at; she was going to ask her about the operations. She didn't want to talk about it; she didn't even want to think about it. How had Ammoo known? The clinics were not at the centre itself, and, though they had not been explicitly ordered to keep their activities a secret, none of the doctors or nurses ever spoke about it.

'You remember Piya?'

Maya nodded. Of course she remembered Piya.

'She was pregnant.'

'Yes, I knew.'

'You knew?' Ammoo paused for a moment, taking this in. 'She wanted – she wanted to get rid of it. She was afraid of the operation, she wasn't sure. She held my arm like this—'

Ammoo turned to Maya and gripped her elbow, her fingers hot, her lips smudged and red. 'And she said, please, I don't want to. And you know, a few days later, she was gone. She disappeared. Why do you think she left?'

'Maybe she changed her mind.'

Ammoo tightened her grip on Maya's arm, and they looked at each other. Maya didn't want to tell her what had happened the night before Piya left. 'Maybe it was better', she said, 'for everyone.'

'Don't you see?' Ammoo's voice was cracked, her eyes swimming. 'They forced her. And she's not the only one. Some of the girls don't want to. But they're ashamed, they're told they're carrying the seed of those soldiers.'

Bangabandhu had promised to take care of the women; he had even given them a name – Birangona, *heroines* – and asked their husbands and fathers to welcome them home, as they would their sons. But the children, he had said he didn't want the children of war. Maya told herself this every day, every day while she put the mask over their faces and told them to count backwards from 100. 'Isn't it better, Ma, to erase all traces of what happened to them? That way they can start to forget.'

'But their children, Maya, their children.' Rehana passed the back of her hand over her eyes and turned away from her. Thick-throated, she said, 'You're not a mother, you won't understand.' She crumpled the letter and tossed it aside. 'Let's go, we're going to be late.'

Maya was worried Ammoo would say something to Bangabandhu, about the war babies, but she needn't have worried; Ammoo was quiet and polite and repeated what an honour it was to meet him. Only she could tell that Ammoo was trying to convince herself, that the thing did not sit right with her, and that, even as she allowed him to hold her hands between his, she resisted him, doubted his sincerity.

Maya offered no such resistance. Bangabandhu was the closest thing to a deity she had ever known, and to have him standing before her, touching her head as she bent down to take the dust of his feet, was almost too much. She thought she might vomit, and gulped down the bottle of Fanta brought in on a trolley by the servant.

He was surrounded by his family – she glimpsed his daughter, Hasina, and Sheikh Moni, his nephew. Mrs Mujib was there too, and although the room was empty when they first entered, it was soon crowded with people, touching Bangabandhu's feet and crying with the sheer joy of it.

He lit his pipe and gave it a few short, shallow breaths.

Sohail sat transfixed, mirroring what Maya imagined was her own fascination.

'You are responsible for the power-plant blast?'

'Ji, sir,' Sohail said, nodding.

'Very audacious of you, my son.'

'Risk was great, sir, but we were determined.' Sohail's head was bent, but she saw the curve of his mouth. He was smiling. She hadn't seen him smile like that in months.

'Shahbash,' Bangabandhu said. 'Come here, let's take a photo. Come, come.'

Sohail had brought his Leica, but a photographer was already stationed, and they arranged themselves on either side of Bangabandhu. Maya put on the face she thought would be most appropriate for the photograph: a serious, determined young citizen, grateful to be in the presence of this man.

As they gathered around him for the photo, Bangabandhu turned to her and said, 'And you, my dear, how did you pass those nine months?'

Maya looked at Ammoo, and she nodded. 'I worked. I was in Theatre Road, sir. It was my honour to serve the government in exile.'

'Theatre Road! Your mother let you go to Calcutta? Well, you are a brave girl.'

'It was wonderful, sir, so many of us, working together.'

He regarded her quietly, gnawing on his pipe. 'I would have liked to see that, ma. I would have liked that very much.'

Maya wondered if Bangabandhu had felt as she had – left out, stuck somewhere safe and unremarkable – when the fighting broke out and she couldn't enlist in the army. He had been in prison the whole time. He hadn't seen a day of fighting or listened to a single broadcast. She hoped he knew that he was there without being there, because they had gone to sleep every night with his name on their lips and woken every morning to his portrait, cut out of newspapers, on their walls, his voice on the radio. It didn't matter to anyone that he had been in jail and not on the front lines of the battle. Though perhaps it mattered to him.

She wanted to tell him all of this, but a group of new visitors came to the door, and Bangabandhu's attention was diverted. By now she really needed the toilet, but she told herself she should concentrate on this moment, because she was going to always remember it, and she tried to fix Bangabandhu's face in her mind so she would be able to recall what he was wearing, and the weight of his hand on her head.

She looked across the room and saw Sohail sitting very straight with his knees in his hands. He rose to get up, but Bangabandhu was telling Ammoo about the other women like herself who had harboured freedom fighters in their homes, and asking if she had known any of them. Maya heard him asking what had happened to her husband, and when Ammoo told him, she saw Bangabandhu hold her two hands between his two hands again and tell her he was very sorry, and that she was very brave to raise her children without a father.

Finally, they gathered around the doorway.

'There's a lot of work to be done, my children,' Bangabandhu said. 'I hope I can trust you.'

'Ji, sir.' Sohail bent to touch his feet again, but Bangabandhu held him by the shoulders and lifted him up until they were eye to eye, then he embraced Sohail, three times, as though they were father and son. He walked them the entire way to the gate, and afterwards all they could talk about was how warm, how genial and how like any other person he had been.

Even Ammoo could not help but praise him, remarking on how, no matter how many people were in his presence, he fixed his eyes on you as if he were telling you a deep secret, as if you were conspiring with him on something, something lasting and great.

1984

September

Maya was astonished by the number of people who came through the door. Mrs Rahman arrived first, fluffed up Rehana's pillows and stuffed the fridge with chicken stew. She was followed by a group of women from the Ladies' Club, all promising to postpone their annual Rummy tournament until Rehana returned. The fish-hawker came, and the butcher she had known for over twenty years, bearing an enormous mutton bone and promising the soup would cure whatever had made her ill. Flowers arrived from the principal of Maya's junior school, and from the Dhanmondi Society. Sufia's sister and her husband came, dressed in formal clothes and bearing a prayer written by their local pir on a tiny piece of paper. Even the German tenant came, clutching a spray of roses. He stayed only a minute, but long enough for Maya to appraise him and find him sorely disappointing. Bald, so tall he had to duck to get through the door and covered in a fine coating of orange hair, he smiled his way through the visit, then passed Rehana an envelope labelled SEPTEMBER 1984 RENT.

After another morning with Khadija and the upstairs women, Maya found Joy sitting at Ammoo's bedside, telling her a story about his new business venture with Chottu. She was laughing, holding her stomach in her hands.

'Ma, be careful, your stitches have barely healed.' She shot Joy an irritated look.

Joy continued to entertain Rehana. He looked breezy, as though he had just stepped out of the bath, with his neat sandalled feet, his closely cropped hair. Slowly, he finished his story, leaning close to Ammoo's ear. Then he took his leave, assuring her she would be out of bed in no time, ready to fry her famous parathas.

'Thank you for coming,' Maya said politely, leading him to the living room. She wanted to say something about the last time they'd met, the awkward goodbye.

'Your mother said you've been visiting the upstairs.'

'Sohail came to the hospital. He sat with her, I think she really liked that. So I wanted to thank him.'

'How did you find it?'

'It's another world.'

'You say that as if it's not so bad.'

'It's different. Totally unlike anything else.' She tried to turn it into words, the feeling of being among those women. Joy's foot had touched something under the sofa, and now he was reaching underneath, disturbing the dust.

'I think I know what this is,' he said.

Maya knew too. And he pulled it out, a piece of wreckage. A relic.

'Still has all its strings,' he said. Maya found a wet rag in the kitchen, and they rubbed it down together, watching as the colour of the wood emerged, honey-toned.

'Does it play?' she asked.

'Probably needs to be tuned. I can try, I'm not very good. It was always my brother.'

'Mine too,' she said.

It isn't fair, she felt him thinking, at least her brother is still alive. What he would give to have his brother back. She imagined him wanting his brother under any circumstances, so long as he were here, even if he shunned his old life and behaved like a stranger. A world of difference, she imagined him thinking, between the living and the dead; not so different, she countered in her mind. There's a reason for phrases such as *you're dead to me*, which she had used against Sohail more than once.

Joy began to fiddle with the guitar strings, turning knobs on the long neck of the instrument. 'I think I've got it,' he said. 'Try it now.'

She ran her thumb down the strings. 'Sounds nice,' she said. 'Like old times.'

'What was that song you used to sing, that Spanish song?'

'We never sang a song in Spanish.'

'You did, something with a very long name.'

'Oh!' He slapped his knee. 'You mean "Guantanamera".'

'I always loved that song.'

'Sohail used to sing it. He said it was a revolutionary song, but when I was in New York I had a Mexican friend who told me the words. It's just like every other song.'

'Oh?'

'About some poor chap who wants to fall in love.'

'You have something against love?'

He leaned back and crossed his legs. 'I'm only a minor opponent. Not like you.'

She plucked at the strings. 'You know nothing, my friend. I'm just like any other girl.' She believed it herself, at that moment. That she was as tender as all the others, as hopeful. He began to strum the guitar.

'Let me show you the chords,' Joy said. He took hold of her

fingers and placed them on the strings. 'You have to press harder than that.'

Zaid came into the room. 'Here's my little tongue-twister,' Maya said. 'Zaid, come and say hello to uncle Joy.'

Joy extended his hand, and when Zaid stepped forward to shake it, he moved it quickly to his forehead. 'As-Salaam Alaikum. Tricked you!'

Zaid collapsed into giggles.

'This one knows every language on the planet. Don't you, Zaid? Tell Uncle Joy something in Spanish.'

Zaid rolled his eyes to the ceiling. 'Oh-kay,' he said, enunciating very slowly. 'Akee yeygo la paz.'

'That's very good,' Joy said. 'Even I know what that means.'

'Did he really say something?' Maya whispered. 'I always think he's pulling my leg.'

Joy picked up the deck of cards on the table and began to shuffle. 'Let me show you something,' he said.

'We can't play cards,' Maya interjected; 'he's not allowed.'

Joy cast a sideways glance at her. 'It's not a game,' he said, 'it's magic.' Nervous, she let him play his trick. Then Zaid climbed into Joy's lap and whispered something in his ear, and then he danced out of the room, ta-ta, ta-ta, ta-ta, ta-ta.

*

Rehana held her hair in her hands.

'Oh, Ma.' Maya took it from her, the tuft like a tiny furred animal. The place where it had been shone like a fragment of metal at the bottom of the sea.

She was in the bath when it happened. There was more, she said, in the towel.

'Ma,' Maya said, 'let's shave it.'

'No, not yet.' Her voice was small and tired. 'Please, no.' She lay her head back on the pillow, turned her face away so Maya

148

could no longer see her crying. 'It's all right,' she said, blowing her nose, 'we discussed this with the doctor.'

Maya was still holding her fallen tuft of hair. 'Throw it,' she said. 'Burn it.'

She tossed it to the floor. Sufia picked it up and disappeared into the kitchen.

Rokeya was on a patch of concrete, sitting with her face to the sun. 'Get out of the glare,' Maya said, 'you'll get burned.' It must have been one of the hottest days of the year. Rokeya salaamed, her voice thready, and Maya saw that her lips were dry, hair feathering out from under her scarf.

'How is your mother?' she asked.

'She is managing,' Maya said.

Rokeya nodded, tears pooling at the corners of her eyes. She placed both hands on her stomach in a gesture Maya recognised immediately.

'Are you pregnant?' Maya asked, bending to get a closer look at her.

Rokeya smiled weakly. 'How did you know?'

Khadija parted the curtain and stepped outside. She cast a light glance at Rokeya and handed her a glass of water. 'Go inside now,' she said. Rokeya grabbed the water and swallowed it quickly, holding the glass with both hands and gulping hard.

'We must do another taleem for your mother,' Khadija said. She turned to Rokeya again. 'Tell the sisters to make the arrangements.'

Inside, the air had stopped in its tracks. With the curtains drawn tightly, and the windows shut, it was unbearably hot. Only Khadija looked comfortable, the shine of sweat on her forehead giving her a polished glaze as she took her place at the front of the room. She opened the Book and began to read quietly to herself. The other women, who had been whispering

149

and fanning themselves, straightened and hushed one another. Rokeya motioned for Maya to sit beside her.

The sun was at its full thrust now, as Maya stared down at her hands, sweating steadily. Here, in this room, was the only place she could believe, really believe, that her mother would live. Everywhere else the possibility of her absence had taken over: every meal Maya ate that wasn't cooked by her, the rooms in which she read and bathed and dressed, the garden, which she had diligently watered but could not save from its yellowish cast.

That was why, day after day, she found herself sitting at Khadija's feet. She did not read from the Qur'an or join in the prayers. She just sat cross-legged with her hands in her lap and her legs slowly falling asleep, for as long as it took for the panic to pass.

When most of her hair had gone, Rehana finally asked Maya to shear off the rest. She propped herself up on the bed, sharp shoulders blading out of her nightdress, the skin on her neck grey and tired. Sufia stood crying quietly as Maya draped her mother with a towel.

She had known this day would come; she had rehearsed it. She would remain calm, her hand steady on the instrument. She began with the scissors. Ammoo had lost her hair in patches: in some places it was gone completely; in others it was thick and clung strongly to her scalp. She cut these sections close, lingering at the weight of them, long ribboning strands, before dropping them on the floor. Sufia followed her movements with a broom. Rehana herself was dry-eyed, holding a newspaper in front of her as if it were any other morning and she were waiting for her eggs. She had obviously rehearsed it too.

Maya replaced the scissors with a blade, dipping it into a bowl of warm soapy water, and lightly, delicately, painting across her mother's head. Now Ammoo was emerging under her hand, shiny, perfectly round. The whole planet of her.

'I used to watch my father', Rehana said, holding the newspaper high, 'being shaved by his barber. He always looked so
relaxed.'

'How does it feel?'

'Nice. A bit ticklish.'

Soon there was very little soap left. Maya rubbed her mother's
head with a thin towel. 'I have something for you,' she said.
She went to her room and came back with a bandana she had
acquired a few days before at a roadside stall. It was red and
white, and fitted neatly around her mother's forehead.

'You look like a gypsy,' she said. 'Or a pirate.'

'Give me an eye patch and I'll rob you blind.' They laughed.

In the evening, Mrs Rahman and Mrs Akram came to play
cards with Rehana. Maya agreed to make up their fourth so
they could play poker. No one mentioned Rehana's hair, except
to remark that perhaps red was her lucky colour, because she
won twice, with a pair of aces and a straight flush.

*

When Ramzaan, the fasting month, began, Rehana insisted that
Maya do all the shopping in preparation for Eid. 'It's the first
year I haven't been able to keep the fast,' Rehana said, her head
light on the pillow. 'So the least you can do is wear something
nice for Eid.'

Ammoo had given strict instructions. How many yards of
cloth to buy for her own salwaar-kameez. Blouse, petticoat and
sari for Sufia. Gifts for Mrs Rahman and Mrs Akram. Something
for Sohail. Now Maya was standing in front of a fabric counter
with Zaid, trying to find cloth for Sufia's blouse.

The shopkeepers, young men with wispy moustaches, hurried
back and forth from the counters to the fabrics behind them.
The bolts of cloth, arranged along the wall like books on a
shelf, contained every shade of colour imaginable. They began

the process of finding matching fabric for the blouse by holding up the sari Maya had bought to the palette of colours that most resembled it. Then they moved along this palette, light to dark, until she nodded somewhere along the spectrum. Maya chose a navy-blue piece for Sufia.

It was time to make their way to the tailoring section of the market. Zaid pulled hard on her wrist, jumping over the cracks that rivered through the cement.

'Do you remember what we learned yesterday,' she asked him, 'the numbers? Let's see if you can count the steps from here to the tailor's shop.'

His eyes were everywhere, taking in the brightly painted hoardings, the women in their shopping clothes, the dogs biting at fleas, the cinema posters, the sharp smell of tamarind pickle. It was a pleasant day, a brief hint of the winter to come, the breeze tickling at their knees, fingertips. Maya couldn't help but think back to all the Eid celebrations they'd had at the bungalow. The crackle of new clothes, pressed and starched by Ammoo until they smelled of wet rice. Waiting for Sohail to return from the mosque, and breakfast, and then on a rickshaw, visiting the homes of all the people they knew, their lives suddenly full, and finally, as the afternoon peaked, stopping at the graveyard, marking another year of their threesomeness and praying at Abboo's grave, telling him again how much he was missed.

'Ek,' Zaid began hesitantly, 'dui.' The cap on his head bobbed up and down. 'Teen.' *One. Two. Three.*

'Here,' Maya said, gripped by a sudden tenderness for the boy, 'hold these.' She gave him the shopping bags and lifted him into her arms. He was light, a whisper of a child.

'What do you want?' she said. 'Choose something.'

'For me?'

'Anything you like. Anything in all of New Market.'

He flashed her a smile, his crooked teeth beautifully white, cleaned, she knew with charcoal and the branch of a cypress tree, because toothbrushes were banned upstairs. He tried to decide what he wanted, looking down at himself, taking in his filthy kurta-pyjama, the crescent-shaped dirt under his finger-nails. She thought he might ask for the bicycle he had spoken of at the graveyard, but he surprised her by leaning close and whispering in her ear: 'Sandal.'

'Really, you just want sandals? I said you could have anything in all of New Market and you want a pair of sandals?'

He nodded solemnly.

'Okay, then we have to turn around.' She set him down and they made their way back through the market until they reached Bata. A thin salesman in a blue shirt spotted Maya before she entered the shop.

'Heel for you, madam? Coat-shoe?'

'We're here for the boy,' Maya said, leading Zaid inside. Into his ear she whispered, 'What colour do you want?'

'Blue,' he whispered back.

'We'd like a pair of blue sandals.'

The salesman brought out a pair of blue chappals not unlike the ones Zaid was already wearing, which were worn down to the nub and already a little too small.

Maya slipped the new sandals on his feet. 'Walk from here to there,' she said; 'let's see if they fit.'

He took a few narrow steps, placing each foot on the shop floor with a careful touch. He shuffled back towards her. His lips were red and his eyes were brimming with tears. She cupped his shoulders. 'It's all right. Go on, see if they fit.' Then she turned him around and pushed him gently away.

'Can't you find him something better, a sandal-shoe maybe?'

Zaid charged the length of the shop, then hopped back towards her, whistling.

'Don't run,' the salesman said, putting his finger to his lips. Turning to Maya, he said, 'How much do you want to spend?'

'It doesn't matter,' she said, 'just show me another style.'

'How very kind of you,' he said, shuffling through the shoe-boxes, 'bringing your servant boy to the market.'

'He's not—'

Zaid was holding the shoes in his hands now, threading them through his fingers and clapping them together, seal-like. She looked at him and she looked at the salesman. He was holding out another crude pair of rubber sandals.

'Let's go,' Maya said, pulling the shoes from Zaid's hands and returning them to the salesman. 'Give us back the old sandals.'

'I've thrown them away.'

'Get them back.'

Zaid began to cry. 'Sush,' she said, impatient, and suddenly angry at him for being so shabbily dressed. She saw the way he breathed through his mouth, and the caked mucus in the corners of his eyes. He did look like a servant boy, his collars rimmed with grey, short scabs dotting his forearms.

The salesman returned, holding the old shoes by the very tips of his fingers. She grabbed them and nudged Zaid out of the shop. By now the boy had dropped into a hard silence, refusing to hold her hand, walking a few paces behind. She tried to tell him *the salesman thought you were a servant boy, the bastard*, but he refused to listen, keeping his back to her and swatting her hand away when she tried to touch him. She finished her errand at the tailor's, haggling unnecessarily about the price of stitching, demanding the clothes be ready in three days even though Eid was still weeks away, and then they left, ignoring each other in the rickshaw. When they reached the bungalow Maya tried again to address him, but Zaid bounded up the stairs two at a time, refusing to look back at her when she called out goodbye.

'Did you get everything?' Ammoo asked. Her voice was down to a whisper, chalk in the dust.

'I did.'

'I need the toilet. Call Sufia.'

'She's washing the pots. I'll take you.'

Ammoo didn't have the strength to protest. Maya slid an arm under her shoulders, and with a soft grunt Ammoo sat upright. She held up her hand. 'Wait,' she said. She caught her breath. Swung her legs over the side of the bed. Waved to Maya to hold out her arm so she could stand up. Together they shuffled to the hallway.

'Keep the door unlocked,' Maya said. She heard the water running, and then a slap against the wall and the sound of retching. 'Are you all right, Ma? Let me come in.'

She didn't hear anything. 'Ma? Let me come in, Ma, please.' Still nothing. She pushed the door open and found Ammoo lying beside the toilet, her arm over her face. Maya tried to lift her up. Her cheek and chin were coated in vomit. Maya poured a mugful of water over her, and then another. Ammoo lay very still, opening her eyes against the cool splash of water. The sounds of the garden came through the small bathroom window. Maya peeled away Ammoo's sari and placed it in the washing bucket. Ammoo lifted her head. They inched their way back to the bed. Ammoo mouthed something and Maya came close, trying to understand.

'Everything,' she said softly, 'did you get everything?'

'Don't worry, Ma,' Maya replied. 'Eid will be just like it always is.'

Shafaat rang, excited. 'We've been getting letters about your column,' he said. 'People like it.'

She didn't care if people liked it. Did they understand it? 'Yes,' he said, 'your message is certainly getting across. We had a letter from the Khatib of Rajshahi Mosque. An upstanding fellow, apparently.'

'Is it threatening?' She didn't care for herself, only for the people of the village, for Nazia.

He told her not to worry. Static through the receiver as he blew smoke out of the corner of his mouth. All right, then. She would keep on writing.

Travelling through the rugged south of the country, I found myself among the Hill tribes, the Garo and the Chakma. Ask yourself, citizen, have you ever met a tribal? Ever sat next to one at school? Ever known anyone who knows anyone who has a tribal for a friend? I thought not.

They know the medicine of the forest. Plants that you soak and paste over a wound. They chew the leaf and smear it over your cut. There is a treasure, they say, in every inch of this land.

In exchange, we raze their villages and let the army rape their women. We take their forests and smoke them out of their villages. This is no kind of freedom.

*

Ammoo grew weaker every day. The change was hardly perceptible, but occasionally Maya would notice something, the angle of her cheekbones, the sleek profile she had acquired. She tried to monitor other things – her eating, her bowel movements, the vomiting from chemotherapy. But Ammoo remained scrupulously private, refusing to talk openly about her disease, always preferring Sufia's help to hers. She was so careful to obscure the details of the cancer that Maya began to wonder if she should be there at all.

But she couldn't imagine being anywhere else. Her time away had dissolved, like sugar in water, leaving no imprint. She rarely thought of Nazia and whether she might call again. The season of mangoes had come and gone in Rajshahi, and she might have spent a few moments remembering the currents of scent that blew into the village and made everyone's mouth water, but she didn't. She thought only of Ammoo, only of banishing the premonition. She was a regular visitor upstairs, sitting on the fringes of their strange world, transfixed by its rituals, the air of calm and certainty that surrounded them. She once asked Rokeya what she thought of President Zia's death, and Rokeya looked at her blankly as though unaware of which Zia she meant. Was there a Zia in the Qur'an, she saw her wondering. A Zia in their extended family? But instead of experiencing the familiar surge of anger, instead of repeating her usual lines – about citizens who do not deserve the freedom they had fought so hard to gain, about how they deserve their dirty politicians, and about how it was people like her who had brought all of this upon the country – Maya found herself relieved. She was tired of letting everything break her heart, the politicians and crooks and the women whose babies died because they didn't make it to the hospital on time. This was a world in which it didn't matter that two of their presidents had been assassinated, and that they were now fully in the throes of irony, with their very own Dictator, their own injustices, their own dirty little war down south. There was just this room, this hot room with its stink of men and its stink of women, and the feeling that she was pulling the end of a rope with all her weight, pulling her mother back as she careened towards death.

Zaid forgave Maya for the incident in the market, and came and went as usual. As before, she fed him and tried to teach him things. Halal things, no card games, no television. She was working on addition and subtraction. His frenzied energy was the only bright thing in the bungalow. He tiptoed into Rehana's room and sat at her feet, radiating a sort of brisk optimism, no matter that she was sinking into the mattress, that she was as frail as a bird in its nest, a trembling, bruise-breasted robin.

1973

July

Even after Sohail declared his love for the Holy Book, after he started making trips to the mosque and wearing a cap on his head, Maya still thought she could persuade her brother to change his mind. She had known him all her life, and all her life he had been the opposite of a religious man. He had laughed and joked about it, and he had been angry at a religion that could be so easily turned to cruelty. He had seen it with his own eyes, the boys butchered because they were Hindu, the university teachers shot and piled into graves because they weren't considered Islamic enough. For all these reasons Maya believed Sohail's conversion was fragile, like the dew that settled between the grasses at the start of the day, gone by the time the afternoon sun vanished into dusk.

She decided to throw him a birthday party. All the old friends would come – Chottu, Saima, Iqbal, the boys from his regiment,

158

their friends from university. The ones who had heard Sohail's speeches at the student union, the ones who had voted him president of his hall and heard his name ringing in their throats when they joined up.

When the day arrived, she ignored Ammoo's advice and said little to Sohail about the party, informing him only that it would take place in the afternoon, and that he would be expected to be there. It was his birthday, after all. She worked hard, setting up the Carrom board on the verandah and squeezing lemons by the dozen and frying lentils for a vast pot of khichuri.

The day was bright and hot, not a hint of a monsoon spoiler. Chottu and Saima arrived first, carrying their newborn baby in a katha they had stitched in the colours of the Bangladesh flag. 'Have you decided on a name?' she asked, knowing that Chottu's mother was superstitious, and that she had forbidden them to name the child before her three-month naming ceremony.

'No,' Saima said, 'the dragon still hasn't given us permission.'

Chottu said, 'I keep telling this kid how lucky she is to be born in a free country, but all she does is fart and eat, eat and fart.'

Some of the boys in Sohail's regiment sauntered in, dressed in their army uniforms. Kona, the one whose shoulders filled his uniform most handsomely, gave her a brief salute. 'Hello, little sister,' he said. 'Not so little any more, I see.'

The garden began to fill up. She passed around the lemonade while people scattered to the shady parts of the garden, leaning against the guava tree, lingering on the porch. A large group of Maya's fellow medical students arrived. Then a trio of women who had always taken a particular interest in Sohail. At university they had been known as the fast girls, sleeveless blouses and lips always curled into perfect, teeth-hiding, air-hostess smiles. It was all coming together, laughter and lemonade and pretty girls – the only thing missing was Sohail. She checked her watch: three o'clock and he still wasn't there. She felt a flutter of panic; maybe he wouldn't turn up at all. He was probably at the mosque, repelled by the whole thing, and then what would she do, what would she tell all these people as they munched on peanuts and traded stories about her brother?

She greeted the medical students, pulling chairs together so they could sit in a circle. At that moment she caught sight of Ammoo in a starched white sari, passing out little bowls of puffed rice, smiling and greeting everyone by name. The boys stood up straight and put their hands to their foreheads or bent down to touch her feet. Around her the talk grew more animated, the atmosphere more relaxed, and although there were occasional chants of 'where is the birthday boy?' no one seemed to mind Sohail's absence.

Maya decided to go ahead and serve lunch. She sliced cucumbers for the salad and heated up the khichuri, piling it on to large platters and corralling everyone into the living room. Then, just as she was about to serve the egg curry, she saw him coming in from the far side of the garden. He stood back for a moment, until someone caught his eye and he waved. He wore a white kurta and a cap; she was right, he had been to the mosque. She gave the egg curry an irritated stir, then she heaved the pot out of the kitchen and into the dining room. The fast girls circled Sohail. One of them, the tallest, touched his arm lightly and giggled with the sound of a spoon against a glass.

Maya made her way around the garden, calling everyone to the table. In Ammoo's room she found Saima lying on the bed with the shutters closed, feeding the baby. She offered to look after the baby so Saima could eat.

'You're a jaan,' she sighed. 'I'm starving! And that rascal has gone off to refill his glass. Wait, let me change her nappy.'

'Refill? Where?' Maya hadn't seen Chottu in the kitchen.

'In Murad's car.' She giggled. 'He's brought a half-bottle of whisky.'

'Oh,' she said, imagining Ammoo's stony anger if she found out.

'You don't mind, do you?' Saima said, pulling up the baby's legs and slipping the cloth nappy underneath, shushing her as she squealed in protest.

As long as no one found out. 'No, I suppose not. Just tell them to be careful. Ammoo won't like it. And Sohail.'

'We'll definitely keep it from auntie. But I've seen Sohail with a drink before – who knows, he might be in Murad's car himself.' She folded the nappy, holding a giant safety pin between her teeth.

Maya couldn't believe her eyes. 'Honestly, Saima, I don't know how you do it, all this baby-handling. Already you're an expert.' Maya was relieved it wasn't her, but still she felt a twinge of jealousy at the thought that her friend was already good at something, while she was floundering, still not sure how she was going to get used to a life without war.

'Oh, it's nothing. Can't be as hard as medical college.'

She was about to ask Saima if she might want to return to the university herself, but she was suddenly given the infant, swaddled into its flag-blanket. 'He's different, you know,' Maya said instead, steering the conversation back to Sohail, her hand warm under the baby's head.

'They've all changed,' Saima replied. 'No one is the same any more.'

She struggled to explain it. 'He's been going to the mosque. Says he's found something.'

'Don't worry, it'll pass.'

'That's what Ammoo said. But you know how he is, takes everything so seriously.'

Saima stood up, waved her hand as if she were swatting a mosquito. 'We won't let him go too far. I'm going to eat now – you'll be okay with the monster?'

The child was asleep again, puffy-eyed, working her fists

against some imaginary foe. Maya carried her into the living room, where Ammoo was passing out plates. 'Not too much, auntie,' she overheard, 'have to keep our figures!'

Sohail was beside Chottu, holding an empty plate in his hand. Maya saw him, forbidding in his white kurta, tall and lean and spotless. She was suddenly acutely aware of how angry he must be. Tightening her arms around the baby, she gathered the courage to approach him. When he saw her, Chottu thumped Sohail's back. 'This guy is full of goodness. He's been telling me some awesome things. Awesome.'

'Come,' she said, 'eat something.' Sohail looked at her with an expression she could not decipher. His eyes were dark and locked on her. 'Bhaiya, please.' But he shook his head, put down the empty plate and made his way to a clutch of guests waving from the doorway. 'Sorry to eat and run,' she heard one of them say. 'Khoda Hafez,' she heard Sohail reply. 'When you are settled, we will talk again.' She had the impression he had talked to everyone at the party, that they were leaving with little buds of ideas that Sohail had planted, and that, throughout the rest of the day, they would worry these ideas, itch away at them until they were changed, and everything would be slightly altered. This is what Sohail's talking would have done, what his talking had always done.

'Here's my little queen,' Chottu said, poking his finger into the baby's mouth.

'Are your hands washed?' Maya asked, catching the caramel scent of whisky on his breath.

'Give her here.' He pulled the bundle from her hands. 'How's my little stink-bomb?' Maya scanned the room for Sohail, but he had gone outside to open the gate for the departing guests. As people were putting their plates away, it began to rain. The fast girls hurried away, ducking under the gauzy ends of their saris. The medical students and the army men crowded into the living room, leaning against the wall or squeezing on to the sofa.

'Let's have a song, shall we?' Kona said. 'Sohail, mia, you on the guitar.'

Sohail shook his head. He appeared agitated now, removing the cap from his head and folding it into his pocket.

Kona began to sing.

Bangladesh, my first and last,
Bangladesh, my life and death
Bangladesh, Bangladesh, Bangladesh!

Everyone joined in except Sohail, whose eyes shifted from the tapping of Kona's feet to the wide sheets of rain that splashed against the windows. Maya wasn't the only one who noticed; after the song, there was a long, solid silence. The baby began to cry.

'Sohail,' Saima said, putting the baby on her shoulder, 'I hear you're becoming a mowlana.'

'Saima,' Maya said, 'not now.'

'It's all right, we can all see for ourselves. Nothing to be ashamed of. Why don't you tell us about it?'

Maya didn't want Sohail to tell anyone about it. She just wanted it to go away. The medical students stood up to leave. 'Oh, please don't run off,' she called after them weakly. But they waved goodbye, promising to see her in the dissection room. 'We have to take out Hitler's kidney,' they said, referring to their cadaver. One of the boys, a rather malnourished-looking one with hair over his ears, paid her particular attention as he said goodbye, holding her gaze for a moment too long and chewing his bottom lip. She ignored him, but when the gate had closed behind them, she heard the others sniggering, and a few dull thumps as they jostled one another.

Now there was only Chottu and Saima and Kona and the boys from Sohail's regiment. Saima's question was circling the room.

Suddenly Sohail stood up, smoothing his kurta and resettling the cap on his head. 'It's true,' he said, his voice the perfect shade of rough-smooth. 'I have been going to the mosque.'

'Watch out,' Chottu said, 'they steal shoes at the mosque.'

'And stand at the back, yaar, otherwise the other men will get turned on by your backside. All that squatting and leaning.' They started to laugh. Chottu got down on the floor, demonstrating the dangers of leaning too far forward in prostration. 'Trouser can come down any time!'

The room erupted. This was exactly what she had wanted, but she realised, too late, what was happening. There was no way Sohail was going to join in, no way he was going to start laughing at himself.

Kona continued to strum the guitar, humming lightly. Sohail did not sit down. He stared straight into the room and said, 'It is not a bad thing, to find one's God.'

'Alhamdulillah!' Chottu said, raising his fist into the air.

Kona put down his guitar and spoke up. 'You remember, Sohail, you told us religion would make us blind – in training you would tell everyone not to recite the Kalma before an operation.'

'That's right,' Sohail said, 'you remember well. And did you listen to me?'

'No.'

'Because you knew I was wrong.'

'Well,' he said, smiling, 'we just didn't want to get our heads blown off, eh boys?'

Ammoo entered with the cake. It was white and square and decorated with blue flowers. Many Happy Returns, Bhaiya.

'Dosto,' Chottu said, 'we didn't know it was a birthday party.'

Ammoo lit the candles. 'Come, beta,' she said, her hand on Sohail's cheek, 'cut the cake.'

They sang. Sohail sliced into the cake and fed a small piece to Ammoo. Usually he would do the same for Maya, but she leaned out of sight, her back against the wall. She saw him putting a piece of cake into his own mouth, and she knew, at that moment, that it would be the last time she would see him this way, pretending to be something of the man she remembered, allowing lipsticked women to dance their fingers on his arm, smelling the whisky on his friends' breath and watching them all shifting uncomfortably as he talked about the mosque; maybe now he would change his clothes and start to grow a beard, and maybe he would make the trip to Mecca and go into purdah. The future was suddenly clear: he was going somewhere, somewhere remote and out of reach, somewhere that had nothing to do with her, and that even if he didn't disappear altogether, she would, from now on, be left behind.

Later, when they had dried the plates and scraped the khichuri out of the bottom of the pot, Maya turned to Ammoo. 'I shouldn't have done it.'

Ammoo nodded, and without a word continued to divide the leftovers into smaller containers, her elbows working hard, lifting, scooping.

'Did you see him? The way he looked at everyone, like he was from another world.'

She was waiting for Ammoo to tell her it wasn't something to get so agitated about, just a phase, it would pass. But, instead, she said, 'It's more serious than we thought.'

'He told you?'

'He wants to use the roof. To talk.'

'Talk?'

'Talk about religion. He's not a mowlana, he says. We shouldn't call him that. He says he just wants to go up there and talk about God.'

'To who?'

'To anyone who'll listen. His friend Kona has already signed up.'

Ammoo put her hand up to her hair and retied her bun, twisting firmly from the wrist. Outside, the rain had stopped, leaving the air heavy with its imprint, and with the occasional sound of leaves dropping their last traces of water.

'There isn't anything we can do, is there?'

Ammoo bent over to pick up the empty pot and take it to the outside tap. She sounded very tired when she said, 'No, I don't think so.'

'Well,' Maya said, 'let's eat this leftover cake, then.' And she squatted on a piri beside her mother and passed her a plate with the last corner of the birthday cake, the flourish now gone from the edges, the frosting matted and smudged.

He recited words from the Torah, the Gita, the Bible. He praised the prophets of old, Ram and Odysseus, Jesus and Arjun, the Buddha and Guru Nanak. They were all messengers of God, in their way. Separate in time, diverse in their teaching, yet equal in their desire for human betterment. He spoke to those, like Kona, who had never thought seriously about their faith; he read to them from the Qur'an, and he told them stories about the place where their faith was born, in the high desert of Arabia, where the warring tribes of the Quraysh came together in the shadow of the Ka'bah.

Other religions had their saints, their icons. They had their churches, their gospels, their commandments, their strife, their exiles, their miracles. We, he said, have our Prophet, and our Book. The Book was the miracle. It was so simple. That was the power of the message. It turned them into brothers and guardians of one another. It promised equality. It promised freedom. It was perfect.

The Book spoke to his every sorrow, to every bruise of his life. It spoke to the knife passing across the throat of an innocent man; it spoke to the day his father died, hand on his arrested heart; and it spoke to the machine-gun sound that echoed in his chest, night after night, and to the hollow where Piya had been. And every idea he had ever had about the world, it spoke to those too. That every man was equal before God – how foolish of him to believe that Marx had invented this concept, when it was ancient, even deeper than ancient, embedded in the very germ of every being; that is what God had intended, what God had created. He wept from the beauty of it.

1984

October

She had forgotten about the trip to New Market when Sohail
came through the door a few weeks later. His face was red,
the air coming hard out of his mouth. He held a small paper
bag in his hands.

'How is Ammoo?' he asked, sitting down heavily.

'She has cancer, how do you think?' She hadn't meant to
sound so sharp, but he hadn't been to see Ammoo since that
day at the hospital. Ammoo asked after him constantly, and
Maya had to tell her he was off somewhere on important
jamaat business, that he had sent his love and blessings. There
were messages from upstairs, informing them that the Qur'an
had been read three times from start to finish in Rehana's
name. Khadija had sent food, sometimes in excessive amounts,
which they'd had to throw away because there was no one to
eat it.

'I've been praying,' Sohail said.

'I know. I heard.' She remembered his sermon, the way he had admonished her.

He rubbed his face with both hands. Then he held out the paper bag. Inside were the Bata sandals, blue and brand new. She felt a cold flood of panic. Sohail tented his fingers and said, 'I would like to know how these sandals came to be in my son's possession.' Maya noticed a ring on his left thumb, a silver ring with a cheap green stone. She stared at it as she tried to decide how to explain it to him – the market, the salesman, the insult.

'They were a gift from me. His old sandals were torn.'

'They were not torn. I have seen them myself.'

'You're right, they weren't torn. But they were too small.'

'You know I regard humility and truthfulness above all things.'

'He wanted—'

'Of course he wanted. He's a child.'

'Exactly. He's a kid – you don't treat him like one.'

Sohail looked at her directly, sword-like. Damn it, he always knew when she was lying. 'Did you give him the sandals?'

'No.'

'Then where did he get them?'

'I don't know.'

'I don't believe you.'

'Look, we went to New Market, and I wanted to buy him sandals, but the shopkeeper thought he was a servant.' Sohail said nothing, just continued to stare at her. 'Did you hear me? A servant.'

'Why do you care about such things?'

He seemed genuinely perplexed. Why *had* she cared? 'Because he was humiliated, that's why. Your son was humiliated. It's the same thing that happens when he walks the streets in torn clothes, or stares at the children coming out of the playground when the school bell rings.'

'If you didn't buy the sandals, then who did?'

'I don't know. Maybe he bought them with his pocket money.'

'You know very well we don't give him pocket money.'

No toys. No pocket money. No sandals. A rattle in his chest. Dirty scabs on his arms.

'I have to do something,' he said, rising heavily from the sofa.

Maybe this was a good thing. Maybe Sohail would realise what he was doing to his son. 'Yes, do something. Please.'

Sohail hesitated. Then he drew a sharp, deep breath and said, 'I'm sending him to madrasa.'

'*What?*'

'In Chandpur.'

She felt her voice narrowing, trembling. 'Where the hell is Chandpur?'

'On the other side of the Jamuna. I thought you knew every corner of this country.' He couldn't resist it, the gibe.

'But that's days away.'

'I hear the Huzoor is a good man.'

'You hear? You don't know him?'

'He comes highly recommended. I need to spend more time at the mosque; I can't watch over Zaid. He – he needs guidance. Even you can see that.'

'Let him stay with us, Ammoo and me. He's lost his mother.'

'I am grateful for the efforts you've made, Maya, but I think we both know the situation is getting out of hand. Can you promise me he won't steal any more? And he makes up stories all the time; the boy lives in his own dream-world. It's not right.'

She couldn't promise him the boy wouldn't steal. She couldn't promise him anything – she didn't even know where Zaid was half the time, or why he returned with bruises on his arms or why he smelled of vomit.

'Ammoo needs you,' Sohail continued; 'your duty lies with her.'

'Zaid needs us too. Please, Bhaiya.' The air closed around her throat. 'I'm sorry about the chappals, I should have asked you first. But madrasa is too much, Bhaiya, even for you.'

His voice hardened, as if he'd just piped a line of metal through it. 'He's my son. The decision is made. He leaves after Zohr on Wednesday.'

There was nothing left to say; his voice left no space for argument. 'And Ammoo?'

'Give Ammoo my salaam.'

He would even shun his own mother. 'You don't want to see her?'

'Tell her we are praying for her recovery, inshallah.'

And then he was gone.

Of course, the boy would never agree to it. He would refuse, and she would have another argument with Sohail. This time, she would be prepared; Ammoo would help. But the next day Maya found Zaid dancing on the rooftop, plucking leaves from the lemon tree that brushed the first-floor windows, sprinkling them over his head. He bounded down the stairs, yah yah yah, wearing a brand new lungi, the starch of it making him look wider than he really was, a half-sleeved kurta and a cap on his head. A small trunk was in his arms.

'I've come to show you my new things.' He laid the trunk on the ground and gently, reverently, hinged it open. Fingernails clipped. Excited hands revealing the treasures within. A comb. A stick of neem for his teeth. A crisp-paged Qur'an. Two new lungis. And the chappals, wrapped in newspaper. His father had gone back to the shop and paid for them. 'It has a lock,' he said, showing her the key attached to a string around his neck.

There was nothing more for her to do. She wanted to give him something for his trunk. What could she give him? Photographs were banned. No books other than the Qur'an. Toys out of the question.

In the end she packed up a few balls of sweet puffed rice. 'Here,' she said, 'some snacks for your trip.'

He placed them delicately in the trunk, careful not to disturb the other objects.

'You'll be all right?'

He smiled, still caught up in the joy of it. School. Other children. The women upstairs no longer worrying he was getting too old to be around them. His father's heavy hand on the back of his head.

'How will you get there?'

'Abboo. He says we'll take a train, and the ferry. And a bus, and a rickshaw.'

She closed her eyes and imagined his journey. Holding his father's hand – had he ever known it before, the grip of his father's hand? Heaven. And the ferry, the syrupy tea, the river wind wrapped tightly around him, the sky open and vast and giving a boy a small piece of the world. And here her imagination reached its limits.

The building's sagging mud walls and patchy green moss. The courtyard strewn with chicken bones, a dirty drain clogged with spit. He swallows the lump of disappointment, his heart lifting, for a moment, at the chorus of sound drifting into the courtyard. His father quickly releases his hand and suddenly the Huzoor appears, unsmiling, taking the key from around his neck, examining his trunk, tossing aside the sweet moori. He nods to his father, yes, he will be instructed in the way of deen, he will not be tempted by the modern life, and all the while he is watching the pale green lizards as they scurry and fuck and lose their tails, and the cane that lies upon the Huzoor's low table, and his knees are starting to ache as his father's speech continues, so he is relieved when he is asked to stand up, and when he is given a blanket and a plate he dreams of what he will be fed. And as he crosses the courtyard, he wonders if he will meet the other students now, and then a door opens and there is another key, and his father's voice says As-Salaam Alaikum, the Huzoor's face retreats and the door swings shut.

He is alone with the blanket and the plate, the grey light from a slit between the thatch and the wall, the scratch of rats, and as the lock is turned he hurls himself at the door and opens his voice to the footsteps fading with every moment, until there is nothing but his own voice, begging to be released, and his fist on the wall, and each cry echoing into the next: Abboo, Abboo, Abboo. At this moment he is more afraid of what is in the room, the aloneness and the rats and the line of light against the wall, than of what is beyond. He is wrong.

1974

January

Whatever else had led Sohail to delivering sermons on his rooftop – Piya, the war, the disappointing ordinariness of freedom – Maya had always believed it was Silvi, his oldest and first love, who had finally brought about the end of his old self.

Silvi had continued to live across the road. After her husband's death, she had started covering her head, and now, on the rare occasions when she left the house, she was seen in a black chador that masked everything but her eyes. Her mother, Mrs Chowdhury, once a great friend of Rehana, was rumoured to have become an obsessive hand-washer, spending hours in the bathroom scrubbing at her fingers until they peeled and bled. More and more rooms of the grand two-storey house were closed off, until Mrs Chowdhury lived in one bedroom, and Silvi in another.

The other neighbours had written them off, but Maya was convinced Silvi was just biding her time. She knew that whatever direction her brother might be taking, it would be Silvi who pressed him further along the journey; after all, Silvi had come to her own conclusions about the Almighty. Maya knew Silvi was watching from across the road. And she knew, though he never told her, that Sohail secretly longed for Piya, and that he had decided that this longing must be erased, must be conquered, so that he could fulfil his duty – the reason why, he believed, he had survived the war.

It was true. For months Silvi had kept her vigil, as the people gathered to hear Sohail speak. She saw the men and women sitting in columns, side by side. She couldn't hear his words, but from her rooftop she saw his rooftop, and the bodies that swayed with the cadence of his voice.

And while Silvi watched Sohail, Maya watched Silvi. She saw the parting of Silvi's curtains whenever Sohail appeared. She saw the black outline of her, hanging up her washing on the rooftop so she could peer across at Sohail and his followers. One day, after the sermon had ended and the Azaan been recited, Maya saw Silvi open her gate and cross the road. Silvi caught the eye of a young woman on her way out. Come here, she said, motioning with her hand. The woman looked very little like a religious supplicant – she wore a plain salwaar-kameez and didn't even cover her head. Maya stood behind her own gate and listened to the exchange.

'What goes on in that house?' Silvi asked.

The woman smiled. 'He is a very wise man,' she said. 'A wise and humble man.' And she gazed directly into Silvi's eye, and Maya knew that Silvi was being told everything she needed to know, because Silvi must remember the hypnotic quality of Sohail's voice, and the way he made people want to believe everything he said, and the deep conviction he brought to every word, and the rising colour in his cheek, and the way he raised his hand, gently, as if he were about to caress you, and the stillness of the rest of him, all his energy, his power, channelled into his voice, its current swift, and long, and steady.

What exactly was he preaching, Silvi wanted to know.

'It cannot be explained,' the woman said, looking more and more as if she were in love, 'it cannot be explained.'

And the woman left Silvi at the bungalow gate, treading confidently away, taking with her a piece of that river voice, that little piece of astonishment. Maya was about to confront her, to warn her away, to tell her that she had already broken Sohail's heart once, and that she no longer had a claim to him. But before Maya could act, Silvi climbed up the ladder, surprisingly nimble in her cloak. Maya never knew what happened on that roof, what words were exchanged by Silvi and her brother. She tried to imagine it and she could conjure up only this: that Silvi approached Sohail, still kneeling from the prayer, and said, 'You remember the slave Bilal. He was punished by Ummayah for becoming a Muslim. He was forced to lie outside in the heat with a stone on his chest. And what did he shout to the sun, beating mercilessly on him?'

'One,' Sohail replied, 'One.'

That is how she dealt the final blow. 'One,' she said. 'There can be only One.'

Sohail and Silvi were married in March of the following year. Maya attended out of pity for her mother, who was pretending it was all for the best. Ammoo suggested to Sohail that, because her first marriage had been hastily conducted, Silvi might want to enjoy being a bride this time around. She might like to have her hair done, or hire a girl to decorate her hands and feet. But Sohail said Silvi didn't want any of it. Quietly, they said. No ceremony.

So Rehana printed a few cards and sent them with boxes

of sweets to everyone she knew. Orange-studded Laddus and curd-dusted Pranharas, the sweet named for heartache.

Mrs Rehana Haque is delighted to announce
the marriage of her son
Muhammad Sohail Haque
to
Rehnuma Chowdhury (Silvi)
daughter of late Mr Kamran Chowdhury
and Mrs Aziza Chowdhury
May God bless the Happy Couple

This was how they came to cross the road on a Friday morning in March, carrying a set of clothes for Silvi and a small pair of gold earrings. It was all the jewellery Rehana could afford. Maya had good intentions as she was getting ready, telling herself there was nothing to be done, that she should try to make amends before it was too late, but halfway across the road, between the bungalow and the crumbling mansion, she was seized with a sudden hatred for Silvi. How grim this whole operation was, Sohail retreating to the woman who had once spurned him, who was taking him back only because his fears had suddenly aligned with her own.

Silvi changed into the clothes they had brought, the earrings obscured by the tight headscarf she wrapped across her forehead. Sohail sat alone in Mrs Chowdhury's drawing room while the rest of them crowded into Silvi's bedroom. Silvi sat hunched under her sari, her face invisible. When the contract was pushed in front of her, she signed it quickly and with a sure hand.

It still surprised Maya how small their world had remained. There were no swarms of relations, no uncles and grandparents. It had always been this way: they had spent Eid with Ammoo and her friends from the Ladies' Club; their birthdays were celebrated thinly, with a few neighbours dropping in. And yet Maya could never remember feeling alone, anxious that they were marooned on their own little island while everyone else was sheltered by their extended circle of relations. It must have been difficult for Ammoo, responsible for constructing a family out of just the three of them. Perhaps this is why she and Sohail, and eventually Ammoo, had attached themselves so much to the war effort. Suddenly it did not matter that they had grown up without a father, that their relations were a thousand miles away and had abandoned them, because all the fighters, and their mothers and sisters, were kin, their very own people, as though they shared features, histories, bloodlines. But all of this was before Silvi and Sohail made their own family, with followers and supplicants. They wouldn't need a war after that, or even their own blood.

After the ceremony, Mrs Chowdhury served tea and luchi-aloo, puffed bread and sour potato curry. Ammoo suggested Maya sing a song to entertain them, but Silvi shook her head and whispered no. Maya noted the way her mother obeyed her. They ate their luchi-aloo in silence.

At the end of the meal Mrs Chowdhury's servant appeared with a red suitcase, which he handed to Sohail. Then the four of them, Rehana, Sohail, Silvi and Maya, crossed the road and returned to the bungalow. Mrs Chowdhury did not even see them to the gate, maybe because Silvi herself did not seem sorry to be leaving home, or her mother.

After loving the girl from across the road, after witnessing her marriage to another man, after waiting, patiently and without malice, for him to die, and after conquering his own desire for the girl he had found in the barracks, Sohail had finally got his bride. Nothing could separate them now. Despite the joyless, quiet ceremony, Maya knew Sohail was revelling in this small bit of satisfaction.

And what of the rooftop? The sermons continued, but they

were no longer about the many faces of God. There was only one. One message. One Book. The world narrowed. Curtains between men and women. Lines drawn in the sand. And Silvi, coated in black, reigned in her brother's heart.

1984

October

By morning, the cell has achieved its purpose. There are no more shouts in his throat. No words remain. He clutches his plate and he is no longer lonely, or broken-hearted by the memory of his father's footsteps, or determined to trace his way back home. He is only hungry. He can think only about what will fill that plate.

He is led to the courtyard, where he blinks at the light and the delicate, feathery aroma of the morning.

The others are already seated, fingers dipped into their breakfast. A circle of eyes follows him as he sits down and places his plate in front of him. They laugh, a moment before a hard, tight-fingered palm strikes the back of his head. The voice says, 'Wazu, prayer, then you eat, bodmaish.'

He locates the square of cement on to which he is meant to squat, and the tiny tap that protrudes from the side of the building. Most of the boys have returned to their meal, but some watch while he removes his cap and circles one hand over another, prods the insides of his nostrils and ears. He prays.

Finally, he is allowed to eat. The rice is cold and overcooked, but he swallows it in great gulping mouthfuls. As he takes his final bite, a boy throws a spray of rocks at him.

He has missed the dawn lesson. After breakfast he is led into a room with long rows of low, wooden tables. When he sits cross-legged on the mud floor, the table reaches his chest and on it he can place his Qur'an. A man sits at the front of the room with a square desk of his own. His Qur'an is raised by a triangular shelf that holds the book open. In his hand is a length of cane that catches the light and casts snake-like shadows across the room.

He pretends to read, his fingers on the Book, his body moving back and forth, as if at sea and battered by the tide, but now his mind meanders back to his father, the cell, the ferry ride, and as the anger heats up within him he is suddenly very tired, his eyes dragging downwards. To stay awake he concentrates on the wiry shape of the cane, the thought of it striking his legs. He wonders if he can sneak into the Huzoor's room and retrieve his puffed-rice snacks. He misses Maya. He looks around the room to see if anyone is trying to catch his eye, but no eyes reach out to his; they are all on the same ship, all battered by the same tide.

Later, he tries to sleep, after counting the different noises in the room, the rats, the hum-snoring, the rustle of mosquito nets as they are tucked into sleeping mats. His father has neglected to give him a mosquito net. The Huzoor has instructed the other boys to stretch their nets over his mat, but they have refused. He counts the number of times a mosquito lands near his ear, its buzzing louder than anything he has heard all day. Even the roar let out by the Huzoor when he discovered the boy didn't know the Arabic alphabet. What comes after alif, ba, ta, sa?

What comes after the walking-stick letter? He doesn't know. The Huzoor strikes him three times across the palm. One, two, three. The mosquito is louder than the strike, beating its wings together, hectic, stereophonic.

He falls asleep in the company of wings.

1984
November

Joy was leaning against his car. She had heard the horn, gone outside to see who it was and found him smiling, his hands in his pockets.

'I haven't seen you in weeks,' he said.

'I didn't call – I've been so busy with Ammoo.' She thought of the last time, with Zaid and the magic trick. Afterwards, the boy had refused to reveal what he had whispered in Joy's ear. She had hardly left the house since then; in fact, as she looked down at herself now, dressed in a loose cotton salwaar-kameez, she imagined he was already regretting his decision to come. She thought of very little aside from the care of her mother. She ferried her to and from the hospital; she oversaw the chemotherapy treatment; she took an advance from the German tenant to pay the medical bills. And with the little energy she had left, she went back and forth with herself about Zaid. At times she wondered if Sohail might have been right to send him away; after all, he was his father, and the child was not easy. Perhaps he needed the discipline, and it was school, in its own way – school was what the boy had always wanted. At other times she was filled with a cold rage; she lay awake at night and imagined herself screaming at Sohail. Mostly she just ached to see the boy; she would turn as if to tell him something, and then remember it could be weeks, or months, before she might meet him again. She tried to ask Khadija where he was, exactly, but no one upstairs was willing to tell her.

'Actually, I've got an appointment,' Joy said.

Was he flirting with her? 'With who?'

'Not an appointment, really – I heard he was at home in the afternoons. After three o'clock.'

So that's why he'd come. She resisted the small pinch of disappointment. She remembered that night, in front of Shaheed Minar, when he had cried and taken off his shoes – it seemed such a long time ago. Whatever had seemed possible in that moment had vanished. He was different, the awkwardness gone. The years in America had fallen away, and the Bengali-ness had reasserted itself – she could see it everywhere in him, in the way he held the key of his Toyota in his left hand, swirling the key ring around his finger, and in the slight shadow of stubble he permitted himself.

'Well, if he's given you an appointment, you'd better not be late.'

'Perhaps you could go up and announce my arrival,' he said. 'I'm not sure what the protocol is.' She saw him wanting to ask how changed his friend really was, to ask whether he would be welcome in his jeans and short-sleeved shirt, head uncapped, mind still barricaded against religion.

Maya led the way. At the top of the stairs, seeing Rokeya perched again with her face to the sun, she motioned for Joy to stop. 'Wait here.'

'Rokeya. It's me, Maya.' Rokeya's eyes were closed. Maya tapped her on the shoulder. She turned around and opened her eyes, swaying slowly back and forth, intoxicated. Maya crouched down and looked closely at her. Lines of sweat criss-crossed her face, and her lips were damp and loose. Underneath the burkha, she could see the rise of her belly. 'Rokeya,' Maya said, 'go inside. You'll get heatstroke.'

'I have to stay here.' She smiled thinly. 'It's all right.' She turned away again, a flower to the sun.

'I've brought a guest. A man.'

Hurriedly Rokeya pulled the nikab over her head. 'This way,' Maya said to Joy, resisting the urge to explain the sight of Rokeya kneeling in the sun, or the rest of the scene, the small piles of rubbish dotted along the ground, the windows papered over, the smell of cooking grease and the sharp odour of urine.

At the entrance to the outer chamber, Maya raised her voice and asked for the Huzoor.

'Who is it?' came the reply.

'His sister, Sheherezade Maya.' Her full name, so infrequently uttered, added to the strangeness of the occasion.

'Wait,' the voice inside said.

'Tell him his friend Joy is here.' What's was Joy's non-nickname name? Farshad? Farhan? 'Farhan Bashir.'

They waited in the shadow of the doorway. Minutes passed. For some reason neither spoke. Joy remained fixed in his place, standing with his back to the building and looking out over the road. Then, a shuffle of feet. The curtain parted and a few men left the room, glancing at Maya and quickly averting their eyes. They were soon pooled at the bottom of the stairs, waiting, she assumed, for the signal to return.

A man ushered them inside. The room was smaller than the women's chamber, but improved by windows on two sides and a fresh coat of whitewash. The floors were covered in a patchwork of mismatched carpets and thick white sheets.

Sohail was waiting for them. He stood as they approached, greeting Joy with a warm pressing of his hands and embracing him three times. 'As-Salaam Alaikum.' He sat down heavily in the centre of the room. 'Bring the lemonade,' he said to the man who hovered close to his ear.

Sohail did not acknowledge Maya, and she wondered if she should leave, but curiosity kept her rooted to her seat. Joy nodded at something Sohail said. He must, Maya imagined, be resisting the urge to look around, his eye automatically searching for signs of the old Sohail. Not a bookcase or an LP could be seen – this he knew, this he had been told. But surely in the way he said his name, or curled his hand around Joy's shoulder as he greeted him, there would remain something of the man he had once been, and since shed, snaked off like a worn scrap of hide.

'I am so glad you have returned. I have thought of you often.' He passed Joy a small green glass.

'I have thought of you too.'

It was like the tender meeting of two old lovers. They were awkward around one another, each looking into his glass of lemonade. Joy turned the conversation to ordinary things. 'I drove a taxi for the first five years, while I completed my degree. It wasn't bad,' he said. 'I met a lot of interesting people. They told me everything, like I was a priest.'

'So you two have something in common,' Maya said, wishing they would stop staring so intently at everything but each other.

They ignored her. 'Why did you come back?' Sohail asked, holding out his hand to refill Joy's glass.

'Everyone asks me that. Because it isn't so great.'

'Sometimes we believe something is important, but it turns out to be insignificant.' Sohail pulled the cap from his head, revealing a full head of hair in black and grey tones that matched his beard. He ran his fingers through it briefly, then returned the cap to its place, fitting and tightening it around his crown. 'There were things I held on to, for a very long time. Too long.'

Maya wondered if he was about to talk about the war; she leaned forward to hear him. Then Joy said, 'I didn't go to America for money. I went for other reasons.'

She saw Sohail debating whether to ask what his reasons were, then deciding not to. 'Did you get married?' Sohail asked suddenly.

'Yes, how did you know?'

'A man should marry. You have children?'

'No.'

'You should have children.'

'I'm divorced.'

Sohail nodded. 'Why don't you marry her?' he asked.

It took Maya a moment to realise what Sohail meant. She thought he might burst out laughing any moment, hold his stomach and apologise. But he didn't. Instead, he continued, 'Why not? She's getting old now.'

'We don't love each other,' Maya said. 'Don't you believe in love any more?'

Joy took a long sip of lemonade. 'Actually, Sohail, you're right, I should get married. But this one won't even let me take her out for phuchka.'

'Well, there are others.'

'Yes,' Maya said, 'the world is full of desperate women.' She was being unpleasant, she knew; she should have treated it casually, said something light and funny. Always too serious.

There was an awkward silence. Maya wanted to get up, but her legs were heavy, and she wanted to know what they would say to one another next, whether Joy would ask the question she knew he wanted to ask. What was Sohail doing here, in this shack on top of his mother's house, raising a son without love, in this beard, this costume, this posture of calm? Instead, he asked, 'Do you think often about it?'

'About what?'

'About the war – those villages we saved, and the ones we didn't.'

Sohail didn't reply.

'And my brother, do you remember him?'

'I remember him every day,' Sohail said. 'Your brother and your father both. And you. You saved my life, Joy. I will never forget that.'

Joy had been captured while her brother ran free.

'It wasn't me,' Joy said.

'God is great.'

That was not what Joy had meant. What he had meant was, it was just a matter of chance, that the soldiers had found him and not Sohail. They both fell silent, remembering that long November night. 'Why did you do it, Sohail?' Joy asked finally. 'What made you like this?'

Maya thought Sohail would have a quick and practised response, something about how his path was the natural one, that the question was not why he had become what he had become, but why Joy hadn't joined him. But instead he appeared hesitant, almost nervous, cupping the glass in his palm. He seemed to have no answer for Joy.

Joy turned his face away and caught Maya's eye. She had thought, until that moment, that he had been fooling around, that he might like to trap Sohail into saying something ridiculous, but now she realised he was angry, very angry, as though Sohail's being there, his having become who he was, had something to do with the death of his brother.

'These are mysteries that cannot be explained in brief. Why don't you come to the taleem? We can speak about it then.'

The man returned and spoke softly into Sohail's ear. 'Khadija-ma asks if your guests will stay long.'

'Tell her they will be going soon, inshallah.'

It was time to leave; there appeared nothing left to say. Maya saw the disappointment in Joy's face. She knew that Joy must have thought often of Sohail, while he was in jail, and later, in New York, when he drove that taxi. She suspected that taxi-driver Joy had not elaborated on his gun-wielding, dogs-at-his-heels past; that he had taught himself the alien politeness of *you have a good day now* and *where to, ma'am*, learned to discuss the weather as though it were both a suitable topic for discussion and a way to avoid discussion altogether.

But in that foreign city, where he had been a cabbie, not a freedom fighter, where his most heroic act had been to run the occasional red light – and with the guilt of surviving the death of his brother, propping him up against a tree while the shelling approached, watching the blood escape from his body like water out of a mountain, long behind him – he must have thought of Sohail, thought about writing letters and making long-distance calls, turning their friendship into an ordinary one of traded news. But he hadn't been able to. And now this, this mystery. Joy wouldn't have known what to expect, though perhaps there was some part of him, some arrogance, which might have led him to believe he could catch a glimpse of it in action, cup it between his hands, because no one, after all, knew Sohail as he did, no one else had shaken the fleas out of his bread, or picked the lice out of his hair, or run with him through the smoke and thunder of bullets. No one else had gone to jail while he had run free.

Joy stood to take his leave. Sohail stood as well. They embraced. 'You will always be a brother to me,' Sohail said, his eyes bright.

'And you to me,' Joy replied. The anger had left his face, replaced now with something else – a kind of longing, even envy. Perhaps there was a feeling at the back of Joy's throat, the feeling that this man slept easier than he did, that he didn't need to suck the marrow out of his memories or escape to a tall city to get away from them. Sohail didn't seem to mind, as he stroked the beard that protruded from his chin, that it was threaded with grey; and he didn't seem to mind about the shabbiness of his house, the stains on the carpets, the cement that scratched your feet as you removed your shoes to enter his room. He didn't seem to mind about anything at all. Not in this world.

'Khoda Hafez,' Joy said, his hands sandwiched again between Sohail's.

'Come again soon.' Sohail turned around, and Maya suspected that she and Joy were forgotten already, trumped by the tasks that lay ahead – prayer, sermon. The afterlife.

They descended the stairs in silence, and when they reached the bottom, Maya was reluctant to let Joy get into his car and drive away. She knew he was feeling something of what she was feeling, unsettled by the meeting with her brother, questions asked but not answered. She decided to ask one of her own. 'Tell me about your time in jail,' she said. 'I want to know what happened to you.'

*

Built with its back to the river, Dhaka city had little to recommend it. The roads were narrow and flooded easily, with no grand avenues or boulevards or vistas to make the heart ache and the poet draw out his pen. Still, after the war, it was awash with people who had nowhere to go, and with even more who had nothing to eat. The smell of burned thatch hung in the air in the villages, so they came to the city to escape it, and remained, as had so many before them, turning their backs on one violence to face the possibility of another. And yet they chose those streets, dusty and narrow as they were, over the river that closed around them every monsoon, and over a life spent staring up at the sky, hoping for rain this week, sun the next, their feet wet from the fields, and backs aching from bending over the paddy.

Joy had little affection for the city, but on the day he was released from jail he fell unexpectedly in love with it. That morning, the young subedar unlocked his cell, turned silently away and joined the retreating army. Joy turned to his cell-mates, Raheem and Sultan and the old Abbass, helping them to their feet. They hesitated, the other three, at the threshold, not believing they weren't being tricked into the firing squad or the leg room. But Joy had recognised the loud passage of Indian fighter jets, had known they were on the brink of victory.

In his three months of captivity Joy had refused to speak. Not a word of assent, or protest, or denial, no shake of the head or movement of the hand. At the guerrilla camp in Sonamura they had been told something – he couldn't remember – about being captured, but, like the rest of their training, it was perfunctory, told casually as though it would never happen. The officers had taken this tone with all matters of disaster, parcelling out instructions with dry voices and short sentences, as though no one would ever get shot in the middle of an oper-ation and need to be dragged by his collar and propped up against a tree so that his brother could watch him die, catch his final words in the spoonful of his ear, lock them in his heart until it was safe to tell their mother.

There were twenty-three of them, captured in November on a hot, rain-thirsty morning. And he watched as they were taken, one by one, into the room next door, the leg room. And encour-aged to speak. And as soon as they spoke – said I am a mukti, yes, I fought against the army, yes, I betrayed the country, yes, yes, I am a traitor, yes, I believe in Bangladesh, yes, I was seduced by Sheikh Mujib, Sheikh Mujib is a pig, I am a pig, yes, yes, yes – whatever was being done to them would stop. And the rest of them, bound together by their equal hatred of the piss-pot in the corner of the cell, the foot beatings, the word 'bastard' attached to the mispronunciation of their name, eased into a quiet night, waking, the next morning, to the call to prayer followed by the snap of bullets.

That the soldiers liked to do their shooting at the hinge of day was another of their incomprehensible habits, like the taking of meat in the morning, which they did daily without fail.

Silence, and then the shot. This was all the schooling Joy needed. So when they took him out into the yard, he did not scream or curse or spit or rage. He pretended he couldn't make any sounds, and soon it became too difficult to utter words at night and forget them in the day, so he gave up speaking altogether. He learned the gestures of animals – the fingers in the mouth, hand in front of his face, the wave to indicate friendship. With his tongue trapped, his hands were freed – to hold the head of the boy who had run away to fight, the soldier with the torn shoulder, the one who feared the current above all other things and, later, his thing, to ease the pain. Beard growing, hands healing, tongue-tied, Joy passed his three months in the belly of a cell, determined he would survive to see what came after.

The soldiers marked time by the sounds they routinely heard. The call to prayer. The splashing of water while performing the Wazu. The unrolling of prayer mats. The screams of the birds, arguing throughout their morning rituals. The prisoner dragged, heels collapsing, in front of the firing squad. His final plea for mercy.

But this prisoner made no sound. Not at the beating of his soles or the putting out of cigarettes on his back or the electrocution of his mouth. They rode him harder than all the others, charged with the suspicion, the hope, that his silence was loaded, that he might yield something special. He must know something, and he must have been trained to keep it, this secret. It was just a matter of cracking him. So they waited, taking him every day to the leg room, the upside-down room, the chair. He didn't cry, he didn't speak.

Finally, it was too much for his captors to bear. On a particularly slow day, they took their revenge. The new prisoners they were expecting had failed to arrive, and it was only the silent one and the old man who had dried up a long time ago, not worth the price of a bullet. The birds were winning. Singing, gurgling, cackling. Aftab, the youngest in the unit, fired a shot into the tamarind tree, sending the birds flapping, raising their voices, and now they moved to the windowsills of the barracks and picked at the remnants of food tossed carelessly through the bars, the dried-up bits of bread. The rest of them cursed him for shooting into the tree, typical Sindhi behaviour, they said, probably shits softer than the rest of us.

They dragged Joy out to the compound. Aftab nudged him with the back of his rifle. 'Make the birds stop singing,' he said. 'Bengali birds, they'll listen to you.'

Joy stood silent as the flap of birds continued around him, like sheets in the wind.

'Do it.' The slap of the rifle, the small rectangle of pain. 'Now,' he said, 'make those sisterfucking birds shut the fucking hell up or I will shove a bullet up your ass, I swear it.'

Joy raised himself to his knees and pointed at the tree. Nothing happened for a few moments: the birds continued to crowd the windowsill, picking and flirting and flapping. Then a small one separated from the others and sailed up, away from the compound, circling the perimeter of the building. The soldiers lifted their eyes to it as it turned and came towards them, landing quietly on Joy's outstretched finger. With his other hand, Joy stroked the bird as it moved up on to his arm, settling on the crook of his elbow. That was the last day he was whole; later they took his finger as payment, so the birds would have one less place to perch, one less reason to sing.

Freed in February, Joy fell in love with the city. Dhaka was the first thing he saw when he opened his eyes, and its air was the first into which he spoke; it was the only place he wanted to be. He walked home, making his way out of the army cantonment and through the live streets, embraced by strangers who cried out at the sight of his scarred arms, his absent finger.

It wasn't until he got home that he learned the war had taken his father too. He walked into the house and saw his mother in a white sari and he knew. She sent him away, then, sent him as far from Dhaka as she possibly could, mortgaging their house and pawning her wedding jewellery. And he had grasped at the chance and fled without looking back, without regret or sentiment.

He never thought about why he had been caught that night. Never minded it. On that November morning when it refused to rain, he had run free for six hours, scratched by close, thin-limbed trees, chased by the sound of dogs until his breath gave out – and in the few seconds it took them to catch up with him he had enough time to contemplate taking the gun to himself but not enough to balance the rifle against his head. So, as the day cracked open, hot and tired, and he walked back into the city with his arms and legs shackled, he thanked the soldiers for their speed, because he wasn't ready to die, not on that day, not in the very year he had watched the blood ribboning out of his brother.

Headmaster Headmaster Headmaster Huzoor Huzoor Huzoor. Your whip is a snake. Why you bracelet my wrist? Why keno por que? I speak all the tongues but Arabic. You take revenge on my Arabic. Revenge on the palm of my hand. Zaid was an orphan adopted by the Prophet. I am an orphan. The Prophet was an orphan. Peace and blessings be upon the orphan that was the Prophet. When my mother died, the Kazi said, *You are now an orphan.* My father took me across the river and he told the Huzoor, he is in your hands now, and Allah's. The Huzoor takes my hand. He puts my hand on his heat. His whip is a snake. His snake is a whip. Hands on the heat. In the Huzoor's hand. In Allah's hands. Because my hands were wandering. Stealing. Coins and notes. Why you hold my hands behind my back? Keno why pourquoi? I always ask them to teach me three things. Hello and Goodbye, peace on earth, and why. They don't like to teach why. I get it out of them. Why why why. Why did you put me in the Huzoor's hands? Why the Huzoor's hand? His hand on my hand. My hand in his hand. It is always like this for the new ones, one of the boys tells me. He is happy I am here, no more Huzoor for him. You are too pretty, he says. Foreign eyes. I am the Prophet's orphan. The Huzoor likes light eyes. The Huzoor's hand in my hand. All the boys laughing. The doors are always locked. The Huzoor carries the key around his neck. The toilet is outside, it is a hole dug into the ground. Deep. Flows into the river. I can hold my breath that long.

1984
December

'The treatment hasn't worked,' Dr Sattar said. He would have to take out a piece of her liver. Rehana laughed at this news, and they all knew immediately what she found so funny. Kolijar tukra, *piece-of-my-liver*, was a common form of endearment; she had applied it many times to her children. My sweet, my heart, piece-of-my-liver. In all those years, she had never thought that she had promised to give an actual piece of the organ away. She said, 'Make sure you leave enough of it in there, Dr Sattar. I believe it's my only one.'

The surgery was scheduled immediately. That night, as she was helping her mother with her bag, packing toothbrush, comb, prayer mat, Maya had the feeling she should have come up with a list of things to say, words stored up in the event of this very occurrence. In the months since her mother had told her about the tumour, she should have been preparing herself. Instead, what had she done? Shaved her mother's hair, sorted through her medication, ferried her back and forth from the hospital, made short, abrupt phone calls to her friends to give them the news: yes, Ammoo is feeling better, yes, she's been eating. I gave her the food you sent, she liked it, yes, I agree, she needs to keep up her strength. Can you come around ten? She is better in the morning.

And she had nurtured a fragile alliance with the upstairs. She could think of her brother without that piercing anger, she could behold the serene, remote man he had become, and she could lie in her bed and listen to the chaotic footsteps above, and she could watch the clouds of men and women go up and down the stairs, and yes, she could even bear to witness the ragged condition of the boy, and tell herself it was all a casualty of the past.

She told herself she was growing up. There was her mother, and there was readjusting to the city, and the lack of politics, and maybe, just maybe, the beginning of a truce with Sohail. But that was all. Silently she folded Rehana's clothes, listening for the rustle of rain in the trees so that she would have something to remark on, so she could make some comment about the garden, how it would flood if they had another downpour. She started a few sentences in her head, but none of them sounded right. She remembered something Dr Sattar had said. 'The disease hasn't won yet.' She clung to this.

Rehana was sitting up in bed, cross-legged, with her right hand on the Qur'an. 'You need your rest, Ammoo, you know how the ward is.' It had finally begun to rain, soft sheets casting grey shadows into the room.

'It says here your lord has prescribed for himself mercy. Do you know what that means?'

'No.'

She closed the Book. 'You never did pay any attention to your ustani.'

Maya flopped down on the bed beside her mother. 'She never explained anything to me. And she told me to shave between my legs.'

Rehana's eyes widened. 'I don't believe you.'

'I'm not joking. She said it was cleaner that way. But you remember, Ammoo, she was always scratching herself there?'

'No, I don't remember.'

'I swear, I thought there was a man hiding under that burkha. Or a hive of mosquitoes.'

'Chi!' Rehana slapped Maya gently on the cheek, but she was laughing now, shaking her head. 'You're still that little girl who pretended to be ill every time the teacher came. You told her you had your period, remember, when you were only eight.'

'She ran out of the house so fast!'

'When will my little girl grow up, hmm? Give me some grand-children?'

'I'd have to get married first, you know.'

She placed her hand on the cover of her Qur'an, her fingers tracing the gold lettering. 'I hardly knew your father when we married. After it was arranged there was a photograph going around the house, but I didn't have the courage to ask for it. Marzia brought it to me one night, and we examined it by candlelight.'

'What did you think?'

'That I wished I hadn't seen it. I had to marry him anyway.'

'Would it be so bad, if I never married?'

'No, it wouldn't be so bad. Look at me, I've spent most of my life without a husband.'

'Men can be so horrible.' She was thinking about Nazia now, the baby that came out with narrow eyes and a foreign cast, and Saima and Chottu, and all the cruelties that might be inflicted on her if she agreed to be someone's wife.

'That's true,' Rehana said, stretching her legs slowly and

leaning back on her pillow. 'But to whom will you utter your sorrows, my little girl?'

'I don't know.' Maya found her mother's foot under the blanket and began to knead it. 'I'll do what you did.'

Rehana smiled. 'I am taking comfort from the love of my child.'

Maya felt it stirring then, the need, deeply buried, for love. The chemo had made Rehana's circulation sluggish; her feet were cold, and Maya heard her sigh as she scrubbed the arch with the palm of her hand. Outside, the rain softened the other sounds of the evening. The crickets and the lizards chirped, the high notes of their calls swallowed by the fall of water. Only the leaves increased their volume, making themselves heard as they clapped against the raindrops.

She had told herself many times that marriage could not be for her. Or children. She saw them coming into the world every day, selfish and lonely and powerful; she watched as they devoured those around them, and then witnessed the slow sapping of their strength as the world showed itself to be far poorer than it had once promised to be.

Rehana closed her eyes, suddenly appearing very tired. 'Say Aytul Kursi with me,' she said.

'All right.' Despite telling herself it was for the sake of her mother, the same thing she told herself of the visits upstairs, Maya felt relief flooding through her as she recited the prayer. The words stumbled out of her at first, then came to her smoothly, like the memories of childhood, her favourite foods, the marigolds on the lawn.

Allahu la ilaha illa Huwa, Al-Haiyul-Qaiyum.
There is no God but He, the Living, the Self-subsisting, Eternal.
La ta'khudhuhu sinatun wa la nawm.
No slumber can seize Him, nor sleep.

'I would like you to pray, Maya. Just once a day, at Maghreb.'

Maya shook her head. 'You know I can't do that, Ma, it wouldn't be fair.'

'To who?'

'To all the believers.' She was crying now, the tears landing hot and soft on her cheek.

'God is greater than your belief,' Rehana said. 'I'm asking you because you might need something, if I am gone.'

'Ma, please, don't say that.'

'You act so independent. You left home, you made your own life. You're a strong girl. But who will take care of you when I am not here? I wish you had something of your own. Your father would have wanted that.'

Something of her own. What could she have? A marriage, a family, a God? She had prepared herself for none of these. And then she realised Ammoo had been encumbered by her daughter's loneliness all this time. She has had to bear me all alone. All my burdens. Perhaps, Maya thought, she should tell her mother that it was all right for her to die now, that she would find a way to make up for the space that would be left behind. But she couldn't do it, she wasn't ready. 'Let's pray some more, Ammoo, if that will make you feel better.'

'I'm tired now, jaan. Let's go to sleep.'

Maya kept vigil beside Ammoo, listening for her breath, her hands ready to shake her if she faltered, if she showed any signs of giving in to her forehead, her fate, or her sense that she had completed what she had come to do.

And she thought about what Ammoo was asking for, a prayer once a day, at dusk, that holy hour. She thought about giving in, and wished somehow she had done it long ago, surrendered to the practicality of religion. If she chose it now, it would be a hollow bargain, shallow and insubstantial. No God she could respect would enter into such a pact, knowing the believer knocking at the door wanted nothing more than a genie, a single wish, and that even if this wish were to be accompanied by a deeper longing, there was no saying if she would ever keep her promises.

*

In the morning Maya found Zaid curled up under the small wooden desk. She peered underneath and saw his knees, wedged tight against his chest.

He opened his eyes. Held out his hands and she pulled him out from under the desk. 'How did you come?' she asked.

'The bus,' he said.

'All by yourself?' He couldn't have chosen a worse time. She had to help Ammoo pack her things for the hospital. He stank of sweat and God knew what else, and his head was shaved so close she could see the pale veins of his neck as they climbed, creeper-like, over the dome of his head. She had waited all these weeks for him, and here he was, dirty and bald and breaking her heart.

He nodded, eyes rimmed with water. 'It's a holiday,' he mumbled.

'Are you hungry?' she said, sounding rougher than she meant. She had known her mother's treatment wasn't working; she knew what it meant, the spread to the liver. Zaid was crying now, his hands pressed tightly to his face.

She grabbed him, and squeezed the breath out of his lungs. 'I've been waiting for you,' she said. 'Did you know that?'

She brought him a piece of toast and a fried egg, which he ate slowly, his mouth trembling as he chewed. Ammoo was awake, calling out to remind her to pack the prayer mat into her bag. She turned to Zaid. 'I have to take Dadu to the hospital.'

'It's a holiday,' he repeated. 'Huzoor let us go home.'

Because she had to, she believed him.

'I'll be back as soon as I can.'

He handed her the empty plate and crawled across the room, tucking himself under the desk again. 'I'll stay here. I'm just going to stay here.'

She told herself he would be all right. She would come back from the hospital and fetch him and they would go to the park and Ammoo would recover and they would all play Ludo together and he would cheat, like he always did.

*

Maya counted the hours of her mother's sleep. Twenty-two. Thirty-seven. Forty. On the third day, Dr Sattar asked Maya to call her brother. And anyone else who might want to see her. She made the telephone calls, and they came, people she remembered from her childhood, neighbours and friends. They brought their children, who tugged at the bedsheets and complained about the hospital smell. They said innalillah, as though she were already dead. Maya called the bungalow, begged for Sohail. *Ammoo is going*, she said into the telephone, *do something*.

'I've done all I can,' Dr Sattar had said; 'now we just wait.'

Rehana breathed, but she hadn't regained consciousness. Her kidneys were failing. Her fingertips had begun to turn blue.

They had put her in a private cubicle, away from the ward and the other patients. Maya greeted the guests, repeated the lines about cancer, her uterus, the liver resection. She was polite; she didn't protest when Mrs Rahman brought a piece of thread from the Saint of Eight Ropes and tied it around Rehana's wrist.

On the fourth day, Dr Sattar pleaded with Maya to go home. Just for a few hours. Freshen up. Change her clothes. When she refused, he offered to let her rest in the doctors' lounge. He held her elbow and led her down the stairs and across the courtyard. She knew the way, through the green corridors, the patients lining up outside, holding ragged bits of paper and files with worn, blackened edges.

'I'll send someone to fetch you. Sleep now.' Dr Sattar shut the door behind him, and Maya focused her eyes on a line of light under the door. Yellow and gold, it glowed steadily, lying about the other side, where her mother lay, blue-fingertipped, dying out of herself. She told the line of light she would stare at it until its colour changed, until it turned from gold to blue, day to night, but her eyes must have closed, because when she opened them the light was there again, steady, unflinching, casting its narrow length into the room, and she thought, then, of her father, of the short line of his life, and of all the boys who had bled into the dust, and of her brother, and his child, and she suddenly remembered Zaid, wondered whether he was still hiding under the desk – how could she have left him there? – and then she worried whether she would ever have a boy of her own, because she might never be able to love anyone enough, love them enough to swallow their loneliness and make it her own.

The line of light shone steadily. Day remained day. Then it lengthened, acquired shadows. She held up her hand to shield her eyes. A nurse in the doorway.

'How long has it been?'

'A few hours. Not long.'

She returned to a roomful of strangers, a ring of men in long white coats. Were they ready to write it up? Fifty-two-year-old woman with stage four metastatic uterine cancer. Hysterectomy. Liver resection. Through the crowd, she saw her mother's feet sticking out from under the sheet, her neat, organised toes, a dark spot under her ankle bone.

Dr Sattar separated from the others. 'Come, Maya, join us.' The circle opened to let her in. Did they want her medical opinion? Now they raised their arms, palms to the sky. She understood all at once, that gesture. Not doctors after all. I put my palms up to you, and ask. O Allah, I beg. I entreat you. Her arms went up. She turned around and saw her brother at the end of the bed, where her mother's feet lay open and lonely, whispering words she didn't recognise. The men in white repeated after him, raised their voices in chorus. Ameen. She knew it was wrong, standing in a circle, facing this way and that, appealing to God. It wasn't done like this. This world, he had told her, was only temporary. Ammoo would reap her heavenly reward. It was selfish to keep her here. He was doing it for Maya, because she had begged him not to let her mother die. He had come, he had brought these men, and they had stood in a circle, not in a line facing Mecca. They knew the words. They had decided to use them.

She caught his eye, and she moved to embrace him, but his face told her to keep apart, that their keeping apart was part of the spell, so she stepped back and concentrated on believing that this was the cure.

Sohail lifted a plastic container of water, poured a small measure into a glass. Water from the Well of Zamzam. He lifted his mother's head and raised the glass to her mouth, tipping it slowly through the slight part in her lips. The drops that spilled on to her chin he did not wipe away. The men continued to recite. Dr Sattar brushed his eyes with a handkerchief.

During the war, the Pakistani soldiers would ask a boy, any boy on the street, to unwrap his lungi. Prove it, they would say. Prove you are one of us. The boy would fumble with the knot of his lungi and hold it open for the soldier to peer inside. It might be night. It's too dark to see, the soldier would say. Take it out and show us. Show us your cut, you dirty Bengali.

Maya had taught herself away from faith. She had unlearned the surahs her mother had recited aloud, forgotten the soft feather of air across her forehead when Ammoo whispered a prayer and blew the blessing out of her mouth. She had erased from her memory all knowledge of the sacred, returned her body to a time before it had been taught to kneel, to prostrate itself.

In her seven years of roaming the countryside, she had witnessed an altogether different form of the faith. The mosques were few and far between; the city, proclaiming itself newly pious, was even further away. In villages the people worshipped saints and the Prophet in equal measure. They worshipped by prayer, yes, and like everyone else they fasted during the month of Ramzaan and kept a section of land aside, if they had it, to sell someday and embark on the trip to Mecca. But in the forest they prayed to Bon-Bibi, the goddess of the trees, and they invited Bauls to their villages – thin, reedy-voiced men who sang the songs of Lalon, turning the words of the Qur'an into song, a tryst between lovers, casting the divine as the beloved, the poet as His supplicant.

Occasionally she had stood at the edge of a concert, mesmerised by the voice of the Baul. But she could not bring herself to step inside, because of the boys on the roadside, and all the things she had witnessed, committed in the name of God.

The men filed silently out of the room. Only Sohail remained, stroking his mother's forehead, whispering to her. Maya sat beside him and he reached out to her with his free hand. The room began to grow dark, the light finally changing to blue-black, and in the breeze was a hint of cold. Winter is here, she thought. Clementines will scent the city. Ammoo has planted a few vegetables this year: shim beans, cauliflower, tomatoes. Her cooking was always best in winter, suited to the bounty of the colder months. In the morning she would boil cauliflower and peas, and they would eat them just like that, with a few slices of boiled egg crumbled on top. Sohail, she remembered, would sometimes douse his plate with ketchup. Her grip on his hand tightened, and he returned her grasp, and they played this game, an old one, a Morse code of squeezes, until she was too cold to sit up and climbed into the bed with Ammoo, curling around her, resting her face against the outline of her shoulder, careful not to touch.

Maya slept, dreamed. In her dream her mother was very thirsty. Water, she said. Water. Then Sohail said it. Water. She's asking for water.

Maya opened her eyes to see him pouring the Zamzam into Ammoo's mouth. Her mouth was open. She swallowed. Maybe he would spoil the moment now by declaring it a miracle, but he just stood up and kissed his mother gently on her forehead. Then he collected his cap from the table and walked away without looking back, as though this was the only way the day could have ended.

She didn't remember to look for Zaid until it had all passed. Searched under the desk and in the garden shed and behind the curtain of cobwebs at the foot of the stairs. He was gone. She asked Khadija if she knew where he was. 'At the madrasa,' she replied. 'The Huzoor sent him back.'

Book Three

$\mathcal{Q}$

God wrongs no one,
Not even by the weight of an atom

1985

February

In winter, the rivers retreated. They sucked themselves back from the floodplain, and what was water became land once more.

The bungalow sank back into its habits. Downstairs, Rehana prepared the garden for winter and took up knitting; Sufia emptied the kitchen of all its contents and scrubbed each surface until it mirrored her hard hands and the sharp line of her jaw. And Maya returned to her columns, attacking the Dictator, the clergy, the Jamaat Party, Ghulam Azam, Nizami. Shafaat told her the letters had multiplied. *Who is S. M. Haque*, they asked. At the medical college, Dr Sattar told Maya that the students had organised a bet to guess which of their professors it might be. But he had a feeling he knew who it was. As she was leading her mother out of his office after her last check-up (I can't see any signs of the disease, my dear. Your brother seems to have frightened it away), he said, with a tender wink, *Be careful, won't you?* And he offered her a job, if she wanted one. *No point in wasting all that training.*

Upstairs, too, life continued as before. Maya stopped attending the taleem. Khadija did not call down to her, and she did not go up. She thought of ten of those visits, of Khadija's warm lap, the enveloping sound of the recitation. She knew she had been seduced, knew she had betrayed something in herself by accepting the solace it had given her. She carried a small wedge of guilt, for her own falsity, the fraud of it. As for Sohail's act, his words into Ammoo's ear, tipping the zamzam into her mouth – she had no way of cataloguing this, of putting a name to his act. The name that came to her – miracle – was not one she could believe.

Joy persuaded Maya to attend another meeting. Jahanara Imam was going to bring up something important, something Maya would regret not having heard. Ali Rahman, the tall actor who had played Hamlet in all the Bailey Road productions, opened the meeting with a recitation from Gitanjali. Beside her, Joy was a solid presence, his hands placed carefully on his knees. She noticed the bigness of him, the great pads of his fingers, the abundant eyebrows. Everything was verdant within this man, ample, alive. She suddenly had the urge to listen to the speeches with her arm woven through his.

After the poetry they all sang. 'Amar Sonar Bangla'. Jahanara Imam pulled herself to the stage and they stood and cheered. She spoke again about the war criminals. This time, Maya listened. Mujib and Zia had failed to punish the killers, and now the Dictator would never push for a trial. The collaborators will continue to live among us, she said, if we don't do something. She had made a decision.

If the state wouldn't give them justice, they would find it for themselves. They would hold a people's tribunal in which the killers and collaborators would be tried and sentenced. It took a moment for people to realise what she meant. A cheer went up in the room. Clapping. The people will pronounce their verdict on Ghulam Azam, and Nizami, and the Razakars who raped our country in '71. They would hold a trial for the killers – a citizens' trial. Not just for the boys who died in the battle-field, but for the women who were raped.

'Right now, across the country, thousands of women live with the memory of their shame. The men who shamed them roam free in the villages. No one reminds them of the sin they have committed. For those women, this trial. For them, justice must be done. If the courts of this nation will not bear witness to their grief, *we* will bear witness. *We* will bring them justice. It is our duty, our most solemn duty as citizens, as survivors.'

Maya had only one thought.

Piya.

Jahanara Imam finished her speech. A discussion began about the details. Who would stand trial? What would the witnesses say? Would there be real victims, real testimony? How would they convince people to take the stand?

She remembered what Piya said about her ordeal. I have done something. Something I regret. Something very bad. *I* have done. How could she have allowed Piya to put it that way? The memory of it came back to Maya, pointed and sharp. She forced herself to remember the moment at the clinic, the desperate look in her eye as she asked her to *finish* it. *Take away the bad thing.* Maya shook her head, trying to evict the memory, and before she knew it her shoulders began to shake and her cheeks to burn with the heat of tears, and she remembered her mother in the hospital, believing she would die, and Piya, who had turned to her for help, whom she had failed.

The meeting broke up, people rising from their seats and circling Jahanara Imam. Maya sat frozen, water falling hard and quick out of her nose. She tried to wipe her face with the back of her hand. 'Let's go,' Joy said. 'I'll take you home.'

She didn't want to go home. He packed her into the car and they sped out of the neighbourhood. Maya rubbed roughly at her face with the end of her sari until her cheeks were raw. Joy turned on Elephant Road and parked in front of a two-storey building. 'Will you stop with me, have a cup of tea?'

There was a café on the first floor, large panes of glass revealing a view of the shoe shops on Elephant Road. They sat opposite one another in a green leather booth. For a long time neither said anything. Joy allowed her to gaze out of the window for a few minutes, to smooth her hands over her face until she was sure the tears had stopped. Then he fixed her with a light, teasing stare.

'So, now that I've got you,' he said, 'perhaps you can satisfy my curiosity about something.'

'Nothing doing,' she replied, matching his tone. She fixed her eyes on the menu, relieved to be there, the waves of feeling slowly abating. 'I'm not telling you anything.' Below them, the cars and rickshaws wrestled silently on Elephant Road. 'Not until you tell me about your American wife.'

'Okay, fine. But let's make a deal. I answer all of your questions – all, and then you have to answer one of mine. Just one. Okay?'

'What is this?' She pointed to something on the menu.

'Oh, they've just misspelled cheeseburger. Have you had one before? It's like a keema sandwich. They can be rather bland – I can ask them to put some chillies on it for you.'

'All right, chillies. But no cheese.'

'You don't like cheese?'

'It gives me wind.'

He laughed.

'What?'

'It's like you missed the lesson at school on how to talk to boys.'

'I'm a doctor,' she said, irritated, 'bodily functions don't embarrass me. And what kind of education did you get? Mine certainly didn't include any life lessons.'

'I went to the same school as your brother. St Gregory's. Those Jesuits told us everything we needed to know about girls.'

The waiter approached and took their orders. Joy was polite to the man, called him Bhai, said thank you after he'd jotted down the order. 'Do you want a drink?'

'Yes, lemonade.'

'It's very sour. Sure you want to take the risk?'

'Shut up.'

'Now,' he said, placing his hands on the table, 'what do you want to know?'

'About your women.'

'There was just the one.'

'Really? I hear rumours.'

'People always trying to set me up – you know, poor injured freedom fighter needs a wife.'

'Perhaps you'll succumb.'

'Perhaps. You want to know about Cheryl. But maybe before you hear that story, I should tell you about all the shocking jobs I did while I was in New York. Just to get it over with – full disclosure. For a year I washed dishes. I drove a taxi, I told you that already. I cleaned hotel rooms for a while, then I moved on to cleaning houses. Rich people, Park Avenue, you wouldn't believe. Offices too. I saw a lot of things in those offices, after dark and all that. But the last job I had was for an old man. He was dying. He had doctors, nurses, everything, but he needed someone to watch him at night. I slept in his room. That's how I met Cheryl.'

'She worked for him too?'

'She was his daughter.'

Maya's eyebrows went up.

'Yes, that's exactly what her family thought. Marrying the help. Big scandal. I needed a passport, she needed to rebel, that was it.'

'Did you love her?' Maya imagined a light-filled room,

cigarette smoke deep in the furniture, and a tall, elegant woman in a man's shirt, the collars wide about her neck.

He seemed to consider the question. 'Maybe a little. It wasn't just a business transaction. We had to live together, learn about each other. But in the end we couldn't stay together.'

'Why not?'

'Because the relationship was incomplete. I couldn't tell her everything.'

The food arrived, a pair of meat patties between soggy layers of bread. Maya took a bite, the grease leaking on to her fingers. It was salty, and fiery from the chillies. She decided she liked it. 'Very good, your American dish,' she said, wiping her mouth. 'So, you ended it.'

'I came home.'

'Poor girl. To be left behind.' She thought of Cheryl, now without the solid bulk of Joy. How hollow her life must seem.

'She couldn't have been here with me.'

'"Never the twain shall meet"?'

He shrugged, confused.

'Kipling, you know? And Forster too.'

'I don't know what you mean.'

'Nothing. Just something I read in a book.' She remembered now, he wasn't the bookish type.

'I'm not very well read.' He crumpled the napkin in his hand and tossed it on to his plate. 'Not like your brother.'

'Don't worry. He burned his books anyway.'

'Burned?'

'Hitler-style. In the garden.'

Joy clapped his hand over his mouth.

'Yes, really.' She had relived the incident so many times in her mind, she had forgotten how shocking it was.

They sat for a moment, picking at the remnants of their meal. Joy didn't ask her why, or how, Sohail had burned his books, and she was happy not to have to describe it.

'I suppose you've answered my question. I wanted to know why you left home, why you stayed away so long. Was it because of the books?'

She made a chopping motion with her hands. 'Everything was finished in that moment.'

'What year was it?'

''77. I waited five years longer than you did.'

'True. You had higher hopes.'

'The famine, and then Mujib dying, and then the army came in and it was like the war had never happened. But when Sohail did that – I mean, he wasn't just my brother. People looked up to him. They worshipped him.'

'They still do,' he said.

He was right. 'Yes, I've seen it with my own eyes.'

'So you ran away.'

'I couldn't bear it. You want to hear what *I* did, what my jobs were? I was training to be a surgeon, you know, before I left the city. Then one day, as I was travelling through some small town, I don't even remember where it was exactly, I heard a woman screaming. She was squatting at the back of a tailoring shop, in labour. I helped her, and I felt – well, I hadn't felt like that in a long time. Like I was finally good for something. After I finished the training, I started doing it full time. I opened a clinic, trained dayyis not to use rusty knives, to boil their instruments. I convinced the husbands to send their wives to hospital when complications came up.'

'Did it make you think of having children?'

Maya shifted in her seat. 'Not really, no. I mean, I suppose I would know what to – to expect, but I don't think it's for me. I was good at it, though.' She flagged the waiter down and ordered two cups of tea.

'Much better than cleaning an old man's pissy sheets.'

'There's dignity in that. You were shepherding him out of this life, that's a noble thing.'

217

'Sohail probably thinks he's doing the same thing. Helping people into the afterlife. And I guess he feels quite noble doing it.'

'Did you know, I went upstairs and attended their taleems when Ammoo was sick?'

He tilted his head. 'I'm surprised.'

'It was – it felt like the only place in the world where I had hope she wouldn't die.'

Joy reached across the table and brushed his knuckles against hers. She was still gripping the teacup, and he moved his hand and circled her wrist with his fingers. She felt the tears coming again. 'Twice in one day,' she said, dabbing at her face with her free hand. 'You might think I cry all the time.'

'No, I imagine you hardly ever cry at all.'

She looked at him closely then, and noticed that one of his eyes was slightly bigger than the other. And his smile was crooked. It was as though his mother had loved one side of his face better than the other. I would love your whole face, she thought. I would love your whole face, and your nine and a half fingers. She caught herself staring at his lips. The last few months, Ammoo's illness, were making her forget herself. She swallowed her tea. 'I must go,' she said, rising abruptly from her seat. She insisted on paying for the meal. And when he offered to drive her home, she refused, rushing into a rickshaw and looking back only when the driver had pulled away, catching sight of his arm as it waved to her, and his eyebrows up, bemused.

*

Rehana was cured. There was no other way to put it. Dr Sattar said the chemotherapy had worked and she was in remission. She had drunk the Zamzam and the cancer had fled out of her, like birds from a tree when a shot is fired. Sohail was the shot. Rehana was cured. She walked around the garden, pulling weeds from the beds of sunflowers and dahlias. She reached between the plants, tearing them out with a flick of her wrist, and then she straightened, and stroked her belly, as if she missed it, whatever had been inside her.

Maya often caught herself staring at Ammoo, wondering what she had done to deserve this second chance. Episodes from their life together came back to her: leaving Ammoo in Dhaka while she and Sohail were taken to Lahore; leaving her again while they went off to war; and later, when she was angry at Sohail but ended up abandoning Ammoo. Leaving, always leaving. That is what she had done. She told herself to think of times she had returned to Ammoo, to this house, and recalled one day, just after the war, when she found Ammoo in the bedroom, sawing her bed in half.

It was the day after the army had surrendered, and Ammoo was holding a saw in one hand and balancing herself against the bed with the other. She had tucked the loose end of her sari around her waist, tied her hair up in a high knot and thrown all of her weight into the cutting.

Maya asked her mother what she was doing, but she ignored her, grunting and moving as though her life depended on it. The streets were filled with people celebrating and Maya was about to join them; she could already hear the radio blasting from a neighbour's window and, in the distance, shouts, firecrackers. She stood and watched, ready to leave her mother to whatever crazy sense of destruction had overcome her, eager to join in the frenzy outside.

Rehana had cut through the foot end and was making her way through the baseboard. The wood was thinner here, which made her work slightly easier, but the position was awkward. Now she struggled to lift the entire frame upright, so she could cut along its length. Maya found herself helping her to lift it, lean it against the wall and hold it steady as she stood on a chair and bore down.

'I'm doing this for you,' she said as she approached the head-board. She descended from the chair.

'What?'

She paused, wiped her forehead. 'I need some water.'

'You hold this,' Maya said, showing her how to keep it steady, 'I'll bring you a glass.'

When she returned, Ammoo was standing where she'd left her, one hand on the upturned bed, the other on her hip. She gulped the water down.

The bed was ornately carved, made of heavy teak, and it had been in that room as long as Maya could remember, one of the few wedding presents her mother had received. An heirloom. But she appeared to take great pleasure in vandalising it.

It took them over an hour just to cut through the headboard; the wood was dense and resisted their efforts. They took turns with the saw. Tiny shavings stuck to their clothes, like field bugs.

When they were finished, the two ends of what used to be Rehana's bed looked like the belly of a ship, pointing down towards the depths. Rehana said, 'Sohail will be back soon, and you'll have to share this room with me again. I thought you should have your own bed. At least.'

'We need legs,' Maya said.

There were a few offcuts of wood in the garden shed, which Maya retrieved. But they had no nails or glue of any kind, or sandpaper to smooth down the edges. Their sawing was reasonably straight but crude.

That night, they made their bed in the living room. It was cold, with just the carpet underneath them, the December chill sunk deep into the red cement floors.

'He will be back, won't he?' Rehana asked, after they had switched off the lights and tucked the blankets under their feet.

'He will,' Maya said. He had to be. He had to be all right, and coming home; too much had been sacrificed for there to be any other ending. She had missed the celebrations, but she didn't mind. Ammoo was preparing her for life after the war: new beds, a room for Sohail. Knowing this, she fell asleep with a quiet comfort in her bones.

They had slept on that sawed-in-half bed for the next few years, through Piya's arrival and Sohail's conversion, through his marrying and moving upstairs. While Maya was away, Ammoo had hired a carpenter and had the bed put back together, and it was whole now, with just a thin line on the headboard, visible if you looked closely, a long, meandering thunderbolt.

*

'There's something I'd like to contribute to the next issue. Under my own name.'

Shafaat was wedged into his chair. 'Of course, my dear, what would you like to write?'

'It's about the war—'

'Oh, would you be a darling and get me a cup of tea? I'm parched.'

Bastard. She decided not to argue, found her way to the tea station, boiled water, brewed, slammed the cup down beside his elbow. He did not raise his eyes.

'Where's Aditi?' she asked.

'At the printers. She's going to try to get us a better rate, so we can print 800 copies next issue.' He started to strike the typewriter.

'As I was saying.'

He stopped, two index fingers in the air. 'You want to write under your own name? I think our readers would prefer to hear S. M. Haque's latest diatribe.' He took a large gulp of tea. 'Did you make my tea with condensed milk?'

'Condensed milk and sugar. I thought you liked it sweet.'

'I do. But I don't like condensed milk. Please make it again. Milk and sugar.' When he saw her face darken he said, 'Come on, it'll only take you a minute. A writer needs his tea.'

As he was sipping her second attempt and nodding in satisfaction, she said, 'Jahanara Imam has called for a trial. For all the war criminals.'

He set the mug on his typewriter. 'Hasn't this been debated too many times already? We should have had a trial, I'm not denying that, but it's too late now, my dear. Too late.'

'It's never too late to seek justice.'

'Darling, it's 1985. Don't you see? We have bigger problems, Dictator isn't going to hold a fair election, we have to get him out. Then worry about other things. Country needs to move forward, not backward.'

She found herself bargaining with him. 'Just a short editorial,' she said, but he was back at his typewriter, his fingers jabbing at the keys. She wondered if she should hang about, wait for him to finish, but she was angry now – he had made her feel old-fashioned, someone still clinging to her war-wounds. She gathered her things together and headed for the door, almost bumping into Aditi in the corridor. She was holding a blue-and-pink box of Alauddin sweets, her face flushed with triumph. 'Celebration!' she said, opening the box to reveal Kalo-Jaam, Chom Chom and a single, extra-large Laddu. 'You're not leaving now, are you? I can't eat these all by myself. Can you believe it? I sweet-talked that printer into letting us do 800 for the price of five.'

Shafaat was still pounding away at the typewriter. 'Come on, Maya,' Aditi said, 'Let's keep these to ourselves. I'll make some tea.'

Maya arranged the sweets on the table beside the Linotype. She liked the smell in here, the dry warmth created by the machine.

'Isn't it exciting?' Aditi said, her cheeks pink with pleasure.

She must have enjoyed the challenge of getting a deal from the printer. He would have been caught off guard by the sight of a woman in trousers, her hair braided tightly to the back of her head, as if she were zipped up. 'What's the matter?' she asked, taking a bite out of the Laddu. 'You peeved at Shafaat? What's he done, asked you to make his tea, did he?'

Maya nodded.

'He's a pig.'

'I want to write a piece about the Razakars, you know, how they should be tried.'

'Really?' A small piece of Laddu clung to Aditi's lip.

'Shafaat isn't in favour.'

'You know how he is, can't see beyond his own two fingers.' And she imitated him, stabbing into the air.

'But he should care. And those people haven't forgotten.'

'Of course they haven't forgotten. All those people who lost their loved ones.'

'And the women.'

'Women too.'

'The raped women.'

'You mean the Birangonas?'

'Yes, the Birangonas. But calling them heroines erases what really happened to them. They didn't charge into the battlefield and ask to be given medals. They were just the damage, the war trophies. They deserve for us to remember.'

'What if they don't want to remember?'

In her years of exile Maya had met many raped women. Some wanted abortions, or came to her to get stitched up, or simply to ask if there was a way for her to wash it out of them. Not one of them wanted anyone to find out. Not one of them wanted to file a police report, or tell her husband or her father. Perhaps it was wrong of her to want them to tell. But she could not get the image of Piya out of her mind. Piya squatting on the verandah, the words bubbling at her lips. She and Sohail had conspired against her that night. They had comforted her and told her it was over, that she was safe – but they had not made it possible for her to speak. It was an act of kindness that had led to the end of everything – Maya knew that now. And there was only one way to make it right.

Aditi popped the rest of the Laddu into her mouth. 'Well, you know how it is. No one wants to stir all of that up.'

'That's not true.'

'Look,' she said, wiping her hands on her jeans, 'if it's important to you, I'll go in there and sugar him into it, okay? Don't look so glum, yaar, you'll get your piece. I'll bring him this Kalo-Jaam and he won't be able to resist.'

Maya followed Aditi with her eyes as she sailed into the other room, the box of sweets in her palm, and realised that this was what everything had been for. The sweets, pretending to commiserate with Maya, the article – all just another opportunity to plead and flirt with him and get her way. Maya didn't want Shafaat to get sugared into anything. There was something sordid, she thought, about this office, the stale stink of cigarette smoke, the belching of the tanneries near by. She remembered back to the time when she and Sohail would talk about people like Aditi and Shafaat, how they had all the right ideas but lacked something, a sort of moral core. She remembered the conversations that took them deep into the night, until Sohail fell asleep with his hands in his pockets, his head falling back, and felt a stab of pain, of longing for him.

Maya often imagined the last day Sohail wore trousers. She wasn't around to see it, but there must have been a final day, a day when he woke up in the morning, brushed his teeth, buttoned his shirt and pushed his feet through a pair of trousers. They may even have been his cherished jeans, handed down by a friend with a relative in America, procured through a mixture of pleading and bribing, like his Elvis LPs and his battered copy of *Lady Chatterley's Lover.*

All day her brother would have walked around with his legs piped through those trousers. He would have sat on rickshaws and brushed against tree trunks, and taken things in and out of his pockets. But at some point on that last day, he would have decided it would be a moulting, changing, skin-shedding sort of day. A day to abandon old fashions and adopt even older ones.

Had he predicted it? Had he known beforehand, and enjoyed those final moments, the stylish figure he cut across the university campus, the looks of admiration from his classmates, the sly glances of women?

Maya didn't think so. The last day was probably as much a mystery to him as to everyone else. It would not have been premeditated. It would have come upon him suddenly, as a revelation: that he should dress in the style and manner of the faithful, that his outward appearance should match the changes that were occurring within, that it wouldn't do to look like everyone else, to look as though he could attend parties and sit behind a desk and be called smart.

He would have decided on that day, and that day would have been the last. He would not have lingered over the trousers, or wanted a few final hours to enjoy them. As soon as he'd made up his mind, that would have been it.

And after:

A starched, white jellaba, the loose cotton pants underneath, pearl buttons on the collar. And, like a hand pressed in benediction, the cap that never left his head. That was what he wore every day after that last trousered day.

It wasn't open for debate, Maya decided. If Shafaat didn't let her write the article, she would send it to another paper. She would send it to the *Observer.* She went home and began to type.

My name is S. M. Haque, and I am here to tell you a few truths about our war. None of us is completely free of responsibility – not when we live in a country that is a living example of what we fought against – a Dictatorship, led by a man who cares nothing for this country, and a refusal to acknowledge the criminals who live among us. If we stand by and allow the crimes of the past to go unpunished, then we are complicit in those crimes. If the Dictator does not hold a trial for the war criminals, he too is a war criminal.

She signed it 'Sheherezade Haque Maya'.

1985

February

The advance rent from the German tenant meant that there would be no money coming from the big house for six months. Maya's savings had dried up. She decided to take up Dr Sattar's offer of a position at the medical college hospital. He asked her to come in for an interview. The committee noted her high marks, her letters of distinction in the final examinations, but they were perplexed by her years in the countryside. Why had she given up surgery? She answered as best she could, making the years sound far more purposeful than they had been. She managed to impress them. She would be a junior doctor, subordinate to the other doctors in her class, but it was a start. She felt a lightness in her chest as she passed through the hospital on her way out. There would be a system here, charts and registers and written prescriptions. Students to boss around. She would not be held solely responsible if a patient died, or know the patient's husband and her three other children, what they'd had to sell in order to afford the trip to hospital. Her world was contracting and expanding: she thought happily of colleagues, hospital politics, gossip in the corridors.

These were her thoughts as she returned to the bungalow that day. When she saw Joy's car in the driveway, her stomach did a little dip.

The living room smelled of perfume. A small, middle-aged woman sat on the sofa and sipped tea from the good cups. Joy sat beside her, loading his plate with biscuits and shondesh. Ammoo was perched opposite, her hands clasped in her lap, smiling.

Because she felt she was interrupting something, Maya knocked on the doorframe.

'Oh!' said her mother, 'come in, beta. Sit down. This is Mrs Bashir.'

Maya avoided looking at Joy and concentrated on the woman who was now standing up and reeling her into a tight embrace. 'My dear girl,' she said, 'I am so happy to meet you. I knew your brother, but this is the first time I'm seeing you. Let me take a look. Oh, you are a beauty, those big eyes. Not so fair as your brother, but never mind, we don't care about those things in our family.'

'Hello,' Maya said, leaning back as far as she could.

'Do feet-salaam,' her mother whispered.

'Oh, no need for such formalities,' Mrs Bashir said, releasing Maya. 'Sit beside me, you must be tired. Joy told me you're a very busy doctor. Very independent-minded,' she said, waving her arms.

Joy crossed and uncrossed his legs. Maya tried to catch his eye, but he was looking the other way. 'Maya,' Ammoo said, her voice like warm milk, 'why don't you tell Mrs Bashir what you did today? Will you have another cup of tea, Mrs Bashir?'

'I have to wash my hands,' Maya said. 'I've just come from the hospital. You wouldn't want to catch TB, auntie.'

Mrs Bashir blinked, smiled through her surprise. 'Please, beta, go right ahead.'

At the sink Maya caught a glimpse of herself. Her eyes were small and tired, and her braid had become ragged. She splashed water on herself and retied her hair.

Joy was waiting for her outside the bathroom. 'TB?'

'Well, there's been an outbreak. I wanted to warn your mother.'

In the living room, more tea had been served. Maya sat as far from Mrs Bashir as she could and stared at the ceiling. Mrs Bashir looked expectantly around the room. Her eye caught the basket beside Maya's chair.

'Do you knit, Maya?'

'No, not me.' Had Joy told this woman nothing? 'It's Ammoo's.'

'I'm just a novice,' Rehana said. 'Something to do with my hands. I thought I'd start with a scarf.'

Mrs Bashir's voice trembled when she said, 'I used to knit too. For my husband.'

They had found their common ground. 'Maya, why don't you and Joy sit in the garden for a while while us mothers have a talk?'

Outside, Joy tried to take her hand. She shrugged him off.

'You want to go for a drive?'

'No, let's walk. We need candles; the electricity's been going off at night.'

They left through the kitchen door. As soon as they had crossed the road, Maya turned to Joy. 'What's going on?'

'Nothing.' He searched his pockets and pulled out a packet of cigarettes. 'I told my mother I wanted to marry you, and she said the proper thing to do would be to pay a visit to your house. She insisted.'

He wanted to marry her. *Marry her.* She suppressed the tiny cheer that went up, unbidden. Marriage was a life sentence. 'Do you do everything your mother says?'

'No.'

Why hadn't he said anything to her? 'And did you think of consulting me first?'

'Of course. But I thought it would be best if I appealed to auntie.'

'That's pathetic.'

'Look,' he said, inhaling sharply, 'there's no conspiracy here.'

'It's pathetic and you are just trying to make me feel guilty. You know how much she wants me to get married – you're just using it against me. She's dying, you know.'

'I thought she was in remission.'

'Well, it's just a matter of time. Don't you know I think about giving her some comfort – wedding, babies?'

'I thought you didn't want any babies.'

'That's not the point. The point is I have never given her anything.' Would it be for herself, or for Ammoo? She might never know.

'Well, then, all the more reason not to delay.'

'You don't care whether I love you, you just want to take advantage of my position?' They were at the park now, where the road curved. She turned, marching towards the small cluster of shops on the corner.

'Maya, please, I know you don't mean that. Why do you always have to talk that way?'

'Because I'm a hard-hearted woman, that's why. You shouldn't want – shouldn't even dream of marrying me.'

'I dream, I can't help it.'

'Well, I can't help myself either. You can't marry me. You can't marry me and turn me into one of those women, with the jewellery and making perfectly round parathas and doing everything my mother-in-law says and only letting nice words out of my mouth.'

'Think of all the nice words you have stored up. Since you've used up all the nasty ones.'

'Don't joke.'

He flicked away the cigarette and stopped in front of her. They had arrived at the shop, which was dimly lit by a hurricane lamp. The shopkeeper recognised her and waved. 'I'm not joking. I want to marry you.'

'You can't. Go now, I have to buy the candles.' She walked away from him and up to the shopkeeper's counter, ordered the candles. She heard his footsteps retreating, and she lingered, buying oil, soap, eggs, chiding herself for listening out for him, for hoping he would come back, beg her again.

When she got home, he was leaning on the bonnet of his car.

'Drive,' she said, flinging herself into the passenger seat.

He was slow, almost casual, as he backed out of the driveway. She pressed her face against the window and the breath dragoned out of her, hot and fierce.

'Where do you want to go?' One hand on the steering wheel, the elbow poking out. It made the blood pound in her ears.

'Just drive. I don't care.' Don't cry, she told herself. It'll be so stupid if you cry. 'You could have asked me yourself, you know.'

'I wanted to get your mother on my side first.'

'She is on your side. Everyone is on your side.'

'There isn't a side.'

'You just said.'

'No sides.'

'Do you even love me?'

He shifted into fourth. Relaxed on the clutch. Smooth as forest honey.

'So you don't even love me.'

'You have something against marriage?'

She turned to face him. 'How old am I?'

'I don't know, twenty-six?'

'Thirty-bloody-two. You think I would be thirty-bloody-two without a husband if I didn't have a problem with marriage?'

'Here I was, thinking it was just a matter of the right man.'

'There is no such thing.'

'No such thing as the right man?'

'They start out all right, but then, somewhere along the way, their egos turn to glass and you have to spend your whole life with your arms around them, making them feel better while your own life turns to shit.' She banged her fist on the dashboard.

'Is this about Shafaat?'

'Shafaat – what? Oh, you're jealous now. Exactly what I meant. Ego like an eggshell. And stop smiling, damn it, this isn't funny.'

'Stings like a bee,' he said quietly, marshmallow-tender.

They were near Paltan now, and she leaned out of the car to see Paltan Maidan, the vast open field she knew so well. The car turned and she saw a brightly lit sign. She banged on the window. 'Stop here – stop. Stop the car.'

He braked, jolted. 'What?'

She wrenched open the door and flew out of the car. 'What's this?' It was dark, and hard to see beyond the gate, but she caught sight of what looked like a Ferris wheel and, beyond, the plastic animals with human faces that told her this was a playground, a children's playground. SHISHU PARK, the sign said.

Maya screamed. 'Shishu Park!' She pulled at the gates. 'Did you know?'

She could see Joy getting out of his car and coming towards her. He must know why she was crying now, and pulling at the gates. 'Who did this?' she said. 'Who did this?'

'I don't know.' He stood a few feet away from her, smoking a cigarette. At first she thought of sitting there, right there in front of the gate, and waiting for someone to come and explain to her why Paltan Maidan had been turned into an amusement park. She dragged her hands across the bars. Joy finished his cigarette and came up behind her and put his arms around her.

Then he led her to the car, opening the door for her before getting in and starting the engine. By the time they had turned around, she had wiped her face on the end of her sari.

'It's just a place,' she said, 'just an open field. They could have done anything with it, they could have left it there.' She was imagining it now, the playground, a place that in the daytime would be littered with the newspaper cones of roasted peanuts, and tiny grains of puffed rice with mustard oil clinging to them, and the ribbons that fell from the braids of little girls as they ran from the bumper cars to the Ferris Wheel and screeched to their parents to hold their hands and the unwound shoelaces and the scraps of Mimi chocolate and pink glucose biscuit wrappers. A playground. Paltan Maidan, the most sacred site of the whole country, the place where Mujib had made all his speeches, and where the Pakistan Army had surrendered, and where he had returned after his nine months in exile and inaugurated the country, wiping tears from his eyes with a handkerchief, which he then waved at the crowd, thousands and thousands of them, as if to say, I come in peace, I am your father.

It was where, for a moment, they had won. Now their history would be papered over by peanuts and the smell of candy floss.

Joy stopped the car again, on a side road. He unbuckled his seatbelt and turned to her. A few feet away was a roadside biri stall. The man behind the stall was asleep, his ankles crossed, his arm flung over his eyes. She started to cry again. Everyone else was passing by this park every day; they were buying tickets and going inside and having a good time. No one else was angry.

Joy peeled her fingers from her face. 'Hey,' he said, 'it's okay. The first time I saw it, I cried too.' He leaned close. He smelled of lemons. She felt the lifting of her senses. She wrapped her hand around the back of his neck and pulled him towards her. Lips yielding. He was saying something but she couldn't hear him. She pulled him closer – now her mouth was scraping his cheek. Smooth, with a hint of bristle. Rough-smooth. Lemonaftershave. She exhaled. She could hear him now, his lips at her ear.

'Let me tell you something about love,' he said. 'They chopped off my finger with a cleaver, did you know that? I don't know where they got it, a heavy big knife like that. Probably got it off some butcher. But you know what I was thinking when they did it? I was thinking that of all the people I knew, you would be the only one who wouldn't mind. And when I got home and found my mother in a white sari, I knew you would understand that too, because you had a dead father all those years. I have loved you this whole time,' he said. 'All this time.' He pulled away, serious now, his hands cupped over her shoulders.

'Promise me' Maya whispered.

'Anything.'

'That you won't ask me to forget. Who we are.'

'I promise.'

He made a fist around her hands. Thank you. He put it to his forehead. Thank you.

*

Maya felt someone shaking her roughly. 'Apa, apa.' A woman stood at the foot of the bed, waving her gloved arms around like a mime artist.

'Who are you?'

'I'm Rokeya's sister. Forgive me for waking you like this, but she asked me to fetch you. She's having terrible pain.'

'Go on, I'll meet you upstairs.'

'Not upstairs. She's at home with us. Hurry, rickshaw is waiting.'

Maya pulled on a crumpled salwaar-kameez, slipped her feet into a pair of chappals and ran through the back door, brushing past Sufia, who had taken to sleeping beside the stove as the nights grew colder.

In the rickshaw, she inspected Rokeya's sister. 'Have I seen you before? You didn't join the upstairs jamaat?' They set off towards the north side of the city, the rickshaw-wallah cycling swiftly through the empty streets, a biri at the edge of his lips.

'I came once, but I didn't want to stay. Khadija was angry because Rokeya didn't bring in the rest of our family.'

The girl was covered from head to toe, with only a small piece of chiffon, like a dirty pane of glass, through which to see the world. The girl lifted the chiffon and revealed her face. In the darkness it shone, pale and perfect. 'Khadija, whatever she calls herself – she's a heartless woman.'

'Don't you like her sermons?' She thought of the rapturous faces of the other girls, the way they fanned the air around Khadija with their gaping, devoted breaths.

'She believes every word she says. That's something. But I can't follow someone like a mule.'

'Then why are you dressed like that?'

'Do you think I could have come to fetch you in the middle of the night otherwise?'

Maya considered this for a moment. A girl like this one, she might never have ventured out if it weren't for the cover of her cloak. The practical reply impressed her. She squeezed the girl's hand. 'How long ago did the labour start?'

'A few hours. She refused to go to the hospital. She was half starved when she came back to us; we thought she wasn't going to make it.'

'What happened?'

'She won't say. She was punished, I think, for something.'

Maya remembered seeing Rokeya twice, out in the sun, kneeling. Why hadn't she said something? She had imagined Rokeya was doing it of her own free will and just shelved it among the other bizarre rituals of the upstairs. Now she felt guilty. 'I'm sorry, I had no idea.'

'Stop here,' the girl said to the rickshaw-wallah. 'We'll have to walk the rest of the way.' She had brought a torch, and they picked their way through the narrowing road, finally coming upon a small house with a curtain draped across the doorway. There was a front room and a back room and, somewhere beyond, a kitchen that was probably shared with the neighbours.

Rokeya's father caught a glimpse of Maya and politely averted his eyes. 'Subhan Allah,' he said, his voice thick, 'please, she's waiting.'

Rokeya was swallowing her breaths. When she saw Maya, she squeezed her eyes shut and said, 'I knew you would come.'

Maya washed her hands in a bowl of water and palpated Rokeya's stomach. Then she told the girl to breathe while she performed an exam. Rokeya winced as Maya plunged her arm deep into her and measured her cervix. 'Just relax now,' she said, falling quickly into the soothing tones she reserved for women in labour. She probed with light fingers, reaching for the soft dome of the baby's head. Instead, she felt the baby's buttocks. Breech. They should have taken her to the hospital, but it was too late now, she was already too advanced. Maya had delivered breech babies before, but they were risky, the delivery slow. And where was Rokeya's husband? There was no sign of him. Better not to ask, not now. 'Listen to me, Rokeya. Open your eyes.'

Rokeya's eyelids fluttered open.

'Your baby is upside-down. Do you hear me? Nod if you understand. It's too late to do anything, you'll have to deliver. Don't worry, I've seen it before. It's going to be slow and it's going to hurt. Understand?' The baby's backside was going to come out first, then the legs. She wouldn't be able to assist; if she laid her hands on the baby, it might extend its arms and get stuck in the birth canal.

Rokeya nodded, squeezing her eyes shut again.

When the time came, Maya pulled her into a squatting position. 'Next pain comes, you push, okay? Push as hard as you can.'

With each contraction, Rokeya put her head down and grunted. Soft, softer than Maya had ever heard a woman grunt. Maya whispered a stream of encouraging words, but the girl didn't appear to be listening, just breathing roughly out of her nose and clenching her hands together into hard white fists.

Her sister came and went, boiling water for Rokeya, cradling her head. The contractions were coming faster now, but without any assistance the baby could descend only a few millimetres at a time. An hour passed. Another. Rokeya collapsed on to her back. 'I can't,' she said, 'I can't any more.'

Maya peered between Rokeya's legs. 'It's not long now, just a few more minutes. I can feel it coming.'

Rokeya shook her head. 'Can't,' she whispered.

'You have to. There's no other way.' Maya tried to pull her up again, but she fell back on the rolled-up mattress, shaking her head. Now the scream came as the baby bore down on her, a low, black bellow. 'Come on now,' Maya said, 'the baby wants to come out, you can feel it, I know you can.'

Rokeya was too tired to move. Maya came up behind her and pushed her into a sitting position. Then she squatted behind her and held her by the armpits. She pushed her mouth close to the girl's ear. 'You know what? It's a girl. I felt it during the exam. This is your little girl. You know how hard it is to be a little girl in this world? Don't you want to let her know you love her, right now, before she's even in the world? Tell her. Tell her now. Push with me.' Maya gripped Rokeya hard while she pushed, and her strength seemed to return as she bore down. Maya saw the baby's legs. With the next surge, the torso and shoulders emerged. Now that the arms were free, Maya tugged, gently, holding the neck in place. 'Just one more,' she said, but

Rokeya was fully in control now, her body dictating every breath. The baby's chin began to emerge, and the bridge of the nose, eyes covered in yellow and green, remnants of an already old world. Maya lifted her up, her arms and legs flopping to the sides while she rubbed the little chest, waiting for the cry, and then it came, high and grand and powerful. Before placing her in her mother's arms, she whispered, as she had at all the other births, *hello, little amphibian.* Someone had to acknowledge the strangeness of this soul, and the distance it had traversed, millions and millions of years, in order to be here.

She had witnessed the birth of so many of these beings, held their hands as they left their sea-scapes and came ashore, but she had never allowed herself the thought that it might someday be hers, this spilling out of life. Now, in the quiet moment that followed, Maya allowed herself a small fantasy. Something of her own. She thought of Joy, and the child they might have, a strange little creature that would be hers this time, all hers.

Bundled into a katha, the baby was handed to the family while Maya attended to Rokeya. She held a needle to the kerosene flame and threaded it with string. 'It's going to hurt again,' she said. 'I'm sorry.'

Rokeya bit down on her lip. 'I have to tell you something,' she said, her fists curled around the mattress.

'Now?'

'Yes,' she said, 'I have to tell you now. It's about the boy.'

About to make another stitch, Maya steadied herself. 'Zaid?'

'Did you know he ran away from the madrasa?'

Maya concentrated on her fingers, reaching, dipping, rising, closing the wound. 'He's run away?'

'It was when your mother was in the hospital.'

He had lied. How stupid of her not to have known. 'You saw him?' she asked.

'Only for a few minutes, then Sister Khadija found him. I asked him why he ran away. He said it was because at the madrasa the Huzoor made him lie down. What did he mean by that, Maya Apa? Because I have been thinking about it and thinking about it, and it can mean only one thing, really. Only one thing.'

Suddenly it seemed to Maya that Rokeya had breathed all the air out of the room. 'You're sure that's what he said?'

'I know the child lies. But I believed him.'

It can mean only one thing. It took every shred of Maya's will to finish stitching Rokeya's tear, give her instructions on how to look after the wound and slip quietly from the room, making her excuses to the family and jumping into the first rickshaw she could find, dawn tapping its feet on the horizon, the sky still black and studded with stars.

1977

November

Sohail was throwing away his books. Maya caught him boxing them into crates and alphabetising, sorting, dusting the spines. It was the loving way he did this, lining each crate with newspaper and placing the books gently inside, that made her angry. She saw the struggle that bent his hand over this title, that spine. The way he opened, read a page – lingered over Ibsen, perhaps considering Hedda, or Nora – then closed each volume with firmness, those women from another age, another world, forbidden to him now.

That's when she confronted him, standing in the doorway of his bedroom, the books clustered at his feet like a dense school of fish. She knew the answer, had known all along, the change in his clothes, the dusting over of the guitar. Silvi, she said, I know it is Silvi.

'She's my wife; you can't speak that way about her.'

'So this is your idea?'

'It was my choice.' He was holding a volume of Rilke and shaking it at her.

Getting those books together hadn't been easy. He had scoured New Market for each of the volumes, sitting on the chairs outside the booksellers, leaning into dusty, spiderwebbed corners for the books they pretended they didn't have. Lawrence, Fitzgerald. *The Scarlet Letter*. He loved the outcast heroines, Lily Bart and Hester Prynne and Moll Flanders. The Rilke, she knew, he had stolen from the university library. The volume had attached itself to him and asked to be taken home, stuffed into the ruck-sack of a boy-soldier, battered in rain, in the water-filled air of the monsoon. It had been read in the pale orange of a kerosene lamp, in the yellow and gold of a candle, over meals of coarse bread and green banana curry. Orange and yellow and gold and green banana. This was what he was pointing at her now, the corner of the stolen volume, about to be closed into the dark of a crate, never to be touched again by the soldier, never lodged in the caress of his throat as he read its verses aloud, because his new love allowed him only one poet.

'It has nothing to do with her.'

'You suddenly have something against books?'

'There has to be a limit, Maya.'

'I agree. There has to be a limit. Isn't that why you joined the fighting?'

'It didn't do any good, did it?'

'I know it feels that way now, but it won't always be like this.'

'It doesn't matter. There is another life after this one.'

He packed away the Rilke, pulled another volume from the shelf and tossed it into the box.

'I want to talk about it,' she said. 'You never told me anything about the war.'

'What could I tell you? We fought, we won. It didn't make a difference in the end.' He peeled off his cap and wrung it between his hands. His hair was cut close against his skin. He looked, as he never had during the war, like a soldier.

Any minute now she knew he could be gone to her. Gone for ever. What could she say to keep him back? Nothing, probably. Silvi's hold on him was too strong, and she had the Almighty to back her up. A formidable foe. But there was one thing, one thing she had never told Sohail. Perhaps now was the time to tell him, something that might shock him into realising he wasn't the only one who was suffering because of what he had done. 'I want to talk about Piya,' she said.

He swerved around to face her, and in a low, secretive voice said, 'That's finished, Maya.'

She knew he was trying to convince himself. She knew he thought of Piya every day. Every day he thought of her and wondered where she had gone. Just as Maya did.

She took the cap from his hands and made a space for them to sit down. He put his palms on the stacks of books and sat like a king, suddenly attentive. She couldn't get out of it now. It occurred to her that if she told him, he might take all the books out of their crates and put them back on to the shelves. And exchange his loose cotton pyjamas for a pair of trousers and buy a reel-to-reel player so they could listen to Simon and Garfunkel.

She swallowed hard and began. 'It was just after liberation, just after Piya came. I started working at the Women's Rehabilitation Board. Ammoo too. We went to the office together, to volunteer. And they gave her the job of talking to the war widows, sorting out their pensions, their property. Negotiating with their husbands' families.' She took a deep breath, steadying herself for the next part. 'And, Bhaiya, because I had medical experience, you know, from the camps, they assigned me to the wards. I performed abortions.'

She folded and unfolded and refolded Sohail's prayer cap. 'I didn't tell you. You thought I was just helping the sick ones but we had a whole clinic at the back, where the women came to get rid of the babies. You remember what Sheikh Mujib said? That he didn't want those bastard children in our country. But some of them – it was hard, you know, I didn't think so much about it at the time – they wanted to get rid of them, but when it came time to do it they would cry. And then they would wake up and ask us to put the babies back. One day, Piya came to the clinic. She asked to see me – Ammoo didn't know, she came straight to the ward. And she asked for a checkup. She was pregnant, Bhaiya, did you know?'

She couldn't look at him. She said to herself, look at him when you tell him. But she couldn't, she couldn't look at him. She looked at the books instead. Her eye fell on *Brideshead Revisited*. To Waugh, she said, 'She was early, you could hardly see. It must have happened towards the end of the war.

'She wanted an abortion. Right now, she said. Do it right now. I was busy, I had ten other patients that morning, but I told her to wait, I said I would do it. Today, she said, it has to be today or I won't be able to. *I'll tell him*, she said. I didn't understand what she meant, but I talked to the in-charge doctor and made the appointment. But by the time I came to her, she was nervous. I'm not sure, she said. She asked for you, she said please call Sohail Bhai. But you were in the cantonment that day, remember, you'd gone to quit the army. There were formalities, you were away all day. I thought she was scared, just scared like the others. I thought about bringing her home but I remembered what she said, that it had to be that day or she would lose her nerve. I knew what to do; I did it all the time, persuading the girls they were doing the right thing, for their families, for the country. If you have the operation you can go home, I said to her, your family will take you back. You are a Birangona, I told her, a war hero—'

The words came rushing back to Maya, the words she had been taught.

'Defiled by the enemy. The child in your womb is a bastard child, a vial of poison. You must not allow it to come into this world. You must not give it the milk of your breast. What has been done can be undone. You must not live with it for the rest of your life. You must not mother this child. Do not think of it as your child, it is the seed of your enemy, I told her. Finally, she agreed.'

Sohail was sweating, thin lines of water bisecting his face. He didn't move to wipe it away. Now he remembered the day he had found her in that prison, how he had carried her out of there, the short stubble of her hair rubbing coarsely against his collarbone. 'Take me home,' she said, 'I want to go home, take me home.'

They were in a small bamboo grove, as far from the barracks as he could carry her. But the land was flat, and every time the building caught her eye she howled, so he propped her against a tree with her back to the prison. He sat in her line of vision, where the sun struck her face, casting a long, elegant shadow across her. 'My village is east,' she said.

They had brought her there in a jeep. 'There was another girl, but she died.'

She told him the name of her village. Dhanikhola. Will you take me? The war is over, he told her. They would walk. At every village they were greeted with tired cheers and the small scraps of the harvest that were leftover from the war. Village after village, Pahara, Mormora, Lalkhet. Every mother wanted him to be her son, returning tired and whole with a woman in his arms.

She was eighteen. 'My sister is the same age,' he said.

'You have a sister?'

'Yes, Maya. She went to work at the refugee camps across the border.'

'All by herself?'

'She's a very spirited girl.'

Piya had wide-apart eyes and a raw, aching quality to her voice. On the third day she waded into a village pond. He watched, worried she would stray too far. The sun struck the back of her, catching her hands as they moved across the water, propelling her forward. When she was neck-deep, she dipped her head under. Her sari floated to the top, flowering. And when she came up again, she was different, as though she had gone under and told all the bones of her to put themselves back in order. That was how she emerged: neat, organised. Wide apart eyes and a bruise in her voice. He asked if she would ever come to Dhaka, if she would visit. They were close now, only a few miles away.

They came to the edge of the village, and it was exactly as she had described it: a patch of trees casting a pale green tinge on neat houses of mud and straw. Round cakes of dung scalloped on to the outside walls, palm-printed by those who had collected it. A pond. Everything hushed, the fog hanging low and swallowing the cries of the koel, the ripple of water.

He wrote his address on a scrap of paper, knowing she couldn't read, knowing every part of her would be examined, explored. She would toss it into the fire. She would never come.

He put his hand to his forehead and said goodbye. Formal. It was Piya who stepped close, who put her palm, scented with water, on his cheek. She who raised her face, kissed him lightly on the mouth, her lip rough and small, like the husk on a grain of rice.

She had learned a few words of English. See you again, she said, expanding the distance between them with her choppy, awkward syllables.

And she did come. She came and they spent their hours in the garden, talking about everything and nothing. The memory of war began to fade. Until that night – now he knows it was after Piya had gone to see Maya in the hospital, but at the time it was just another day. He had gone to the cantonment to surrender his gun. In the last few weeks of the fighting they had given him a uniform, with a green-and-red badge sewn on the sleeve. At the cantonment he saw the other boys in his regiment, Farouq and Shameek and Kona, all of them signing up to remain in the army. They told him it was no surprise that he was quitting; they had never taken him for a company man. Without a cause to fight for, he didn't belong. He had listened to the official speech and been discharged, without dishonour, from the Bangladesh Army. And he had returned still dressed in his uniform. He could give it back later, they said.

It was late and the house was quiet, everyone asleep, or so he had thought until he caught a glimpse of Piya in the garden. He could barely see in the dark, but it was unmistakably her, the straightness of her back just as it was when she had emerged from the village pond.

'Marry me,' he said, whispering into the dark.

She turned around, her gaze drifting to the other side of the wall. 'Who lives there?' she asked, pointing to the two-storey house.

'No one. We have to find new tenants.'

'It belongs to you?'

'Ammoo built it. We lived off the rent after my father died.'

'It's very big.'

'Two storeys.'

'Have you been inside?'

'Yes. Do you want to go?' He unlatched the small gate built into the wall.

She was sure-footed, even in the weak light of the half-moon, slipping through the gate and on to the lawn on the other side. She climbed the three short steps and waited for him in front of the large dark double-doors.

'It's locked,' she said.

'Yes, of course. I forgot. I'm sorry I don't have the key.'

She cupped her hands against a window, peered inside.

'Piya,' he said, 'there's something I have to tell you.'

'Me too.'

'I want to get married.' He tried to see her, but the light was too weak. 'I want us to get married – what do you think?'

'If that is what you wish,' she replied, sitting on the top step.

'Is that what you want?'

'What will everyone say?'

'Who cares?'

'They'll say I did it to get your things, this house.'

'It doesn't matter. You love me, don't you?'

She didn't say anything, only sat perfectly still, caught in the yellow tinge of moonlight. 'If you want, I will be your wife. But I am not a good woman.'

'What happened to you – it's not your fault.'

'I'm very tired,' she said.

He sat down beside her. Laced his fingers through hers. 'It's all right, I'm tired too. I don't care about anything, what anyone says. Do you understand? I'm tired too, I'm so tired. I want to lie with my head in your lap – forgive me – I want to kiss you again. I want to forget everything that happened before. I want our children to live in the country, free children in a free country. But you decide. Don't choose me because you're here, because you can't go home. Choose me if you love me – do you under-stand? That's what I believe. You have to love me.'

Her grip tightened, and then, abruptly, she let go and sprang up, light on the grass, like a girl who had grown up without shoes. She disappeared across the lawn.

Buoyant, he imagined it was a skip of joy, that flight across the lawn, but it was the lightning speed of departure, a farewell without ceremony.

By the morning she was gone. Her small bundle of clothes, her plastic comb, the stick of neem she used to clean her teeth. Her extra sari, drying that morning on the washing line.

He set out to look for her. He didn't mean to, but he found himself travelling all the way back to her village, taking a bus to Mymensingh, a rickshaw the rest of the way. We never saw her again, an old woman said, spitting betel from the side of her mouth. The village was no longer beautiful, the houses ragged and dusty in the rising heat. He returned to the city and walked aimlessly from street to street, asking strangers if they had seen a young brown-eyed girl, walking alone. All the walking-alone girls had brown eyes. What was her father's name? A girl had drowned herself in Dhanmondi Lake. It could have been her. He arrived too late at the morgue; someone had already claimed the body. She was on a bus bound for the border. Or she had boarded one of the planes taking the Pakistan Army back to Islamabad. There were women on that plane? Our women? Yes, there were women. They had been promised marriage. She could have gone with them.

'Bhaiya,' Maya said softly, 'it was your child?'

He sprang up, knocking over an open crate. 'You can ask me this, after everything?'

'It's all right.'

'I didn't touch her, you understand? I wouldn't touch her. Not after what happened to her.' He was shaking now, his arms hanging limp at his sides. 'You gave her the operation, without asking any of us, me or Ammoo?'

'But I didn't do it, Bhaiya. I didn't do it – she changed her mind.'

He started to cry. She could see his eyes welling up and he turned his face away from her.

'You thought I was enjoying the days after liberation. But they were blood-soaked, Bhaiya, for everyone.'

He shook his hands at her, as if they were wet. 'But I killed, Maya. I killed.'

Of course she misunderstood. 'It's all right, Bhaiya, it was the right thing to do. It was a just war, a right war. For us, for our freedom.'

He shook his head. 'I didn't mean to. I was so angry.'

'If they had let me fight, I would have shot them in the knees and let them die slowly.'

'He was innocent.'

None of them were innocent. She told him that.

'You want to talk about saving – Silvi saved me. You were too busy killing those children.'

So he had chosen. His wife, a future without books. The thought unleashed a fury in Maya, a tight, searing fury. 'You put those books in crates, I'm going to take them out and lay them open for you. Every book you put away I will unpack and leave at your doorstep. I'll read them aloud. Remember when Ammoo used to read the Qur'an to you? I'm going to do the same thing. I'm going to keep bringing the books back until you can't ignore them any more.'

His hand was dipped inside a crate. Slowly, he straightened. 'I'll have to find something else to do with them,' he said softly.

He'll give them away, she thought. He'll give them all away. Damn it. She slipped out of the room then, without a word, stalked through the garden, loosening her braid and running her fingers roughly through the tangle of her hair. Do something, she told herself. Do something. Your brother is turning, turning. Soon you won't recognise him. He had been her oldest friend, all the things a brother should be: protective, bullying, pushing her to be better. He knew all her frailties, knew she tended towards the hysterical, the dogmatic. That she was angry most of the time. He pushed her against herself. She needed him. It was selfish, but she needed him. No, it was not selfish. They all needed him. He was the lighthouse. The country needed him. Sheikh Mujib had said so himself. Oh, God, Mujib was dead. Sohail could not be gone too, it would be too much. The world would collapse. What could she do? Silvi was in command now, Silvi, whose thin lips and foreign eyes had turned a wounded man into a prophet.

She thought of all the things he liked to do. Before the war, before Piya and Silvi. Cricket on the shortwave. Mangoes and ice cream. Dante and Ibsen. Jimi Hendrix and John Lennon. Her voice on the harmonium. Her voice. When was the last time he had heard her sing? She could sing to him. She could play the harmonium and open her voice. She had sometimes watched people's eyes widen when she sounded her first note, and afterwards, even if they knew her, she would see that a new formality had opened up between them, because her voice would have altered her in their eyes. Such tenderness out of such a hard girl. Small woman, big voice.

Silvi could go to hell. She would sing. She pulled her harmonium out of its case. It had been a long time since she'd pushed open the bellows at the back of the instrument, since the war, probably.

She was at war now. War with Silvi. She had the books on her side, and the harmonium, and Tagore, and she would fight. Already she felt flush with victory, her hand in a fist, pacing the garden and punching the air. She couldn't rely on her friends any more, not after Sohail had converted Kona on the spot. Weak souls! She would have to do it herself. Sohail was still in his bedroom, probably wondering what to do with his books. This would be the perfect time to strike. She dusted off the top of the harmonium. Laid out a jute pati in the garden. She would do it right there. Ammoo would come home to find her singing in the garden and she would agree that they had to use all the weapons in their arsenal to battle Silvi. They would fight fervour with fervour. The sun was beginning to go down for the night, the evening sounds taking over the daytime ones. Crickets, mosquitoes. She already had a few bites on her arm. She didn't care. She lit a mosquito coil. All right, here we are. She started with one of Sohail's favourites,

'Ekla Chalo Re'. 'Jodi tor daak shune keu na, tobe chalo re.'

She faltered with the harmonium a bit at first, her fingers getting tangled in the keys, but she soon caught up with herself, pumping the bellows with her left hand, pushing the keys down with her other. Tagore, just the man for the job.

The song ended. She heard the swish of a takoo lizard, its low staccato call. Should she have brought a lamp? Keep singing. A revolutionary song, 'Amar protibader bhasha, amar protirodher agun.' This one was getting her blood pumping. Her fingers moved and twisted and battered the keys. Sohail had loved this song. It would bring it all back for him. She kept an eye on his door, but it never stirred, not for the whole length of the song. A poem, then. She recited as much as she knew of Nazrul's 'Bidrohi', keeping the tempo with three fingers on the harmonium. When she faltered on the second stanza, she imagined he would burst out of his room and finish the line for her. Still nothing. She switched to the tenderest Tagore song she knew, 'Anondo Dhara'. *Stream of Joy*. She heard something. The creak of his door. A column of light, his shadow encased within it.

He was coming out. Her voice soared in anticipation. Something in his arms, it was too dark to make out. Just close your eyes and keep singing. 'Anondo dhara bohichey bhuboney.' Out he came, walking through the hallway and into the driveway. The shuffle of things. His books. Oh, he was moving them out. Don't falter, just keep on going. He is only doing what he said he would do. Someone must be coming to collect the books. Whoever it was, she would stop them, convince them to leave the books in front of the house. Ha! What would he do then? Perhaps he just needs to hide them from Silvi – yes, that may be it. He's protecting them. Never mind about the books. Keep singing. Bohichey bhuboney. In and out of his room, in and out; she could hear him occasionally grunting with the weight of the crates as he moved them to the driveway.

She was singing without thinking now, whatever song came to her. She started one without finishing another. Her body swayed with it, fingers and breath and tongue obeying. Eyes squeezed shut, believing that when she opened them, she would have sung them back to another time. A time when her brother wasn't packing his books into crates. The singing was heating up the garden. This is how Tagore must have meant his songs to be done. Warming the spirit and the body. Words coming out with the roar and spit of a fire.

She opened her eyes.

The garden was orange black and Sohail stood in the middle of it, tossing books into a pile. Arm up, fling, watch the fire grow, fling. Was she still singing? She had stopped. Nothing but the sound of burning now, a low growl, and she wanted to move but she could not. The bucket was under the garden tap. She could attempt to fill it up, douse the fire. But its colour was speaking, its colour was saying, I am greater than you. My fire has silenced your fire.

It must be a dream. A great calm flowed through her. She took up the song again. While Ammoo dragged her into the house, while Ammoo filled the bucket and doused the flames, her voice remained tied to the verse. It was only when she heard Ammoo shout that she was roused, because Ammoo was saying it was all her fault, as she picked the floating scraps of paper out of her hair, as she rubbed her cheek, black with print that had turned back to ink. Only then did she realise what had happened.

Sohail had burned all the books.

'You pushed him,' Ammoo was shouting. 'You pushed and you pushed.' And Maya heard herself protest: 'What could I do? I was only singing.' But her mother, eyes as big as eggs now, said, 'Did you listen to anything he said, up on that rooftop? Did you listen? No. You mocked him. You turned deaf and you mocked him.'

'Because I knew where it was going.'

'It didn't have to. It did not. You led him here, calling him a mullah. Why? You couldn't stand for him to be different.'

Et tu, mother.

Maya made the arrangements that very night, telephoning Sultana and packing her bags, her lungs full of the fire. In the morning, she disappeared. Two months later, the sermons on the roof were stopped. The little tin shack went up, and Sohail and Silvi built their world on top of the bungalow. Mrs Chowdhury died, silently and without a tear from her daughter. Zaid was born, brought into the world by a midwife whose face was covered by a piece of black netting. He opened his eyes to that, an empty space where the welcoming laugh should have been.

*

Maya took the bus to Tangail. Without unpacking her bag or greeting her friend, she began a shift at the clinic. The duty doctor was hassled, a spray of blood clinging to the collar of his shirt, as if he had bled there himself. 'What are you doing here alone?' he asked, rolling up his sleeves and bending over a sink, cracked, grey-rimmed.

'I'm a friend of Sultana,' she said. 'From the medical college.'

He appeared too tired to ask any more questions. 'There's a cholera epidemic.' The hallways were crowded; people threw down their gamchas and waited in the corridors. 'You know what to do – ORT.' He handed her a white jacket. She was dismissed.

She raced through one shift, then another, filled with a restless energy, and with the fear that if she sat down, if she thought about what she had done, she might be forced to run back to the bungalow. By the second night, she had found a stray stethoscope and wrapped it around her neck, and when she looked in the mirror she was glad to find a drawn face staring back at her, all signs of her heartache obscured by physical exhaustion.

When Sultana caught up with her the next morning, she was weaving through the ward, skirting between the patients on the floor, between the beds.

'Time to stop,' she said.

She blinked, taking a moment to recognise her. 'I still have a few from last night.'

'It's been thirty-eight hours. Let's go home.'

She blinked again, salt stinging her eyes. 'Thank you,' she said, turning her face away so her friend wouldn't see her tears. 'My things are in the other ward.'

She stayed until the cholera had done its worst. When it was time to go, Sultana's husband said, 'My friend Ranen has a clinic in Rangamati. They're always shorthanded.'

After a fortnight in Khulna, and a week in Khagrachari, she found herself on the train to Rangamati. On the ferry she heard the sound of other languages, syllables with hard edges, and further still along her journey she saw women in long skirts and tunics, their faces small and squarish, babies tied to their backs with lengths of homespun, dark blue and yellow and red. They were called tribals, the Chakma and the Marma and the Santal, there before anyone else, before maps and Pakistan and the war. She saw a young girl and her mother eating with their fingers out of a leaf-wrapped parcel. They laughed with their jaws open and slapped one another on the cheek, gently, in admonishment, affection.

She finished her stint in Rangamati and took the train south again. When she stopped moving she found herself at the edge of the country, past the Chittagong port, and wandered on to an abandoned, tawny-sanded thread of a beach. Cox's Bazaar. The water was cloudy but pleasantly warm, and as she dipped her ankles she found she could no longer taste the cinders, the tarry blackness that had got under her tongue and between her fingers. Now her tongue was clear, and as she squatted in the water, allowing her kameez to soak, she scrubbed between her toes, and the backs of her knees. At the guest-house, she continued to scrub at herself, this time with soap, splashing buckets of water over her head, attacking the dirt beneath her fingernails. She emerged red-faced, her hair wound into the thin striped towel that had come with the room.

She thought, for the first time since her departure, about her mother, and decided to send a telegram. After grappling with the words, she finally settled on *I am fine. Please do not worry. It is better this way.*

And that is how it happened. A few weeks here, a few weeks there. Rangamati, Bandorbon, Kushtia. She finally travelled back up, avoiding the city, weaving up the Jamuna, the Brahmaputra, and into Rajshahi, where she settled, where she had her dreams of orphanhood, and where she found herself eating purple berries under a jackfruit tree, waiting for the postman.

1985

February

Kakrail Mosque had none of the beauty of the mosques in the older parts of town. It was just a concrete structure, rectangular, with a minaret protruding upwards from its middle. Through the square-patterned grille, she could see men going about their business, kneeling down to pray, ducking under the taps to perform the Wazu, standing with their hands crossed in front of them, listening to a munajaat. So this was where Sohail spent all his time. Rising before dawn and making his way through the grey and sleeping city, to this place of fellow men.

She had woken Ammoo and told her she had to meet Sohail. Sohail, Ammoo said, sleep heavy in her mouth. You won't find him. She had rushed out of the house, still wearing the grey cotton she'd had on since the night before, the birth fresh in her memory.

She entered through the gate and found a few men milling around outside the building. They looked at her, turned away, looked again. Stared, scratched behind their ears. She held back a smile. It's all right, she wanted to say, I won't bite you. Finally one approached her. 'Women are not allowed,' he said, clearing his throat.

'I won't stay long,' she said, resisting the urge to stare him down. He couldn't be more than fifteen or sixteen. Beard coming in spare and reluctant. His shoulders still narrow, frame still folded in on itself. He was about to say something to her, but an older man came up behind him and put an enormous hand on his shoulder.

'Begum, I'm very sorry but we have no provisions for women. You must leave immediately.' His voice was as big as his hand, deep and rough, as if scraped along the road.

'I have business here,' she said. 'I'm looking for my brother.'

'The Jumma prayer will begin soon. You must go.'

She was so tired. How hard could it be to find your own brother? 'Sohail Haque – I'm looking for Sohail Haque.'

The man hesitated. His mouth opened and closed, a great, gaping hole surrounded by a pelt of beard. 'He isn't here.'

He was lying.

'But this is where he comes, every day. Every day he is here.'

'He is no longer with us.' The man moved his arm, and she could tell he wanted to push her but he couldn't, not in front of the others, standing around now and nudging each other, the crowd growing as people arrived for the Friday prayer.

'No longer? Where is he?'

'I don't know,' he said, giving her a look of undisguised impatience. The muezzin began the call to prayer. A megaphone sprang to life. Allah-hu Akbar Allaaaah hu Akbar.

The crowd around them began to line up for the prayer. The man cupped her elbow in his palm and led her to the gate. 'Please – I must find my brother.' She raised her voice. 'Sohail,

Sohail!' But they were already at the gate, and with great force he hurled her elbow out on to the street and slammed the gate closed. 'What are you all looking at?' she heard him roar. 'Get back to your prayers, go!'

He must be somewhere inside. She rubbed her elbow, and the night came back to her, Rokeya straining with her breech birth. Her confession. She considered the possibility of Rokeya's being overcome by the pain of labour – but, in her experience, women were often at their most lucid at the moment of delivery. No, it had to be true. As soon as she had said it Maya knew it was true. The truth of it stopped the air in her throat. Zaid had lied about coming home on a holiday. She remembered Khadija's words. *We sent him back.*

She heard someone behind her and turned around to see the young man she had first addressed. He leaned through a crack in the gate. 'Your brother is at a mosque in Kolabagan. Take Elephant Road to Ghost Road. It's a small place, next to an empty plot of land. A new building.'

'A new mosque? But why?' She wanted to reach through the gap, but he was already gone.

*

She followed the directions, Elephant Road to Ghost Road. She asked for the new mosque, waving down passers-by on the road. They pointed, directing her to smaller and smaller lanes. The people of this neighbourhood were intent on their tasks, the women dipping into buckets and coming up with pieces of washing, and the men carrying heavy things with agility, drums of water and boxed-up parcels and bags of cement. Even the telephone wires seemed to dangle over the pavements with lightness and grace.

When she saw the gate she knew it must be the one. Painted green, with a small star and crescent etched in white. She could smell the freshly laid cement, taste the white dust it imposed on the air around it. There was no bell to ring. She banged on the gate. No reply. She banged again. She turned the corner, looking for another entrance. A man walked past with a stack of bricks piled on his head. 'Is this the new mosque?' she asked him.

The man could not nod but called out: 'You have to wait,' he said. 'They don't open the gate.'

More waiting. She found a small cut in the high wall that surrounded the building and wedged herself into it, shielding her eyes against the sun with her hand. The Ghost Road residents drifted past. She thought about finding a telephone and ringing Joy. What would she say? He would drive up in his Honda and try to rescue her. She did not want to be rescued. The sun battered her arm, the lower part of her leg that was out of the shade. She dozed, waking blearily to catch the curious glances of people walking by.

The afternoon opened up, then fell away again, the streets quietening and slowing down, the shops shuttered or lit up for the evening, fluorescent bulbs and kerosene lamps and tiny open fires.

Sohail's building did not stir. She hadn't seen anyone go in or out. There was no call of the muezzin, no shuffle of bodies preparing for the prayer. Ammoo would have started to worry. She realised she hadn't eaten all day, a throb in her stomach. She thought again that she should have waited for him to come home. Then the gate swung open and he was in front of her, his hands crossed over his chest.

'How long have you been here?'

'A long time. Can I come inside? I'm very thirsty.'

'Wait.' He dipped back through the gate and emerged with a tin mug of water.

The water was lukewarm, metallic. She drank it down. 'So, this is your new place? What is it?'

'A meeting house.'

'Can anyone join?'

'If they wish to, yes.' He sighed heavily, then surprised her by putting his hand on her shoulder. 'Is something troubling you, Maya?'

She decided to tread lightly. 'That day, at the hospital,' she said, 'what did you whisper to Ammoo?'

'Surah Yasin.' His voice was tender, heavy with love. 'Waalqurani alhakeemi, Innaka lamina almursaleena . . .' It must have been this that roused Ammoo, the call of her firstborn. The miracle of his voice.

'She's much better, you know. She's walking around and everything.'

A rickshaw pulled up in front of them. 'Jaben?' asked the driver, ringing the bell.

Maya was about to wave him away, but Sohail said, 'Wait over there. Apa will need to get home soon.'

'Sohail, please, let me come inside. I need to speak with you.'

He said nothing, just stood in front of the door as if he were guarding what was inside. She realised she would have to tell him right there, on the street. 'It's about Zaid.' She checked his face to see if he knew, if he had any idea. 'I heard he ran away. When Ammoo was in the hospital.'

Sohail sighed. His hand was heavy on her shoulder.

'Did he tell you why he ran away?'

He shook his head. A weary, resigned shake. 'The Huzoor said—'

'It's the Huzoor I want to talk to you about. There's something going on, something not right – I saw Zaid, he didn't look well. Ammoo was going into hospital that day, or I would have come to you.' She was making excuses for herself. If only Zaid hadn't arrived at that moment, if only she had taken him to the hospital with her. 'The point is, you have to get him out of there,' she said. 'It's not a safe place, not a place for children.

260

That Huzoor is doing things, I don't know exactly what, but the children have no defence against him. Do you understand what I'm saying?'

He turned away from her. Across the road, the rickshaw-wallah had curled up on the seat of his vehicle. The city sounds faded in and out, lorries labouring in the distance, the wheeze of carriages on the railway line. She reached for his hand, imagining the shock of it sinking slowly through him. When he turned around and spoke, his voice was cracked. 'He lies, you know that. He lies all the time.' A deep furrow between his eyes.

'I know, but you can't take the risk. Even if there's a slight chance he's telling the truth, you have to get him out of there. And I'm telling you, he didn't look well. Rokeya said—'

'You've seen Rokeya?'

'I delivered her baby this morning.'

'Sister Khadija was insulted by the way she left the jamaat.' The evidence was getting shakier, less reliable.

'The madrasa is not a good place, Bhaiya.'

'You're hardly objective.' He was using both hands to smooth down his beard. The purple bruise on his forehead reflected the dying light. The devout believed that on the Day of Judgement, it would shine like a beacon, and she imagined it now, light pouring from his forehead, like a miner's headlamp.

'You'll go tomorrow, then?'

He paused, pulling harder on his beard, taming the curl of it. 'He is my son. I will ensure his safety.'

'Promise me you'll go tomorrow.'

'I cannot promise you that.'

He could not mean what he appeared to be saying. He wouldn't go, he wouldn't rescue his son from whatever hell-hole he had sent him to. 'You want him to be just like you, is that it?'

Sohail took a step towards her, and he was close, very close, when he said, 'I want, more than anything else, for him not to become like me. That is why I sent him away.'

It didn't make any sense. She told him so. 'You wouldn't understand.' He kissed her gently, missing her forehead, his lips landing on her eyebrow. She held herself stiffly, wondering what to do now. All this time she had been waiting for something noble to come out of him. At the hospital, she had had an inkling of it. He had gone to Ammoo's bedside, he had recited the words. At the time she had thought this might be enough. But he had not believed her. He would not rescue his son.

By the time she got home, Ammoo was already asleep. Maya packed a small bag. A toothbrush, a change of clothes. Then, thinking of Rokeya's sister, she climbed up on to the roof and quietly pulled a long black chador and a nikab from the washing line. She wrote a note and left it on Ammoo's bedside table. 'I need to go back to Rajshahi for a few days. A few things to collect.'

Before slipping out into the morning, the sky pink and amber, she dialled Joy's number. 'What's the matter?' he said, sleep thick in his voice. 'Changed your mind?'

'No.'

'Good. We can elope, you know. Kazi offices all over the country. Slip them a few bucks and they'll do it on the spot.'

She told him she was going to Rajshahi for a few days.

'Let me come with you.'

'No. But I need a favour.'

'Anything.'

'I want you to find someone for me. Someone I lost in the war.'

The Following Day

There was always this: the Jamuna River, even in its diminished winter state, beating powerfully against its banks. Although she had raced here, Maya paused now for a moment before boarding the ferry, savouring the loam and brown silt of it. Little, in this country, inspired awe, but this river, thick and dangerous, was a wonder.

The ferry was crowded on this Saturday morning. Maya took her seat on the lower deck. A blaze of the siren, and the ferry picked up speed, tilting like a rocking chair as it hit the Jamuna current.

She knew little about the madrasa apart from the few clues she had been able to piece together. Sohail had told her he was taking the boy to Chandpur, and Zaid had said the madrasa was on its own island in the middle of the river. She had looked on a map, and found three different Chandpurs. Only one was near a river.

At dawn, before she departed, she had gone upstairs and questioned Khadija, who had told her nothing. You no longer visit us, she said.

Maya had allowed herself to be duped. All those afternoons she had spent, drunk on the possibility that there might be some other hand in her mother's illness, a divine hand she could manoeuvre with the help of Khadija and the jamaat. How could she have been so foolish? She should never have allowed Sohail to take Zaid to the madrasa. Ammoo's illness had clouded her judgement. And when Zaid had come to her, she had swatted him away. What kind of mother would she make? She couldn't even see the thing that was right before her eyes.

The cabin was packed now, and thick with heat. Being inside was making her thirsty. She stepped on to the deck and leaned her arms against the railing, tiny droplets of water landing on her face.

She found a cold-drinks stall. A boy with a lungi hitched up around his thighs squatted in front of a tub of ice and soft drinks. 'Coke, please,' she said. He looked about twelve, strong arms protruding from a vest that used to be white. He pulled a bottle out of the tub, wiped it with a cloth and opened it against the battered wooden table in front of him.

She gave him five taka. He caught her eye and smiled so broadly, so hopefully, that she found herself asking him why he wasn't in school.

He shrugged, still smiling.

'Where do you live?'

'On this ferry. The driver is my uncle.'

A large family approached the stall and ordered their drinks. 'Three Mirindas and seven 7 Ups!' the father shouted, thrilled by his own joke 'And hurry, na.' The boy rushed through the order, fishing the bottles out of the icy water, throwing in new ones from the crates stacked up alongside. Maya lingered, watching him work. The man took his drinks, throwing his money at the boy, dodging the thin, pointy straws as they bobbed in the open bottles.

'Do you live in Dhaka?' he asked her.

'Yes,' she replied. 'I'm a doctor.'

He pushed out his lower lip and nodded, impressed. 'Dakhtar.'

They were in the middle of the river now, the shores disappearing on either side. A muezzin announced the Asr prayer. The ferry slowed down, the engine coughing. Then it suddenly stopped, and everything was quiet; only the lapping of the water against the boat.

'Sometimes the engine breaks,' the boy said. They heard shouts coming from below, and the sound of running feet. There was no longer a breeze. Passengers crowded the walkways, squeezing themselves against the railing.

'Come with me,' the boy said. 'I know a better place.'

'Oh, it's all right.' Maya shook her head. 'Really, it's all right here. And you shouldn't leave the stall; people will be wanting their drinks.'

He was already sliding the tub under the table and folding down the small cubicle. She followed him as he led her up a set of steps, then through the ferry and up a narrow ladder. He climbed up quickly, his bare feet curling around the metal rungs, then turned and held out his hand to Maya.

It was bright, the sun reflecting off the painted white roof, but it was also cooler, the wind open and rough. There was a tiny ledge on the eastern corner, and they perched there together. The muezzin called again. There were a few others; a man rolled out a small rectangle of cloth and began to pray, dipping his head to the west. Unbidden, the words of the prayer came to Maya's lips. She remembered her mother patiently teaching her the verses, and how reluctantly she had submitted at the hospital. An hour passed. The boy took his leave. 'I have to sell the drinks,' he said.

'What is your name?' Maya asked.

'Khoka.'

'Goodbye, Khoka.' She waved, then added, 'God be with you.'

The ferry gasped to life, the siren blaring as they began to move.

Soon they approached the other side, floating towards the embrace of land, the sun light, high-spirited, on the horizon.

As she was leaving the ferry, Maya found Khoka waiting for her, hugging a small bundle. 'Dakhtar, where are you going? Let me come with you. I can help.' She saw him clearly now, in the full brilliance of the afternoon. He had dark, luminous eyes. He would be handsome one day, if he were fed properly. If his shoulders weren't burned and bowed from long hours on the dock. But she didn't want to be burdened by anyone; he would ask questions and she would not be able to answer them. 'No, it's all right.' She reached into her bag for a few notes.

He shook his head, refusing the money, suddenly shy.

As soon as she hit the ferry ghat, she was surrounded by porters, tea-wallahs, chotpoti-vendors, boatmen, and all manner of people wanting to buy, sell or rent things. Dusk was already falling, but she wouldn't stop here; she wanted to start travelling north, towards Chandpur. Clutching her bag, she scanned the shore for an empty country boat. The boatmen saw her and called out.

'Apa, you need to go somewhere, come with me!'

'Upstream, downstream, anywhere you like, apa, come, come.'

She hesitated beside one boat, suddenly unsure of what to do. She had travelled alone so many times, but as she looked around now and saw that she was the only woman on the shore, she found herself wishing she had brought Joy. You're going soft, Comrade Haque. Irritated by her sudden lack of confidence, she waved to one of the boatmen.

'I need to travel upstream,' she announced.

'Yes, yes,' the boatman nodded, 'let me take your things.'

'Tell me the price first.'

'Don't worry about the price, sister.' He reached out again, grazing the strap of her bag.

She pulled back. 'Never mind,' she said. 'I've changed my mind.'

The man skipped lightly off his boat and came to stand beside her. 'Don't worry, sister, price will be fair. And anyway' – he fished something out of the corner of his mouth, chewed on it, then spat it out – 'a woman should not travel alone.'

She turned away, thanking him for his assistance. The other boatmen watched. 'Lady doesn't know where she wants to go!' the man called out after her. 'Letting a poor man go hungry, chee chee. At least leave us something for our trouble.'

The ridiculousness of the demand made her turn back. 'What trouble? You should pay me, harassing me like that.'

His face darkened. 'You think you can talk any way you like?' He grabbed her arm. 'Because you have money and I'm just a boatman?'

Her anger swelled. 'You think you can talk to me any way you like, just because I'm a woman?' She twisted away and headed back in the direction of the ferry, the man continuing to call out to her. People stopped washing their boats and stared. She was a spectacle, running up and down the shoreline all by herself.

Khoka was carrying a crate of Coke bottles on his shoulder. 'I've changed my mind,' she called out, trying to stop her voice from trembling. 'Find me a boatman, an honest one, who will take me upriver.'

'It's too late, Dakhtar, no one will take you now. They're all leaving the ghat, see, it's getting dark.'

She gathered herself together, unbearably hot now, even though the day was turning from yellow to grey, and she wondered if she were doing the right thing, feeling the urgency of it, the black panic of not knowing where Zaid was. This boy, this cold-drinks boy, was so poor he had to spend all day stuck between one shore and another, opening bottle after bottle and never going to school. But he had that open sky above him, he could walk away on his own legs, with his own will.

'Please, you have to find me someone. I'll pay, I've got money. But it has to be tonight.'

'All right, I will try.' He relieved her of her bag and led her further down the shoreline. The boatmen were packing up their things, cleaning out their engines and bailing water. He left her at a small shop. She bought a packet of Nabisco and a cup of tea. He returned a few minutes later, leading her to a simple country boat. A very old boatman greeted her. 'Chacha will look after you,' Khoka said, 'won't you, Chacha?'

Khoka reached out to steady her as she stepped on to the boat. 'With your permission, Dakhtar, I would like to come with you.'

'You think I can't make it on my own? I've done it before, you know. I was in the war.'

'You were in the war? My uncle too. He has a scar here', he said, running a finger along his cheek, 'from a bullet.'

He smiled again, as though there were no tragedy in the world he hadn't heard of, and conquered. 'All right,' Maya said, 'come along, then.'

They set off as the sun whispered towards the horizon, moving against the current, the people on the shore growing smaller, into bright yellow specks, like lit cigarettes in a dark room. Through the slats in the bamboo she could see the water rising against the boat. They passed the first hour in silence. The boatman hummed as he rowed. Then Khoka said, 'Dakhtar, I shouldn't ask. But you're in trouble?'

Maya hesitated, wondering if he would understand any of it. 'I'm looking for a boy. My nephew.' As she started to speak the story poured out of her, about how she had returned, after her long absence, to the bungalow in Dhaka, her mother's illness, the appearance of Zaid.

Khoka's face moved with every episode of the story. She could tell he was thinking of himself, comparing his life and his miseries with those of the other boy. He was adding it up: the death of his parents, the long days he spent carrying the crates of drinks up and down the ghat. All the other hidden injuries. By the end, she had almost forgotten where she was as she described Rokeya's disclosure, her meeting with Sohail. When she looked up, she saw Khoka's eyes were shining. He leaned over the side of the boat, took a handful of water and splashed it on his face.

It would not have been appropriate for him to embrace her. But when he wiped his face roughly with his palms, it was as though he held her; as if he had said, you are right to be here, to be on this boat, to be travelling upriver in search of this boy. When you find him, you will also find me.

And this is how they passed their journey upstream, with the Jamuna pounding its banks, demanding its passage, breaking and swallowing pieces of the shore as it went, propelling them towards their destination, at its own pace, its own command.

She told Khoka what she knew of the madrasa.

'You don't know the name?'

'No. I'm not familiar with these parts.'

'You don't know the village?'

'No. I'm sorry.'

'Then we will go to every madrasa in every village near Chandpur and we will find him.'

Zaid had said it was surrounded by water. She hadn't understood before, but now she saw what he meant. The river was so vast, and so fierce, it created islands of its own. She had heard of these but she had never seen them. Khoka told her they were called chars, and he pointed them out to her now, shallow, floating cakes of land, rising just inches from the water, scattered with pale shoots of grass.

'These islands come up every year, after the monsoon. They might stay, they might get eaten by the river in a few months. That one over there' – he pointed to what looked like the shore – 'is old, it's been around for years. Your madrasa must be built on one of the older islands.' He said something to the boatman. 'Let's stop here and ask.'

'Too late,' the boatman said. 'We'll stop now and try tomorrow.'

Maya checked her watch. Seven o'clock, but it was fully dark already, the river grey and black and suddenly quiet.

The boatman boiled rice on a makeshift stove beside the engine, and Khoka fried a few shrimps he had caught over the side of the boat. They ate in silence, Maya surprised by the delicious, salty crunch of the shrimp. After the meal, Khoka said, 'The boatman wants to ask you a question, Dakhtar.' He guided the old man towards her. Deep folds sectioned his face and made it kind. 'My wife,' the boatman said, 'it's her throat.' He moved his hands up and down his own sagging neck. 'It's round, like this.'

'You mean it's swollen?'

'Looks like she swallowed a pumpkin.' His own lips were rimmed with orange from betel nut, his mouth black.

'It's called a goitre,' Maya said. 'She needs iodine. When you go to the shop to buy salt, tell them you want salt with iodine.'

'Will it cost?'

'Same as the other salt.' It was the law now that all salt must contain iodine, but not every producer complied. In Rajshahi she had persuaded the salt-sellers to convert to iodine salt. There were no swollen throats in her village.

The boatman raised his right hand to his forehead, thanking her. Then he signalled for her to stretch out along the boat; he and Khoka would find a dry spot on the shore. She fell asleep quickly, hugging her arms tightly over herself and using the burkha as a blanket.

In the morning Khoka hailed a group of men heading towards the fields. Yes, they were told, there's a madrasa here. They trudged between a few patches of paddy and came upon a blue school building made entirely of wavy sheets of tin. A handful of children loitered on a rough patch of grass outside the building. 'This can't be it,' Maya said, turning away.

'You don't want to find the headmaster?'

'Look,' she said, pointing to the children. 'Girls.'

They continued upriver, the boatman straining against the current. They stopped a few more times, turning up at makeshift schoolhouses and outbuildings on the grounds of mosques. The islands had an air of impermanence about them, the people appearing light and carefree as their saris and lungis ballooned out with the force of the river wind. Perhaps, Maya thought, as the sun dipped once more under its watery horizon, I will return here someday with a happier heart.

The next morning they stopped at a large island that rose several feet from the river. Maya and Khoka followed the path that began at the water's edge, their toes sinking into the silt. After a few steps the ground grew higher and became dry, and then the going was comfortable, Khoka swinging her bag as he walked, the koel and the bulbul singing in chorus, singing them on.

Two more false starts and they were standing in front of a small blue door worked into a solid, windowless wall. Maya felt a hollow throb at the pit of her stomach. 'This must be it.' She pulled the burkha out of her bag and slipped it over her head. She tied the nikab over her head and face, surprised by the feeling of her own breath against her cheeks. 'Wait by the boat,' she told Khoka. 'We may have to leave in a hurry.'

She circled the building like a thief. There was a high wall going all the way around the compound, and several smaller buildings around a central courtyard. A deep smell, of unwashed boys and rotting bananas, coated the building like a mist. Finally she gathered up the courage and knocked. A boy, older than Zaid, opened the door immediately. 'Where is the Huzoor?' she said. 'Take me to him.'

He hesitated. 'Big Huzoor or Small Huzoor?'

She didn't know. 'Doesn't matter. Big, I suppose. Whoever's in charge.'

The boy straightened, as if remembering something. 'Women are not allowed,' he said.

'It's all right, he's expecting me.' She reached out and patted the boy's cap, but he stiffened, stepping back into the darkness.

'No,' he said, and made to close the door.

She grabbed his shoulders. 'The Huzoor will see me,' she said. 'Take me inside.'

He pushed her and slammed the door. She banged with her fist, knowing he was waiting on the other side. 'Open up!'

She circled the building again, looking for an entrance. It appeared deserted, no footsteps, no sounds of any kind. She went back to the door. Banged again. The inside of the nikab was black and searing. The breath roared out of her.

Nothing. She turned around, ran back to the river. The boat was unmoored, Khoka and the boatman waiting with the oars on their laps. 'They won't let me inside,' she said.

'How many?' Khoka asked.

'Just a boy. The classrooms must be at the back, but I couldn't tell.'

'Let me come with you,' Khoka said. 'I can try and find a way in.' He waded to shore.

They tried the door again. The boy opened, and Khoka spoke. 'We need to come inside,' he said; 'it's very important.'

The boy pointed to Maya. 'No women allowed.'

Khoka pushed the boy aside and stepped through the gap in the door. Maya was about to follow, but Khoka closed the door behind him. She heard a scuffle inside, footsteps, muffled, tense voices. *Right now*, she heard. *Right now*.

The door opened. Khoka was holding the boy by the elbow. 'Come in,' he said. 'I'll stay here.'

'What did you tell him?' she whispered.

'That you are the sister of Huzoor Haque and you have come on important business, and that, inshallah, if you are allowed inside, great blessings will fall upon the madrasa.'

'Really?'

'Actually forgive me, Dakhtar, I told the boy I would beat him till the blood ran out of his ears if he didn't do as I said.'

The boy sniffed angrily, turned around and led her through a corridor and out into the open courtyard. He asked her to wait while he spoke to the Huzoor. 'Tell him I'm Mrs Haque,' she said. She waited, trying not to fidget in the heat. The boy emerged and led her into a small chamber. A very thin man with a neatly trimmed beard sat behind a desk with a pen in his hand. Glasses high on the bridge of his nose.

'I'd like to speak with the Huzoor,' she said. 'Which one are you?'

'I'm Choto Huzoor.'

'Where's the Big Huzoor?'

'Travelling.'

Maya appraised the man. Rokeya's sister was right about the burkha: from inside, she could stare freely without being noticed. She saw the man's tapered, unworked fingers, the dark pools of his eyes, with their trace of surma. His jellaba was long, sweeping his ankles. She swallowed a fist of fear, remembering the man who had put the knife to her throat.

He set down his pen. 'How can I be of service to you, sister?' He smiled with narrow teeth.

Maya approached, put her hands on the table. 'I want someone. A boy.'

The Huzoor looked down at his shoes, and suddenly she wasn't afraid of him; he knew why she was there, knew it from the way she stood and pointed her face at him now, and his fingers trembled and the pen shook, like the line of an irregular heartbeat. She said, 'I won't stay long. I've come to collect Zaid Haque. You will give him to me and I will not trouble you further.'

She prepared herself for an argument, but he sat frozen at his desk, the pen hovering in mid-air. She noticed his fingernails were dyed red with henna. She repeated herself, raised her voice. She heard herself threatening him, telling him she would tell the Big

Huzoor and he would inform his superiors. He would be disgraced. Then she would call the police and have the madrasa closed down. He would be arrested. Have you ever seen the inside of a prison, Huzoor? He stood up now and blocked the door, and she stepped up to him, placed her hands on his chest. 'I know what you've done,' she said. 'I know and God knows and you'll burn in dosok for it.' There was a tremor in his voice as pointed to the back of the compound, mumbling something about a shack, a locked door. 'I know what you've done,' she said again, as he pulled a key from around his neck. 'I know and God knows.'

She follows the outline of the building, turns around a bend and finds herself on a path leading through the bush. She sees the school building, a rectangular room with a tin roof. And, from within, a hum, many-voiced, like the sound of bees.

Just as the man said, there is a small square shack, the size of a chicken coop. There is no roof but the walls are high. She bangs on the door before attempting the lock. She is afraid to cry out, afraid she will be heard, afraid of what she will hear. The door replies. It is not a voice, only a soft rap, rap rap, not even from knuckles, more like the press of a hand. The lock is attached to a bolt on the door.

She uses the key.

The door swings open and he is inside, squatting over a pit dug into the ground. She holds out her arms and he leaps into them, and she thinks he is calling her name, Maya Maya Maya. Her heart sings along to it, but then the words come into focus, and she remembers she is still in her disguise, and that he has mistaken her for his mother. Ma, ma, ma.

She packs him into the boat. He clings to her. *The Arabic alphabet*, he says. *Alif-ba-ta-sa. I know it*. They make it to Gaibandha. On the boat, in darkness again, Maya pleads with Zaid to eat something. He refuses, gazing through the thin bamboo netting that arches over the boat, his eyes searching for the night sky. *I know the Arabic alphabet,* he repeats. *Where is my mother?* She isn't here, Maya tells him, you know that. *Bismillah ir-Rahman ir-Raheem,* he begins, reciting the words he has been taught. *Nauzubillah hira-shahitan-ir-Raheem.* A small lizard has made its way on board, and scuttles back and forth among the curved roof slats. He settles for this, chasing it with his finger.

His grandmother is waiting at home, Maya tells him, she will be so happy to see him. His father too. At the mention of his father he says, *I don't want to go home. I know the Arabic alphabet. Alifbatasa. BismillahirRahmanirRaheem.* There is a cut on his cheek. A bruise on the crease of his elbow.

She feels a sharp twist of guilt now, for the chappals she never bought him, for allowing him to be caught stealing, for not treating him more like he was hers, like something of her own. She expects to be angry too at his father, expects the rage to have thundered into her by now, but at this very moment she can only summon reproof for herself.

Khoka cannot take his eyes off the boy. He stares and stares, chasing Zaid's hand as it picks up the lizard, pulls off its tail and flings it into the water.

As they approach the shore Zaid's recitation gets louder and louder. *I like oranges,* he says. *Bring me an orange. Bring me a bicycle.* He starts reciting the call to prayer. *AshahadullahMuhammadur RasoolAllah.* He stands up and leans his weight this way and that. The boat tilts. The shore is crowded with boatmen and fishermen and people like them, people between one place and another. Closer now, and he begins to wail, banging his fists against Maya as she throws her arms around him. 'You want to stay on the boat, Zaid, is that what you want? You want to stay the night here? All right, all right.'

They turn around again, moving away from the ferry dock, and the boatman moors them against the river bank.

Khoka and the boatman make their way to the shore, leaving

her alone with Zaid. It's getting chilly and she unzips her burkha and envelops the boy within it. He turns his back to her and she curls herself around him, her hands gently stroking his hair. His breathing slows.

'We'll go home,' she says. 'Tomorrow we'll be home.'

'I don't want to.'

'Don't worry, it won't be like before.'

'I tried to run away.'

'I know, Rokeya told me.'

'But Abboo sent me back.'

'He won't, once you tell him everything. He'll never send you there again. Sleep now. Tomorrow we'll be home.'

She is tired now, so tired. She thinks he is saying something to her, but she isn't sure. *I want a bicycle. I already told him.* 'Don't worry,' she mumbles. 'I'll talk to him. Nothing bad will happen to you now.'

Alifbatasa.

It is only a few moments of sleep, but she will remember them as the sweetest she has ever known, because the boy breathes beside her, the years unmarked ahead of him.

She is dreaming when she hears it, the small splash, little more than a hiccup in the water. But she knows, she knows it is him. She plunges in, the burkha billowing around her, the current pulling her away from the boat in an instant. She calls out to him, she opens her eyes underwater, tries to gaze through the darkness and the liquid silt of the Jamuna, falls deeper and deeper into the night of it, and, then, a pair of strong hands on her shoulders. She opens her eyes. Khoka. She struggles, pushing against him, but they are already on the boat now. How strong he is. How rough the current, how hungry.

She wakes to a slap on the head, and hands that grab her, pulling her arms apart. She discovers something about the police at that moment: that they divide the body so that one side cannot collude with the other. They raise her up, off her feet, and she screams WHEREISZAID, before her head hits the floor of the truck and all is black.

Cold and not a speck of light. In the dark, she fumbles for her face. Nose, broken. Lips like burst fruit. She presses, examines, the pain spreading to her cheeks, her temples.

She tugs at the burkha. It's a cruel joke, the way she has clung to this garment. The other prisoners are nearby but she can't hear them. She was with them at first, crammed into a room where the women slept in shifts. But she started screaming and wouldn't stop. The women surrounded her, making noises of comfort. Still she screamed.

ZAIDWHEREISZAID.

Finally a policeman came into the cell, threw her to the ground and pounded her into blackness. She opened her eyes to this: a coffin of a room, no longer anyone to shout at.

The slide of metal. A plate, a glass of water.

She drinks the water but when they come to collect the tray she throws it at them. Let her body taste hunger. Better if her head is light, her limbs heavy. Better not to remember the deep underwater sound.

They send her a woman. Soft voice. You haven't eaten in three days.

Where is Zaid?

Are you on hunger strike? Tell us why you're here.

Of course they know why she is there. Why else would they have brought her in? A pre-emptive strike by that slant-toothed Huzoor.

Where is Zaid?

How very stupid she has been. Wanted so badly for her brother to return to her that she had ignored her own oath. First. Do. No. Harm.

A small hand collides with her cheek. The lip opens up again. 'Eat, bitch. I will not have your death on my hands.'

Days later, maybe a week, she cannot tell, she is packed into a van. Hands tied together with rope and the smell of the country in her nostrils, grass and paddy and drying cow dung all the way to the edge of town. A man writes her name into a ledger.

In Rajshahi, she was surrounded by children. She lost count of how many she had helped to bring into the world, but she kept a tally of the ones she buried, dead because of cholera, or snakebite, or the sudden rise of a nearby river, or because the tin of milk was too dear when the mother dried up, or for no reason at all. For no reason at all she had seen one hundred and thirty-seven to their graves.

She had loved every one of them, even if she had known them only long enough to pronounce their deaths, putting her ear to their little chests and telling their mothers it was over, there was nothing more to be done. But none had pounced on her heart with such ease, not a living or a dead one. A tongue-twisting, card-cheating, disappearing phantom of a child.

*

Dhaka Central Jail. A big square room, packed with women. Smells of piss and the air is cloudy with the breaths of too many. Like country, like jail. Everybody poor. Death a few feet away. Birth too. A woman in labour is dragged away, head lolling. Maya could have helped, but she does not. An old woman is combing her hair. It hurts, there are bruises on her head. Stop, she says. Water is sprinkled on her eyes. Food passed through salty, wrinkled fingers. She opens her eyes. The woman is a dark shadow, white irises painted into her face.

Scraps of her life come back to her. Swimming in the pond with Nazia. The smell of sesame trees. The books burning in the garden. Sohail's voice. *I killed, Maya. I killed.* So that he won't become like me. It wasn't Piya, it was Silvi. It was the war. War made it too late. *I killed.* Now she knew what it was, the heaviness of death.

Someone calls her name. She is led to the bars at the front of the cell. Joy is crouching on the other side. She raises her eyes and sees that he is crying. She considers lightening the mood, saying something about how they are even now, both jailbirds, but the only thing she wants to say is 'Where is he?'

Joy drops his head. 'They haven't found him yet.'

The light shifts. She can see the full length of him, his sturdy shoulders, his thick-soled shoes. She hasn't been aware of being afraid, all this time, but now her fingers are reaching out and she is grasping and animal-shaking the bars.

'I'm going to get you out,' Joy said. 'It will take a few weeks.'

She stops. Outside, she will have to face it. She is afraid to ask what Ammoo said when she heard. And Sohail. What had Sohail said? 'I don't want to come out. I want to stay here.'

'Don't talk nonsense, Maya. I have a good lawyer working for you.'

'You don't want to marry me any more, I know it. What will your mother say?'

'She knows everything. I told her you just wanted to get the boy out of there. It wasn't your fault.'

He wraps his fingers around hers. A question comes to her lips. 'Were you angry, after your father died?'

'Why?'

'I just want to know.'

'I was so angry I went to the street with my gun, ready to kill anyone who looked like a Bihari or a Pakistani. That's why my mother sent me to America – because I could have murdered someone.'

She understood now, why he had left so abruptly. And how cruel she had been. Stings like a bee.

'The lawyer is pushing for a quick trial. Do you need anything?'

'No.'

'I'm having them check your food. You have to eat.' He is trying not to cry again, his face wound tight with it.

The lamplight follows him for a few steps, and then he is gone, swallowed into the maw of the prison.

The next time, he brings her mother. She is allowed into a room with a table and two chairs. Ammoo is wearing a dark blue sari, and her face leaps out in the darkness, pale, round. She is wearing glasses. Gently, she lowers herself on to a chair. Joy's hand hovers over Maya's head. 'I'll be outside.'

'I've come to tell you something,' Ammoo says.

Maya cannot meet her eye. She reaches up over her head, pulls the nikab over her face. I cannot bear for you to see me.

'I know you have always blamed Silvi for what happened to your brother.'

Silvi. Silvi had reached from across the road and put her hands around Sohail's neck.

'Did you know about Haji Mudassar?'

Maya searches for her voice. She nods.

'He's the imam they worship in Kakrail. But back in '72 he was at the mosque on Road 13.'

The mosque by the lake. The Eidgah, where the men of the neighbourhood gathered on Fridays.

'Sohail started to go there soon after the war.'

Maya's voice emerged thinly from inside the nikab. 'What are you saying?'

'Haji Mudassar was like a father to Sohail.'

'He never said anything to me about him.'

Ammoo leans her elbows on the table. 'You know, I have always wondered which of you two missed your father more.'

It was me. It was me.

'At first I thought it was you. A girl needs a father, I know that better than anyone. And I always thought, if your father were alive, he would not have let you go off to war. Or to Rajshahi. We would have been together, all of us. But when he died Sohail was only eight, you know. He was only eight and he became the man around the house. I used to send him to get the ration card, to pay the bills at the electricity office. You don't remember. I had to, you know, I had no one else. And after what happened in the war, Sohail found Haji Mudassar.'

'After what happened?'

'He was coming back,' she says, 'and there was a man on the road – it was more like an accident, really.'

Why is she the last to know?

'He told me that you knew,' Ammoo says. 'That night, when he burned his books, he told you.'

No, he never said. He never told her anything. *I killed, Maya. I killed.*

'Anyway, the reason I'm telling you this, Maya – the reason

I'm telling you is because a thing like that can destroy a man. It can take away years, your whole life.'

It isn't the same. Zaid was just a boy.

'And another thing – about Silvi. You mustn't blame her so much. Towards the end she was – I think she understood.'

Forgive Silvi? She had started all of it. *There can be only One*, she had said. And the world had narrowed. Her guilt did not make Maya more forgiving.

'Have they found him yet?' she whispers.

Ammoo winds her fingers through Maya's. Her grip is strong. 'No, they haven't found him.' Her hand tightens. 'You didn't believe Zaid, when he told you his mother played Ludo with him and promised him he could go to school. But it was true.'

She does not want her mother to go. She clings to her and they have to pull her arms away.

Ammoo told her everything. Now she knew. Sohail rescued Piya from the barracks. Unshackled her and took her to her village. Only then did he consider going home himself. He walked south, on the Jessore Road, refugees crowding on either side of him. The peace was only a few days old and already they were flooding back. All day he walked, resting on the side of the road like everyone else, his arms folded under his blue-and-red checked shirt – a treasure, it had belonged to his friend Aref. After dark one night, he saw a man on the road. He was unlike any of the others, well fed, wearing a thick wool jacket, a scarf wrapped tight around his neck, his chin. Why was he walking with such confidence – striding, even? Sohail wanted to see him up close. Was he an enemy officer, trying to blend in with the crowd? Was he the officer who had held Piya? It didn't matter. They had, in their own ways, all held Piya in the storeroom at the back of their barracks.

Sohail approached the man, and the man looked at Sohail, and Sohail thought he heard him say something; it was difficult to hear, because the man's mouth was obscured by the woollen scarf around his neck. He came closer, his hand folding around his rifle. *Beta*, the man said, *beta*. Beta. That was the word Ammoo had always used to address Sohail, a tender word, a word from her past. An Urdu word. And before he knew it, he had released his rifle and embraced the man, embraced him as if he were his long-dead father, and the instant after that he took out the knife he had tucked into his lungi, and when the man saw the knife he kneeled and wrapped his arms around Sohail's knees and said *Bismillah ir-Rahman ir-Raheem*. The man begged for his life. He begged but Sohail could hear only the words of the Kalma as he took hold of the man's neck and replied *There is no God but God*, and before he knew it they were speaking in chorus, killing and dying, dying and killing, his palm sure as it handled the knife, and in the glint of that knife he saw the eyes of the girl in the barracks, her head round and with a dusting of hair, and he was gripped by all the things he had seen and could now imagine, things that necessitated his hand across the man's throat, as he recited *God is Great, God is Great, God is Great*.

Blood flowed from the man's neck. Sohail picked up his scarf and unwrapped the man's face, and as he looked down the realisation crashed into him with the force of a bullet. *Beta*. This man was not a soldier. He was not a soldier or a Bihari or any kind of enemy. He was just a very old man, salt-and-pepper hairs on his stubbly chin. And he had the face of a father, a kind, unremarkable, worried face. A nothing man. A man who had done nothing. Walking home from the war like everyone else.

Sohail's life, in exchange for that death. Paying for it in flesh and blood. It must be there, ticking within him. It was why he had shunned Ammoo, because she had not taught him well enough. If she had given him the Book sooner, he might have known better. He might not have done it.

*   *   *

The next day Maya is visited by a stocky man in a tight-fitting suit. He introduces himself as her lawyer. 'Now,' he begins, 'I'm afraid the situation is a little more complicated than we thought. The mullahs have ganged up against you.'

She was right. It was that Huzoor, acting meek and plunging the knife into her back.

'Problem is, the Dictator has been trying to cosy up to them, so he's taken against you. And you didn't help your case, by making him look like a fool.'

The Dictator? She is confused. 'I thought I was in jail for kid-napping my nephew, Zaid.'

'I heard about that, madam, and I'm very sorry. But this is far more serious.'

What could be more serious?

'They are trying to decide whether to bring a charge of slander or a charge of treason against you. As you can imagine, treason would be far worse. Luckily, the public is on your side – there is a protest march at Shaheed Minar tomorrow. For you and Shafaat.'

Shafaat? It comes to her now. She is in jail because she wrote that article, because she called the Dictator a war criminal. The lawyer tells her the whole story. Shafaat and Aditi have been arrested too. Were they angry, she wants to know. He laughs openly, because being arrested is exactly what Shafaat has always wanted. He's a hero, she's done him a favour.

She buries her face in her hands. They had not come for her because of Zaid. No one had cared about that little boy. She tastes it again, the dark purple water.

*

In the courthouse her hands were untied and she was instructed to take her place beside the lawyer. Joy was sitting in the front row in a crumpled kurta. For the last few weeks Maya had felt herself turning into a thing of little substance, her wrists becoming brittle, her cheeks hollow and grey. How ugly she must look. She caught his eye as he stared at her, unblinking.

The lawyer placed a helmet of curls on his head. The judge entered and they all stood up.

'Your honour,' the lawyer said in perfect, foreign-learned English, 'I have come to plead for bail for Miss Sheherezade Haque.'

'The charge is not bailable,' the judge said, clearing his throat and making as if he were about to spit. Of course the charge was not bailable. It should not be.

'Your honour, we dispute the charge of treason. Miss Haque – if it was, indeed, Miss Haque – was merely exercising the freedom granted to her by the constitution of Bangladesh.'

'We are under martial law, sir, may I remind you?'

'Yes, your honour, but I have taken the liberty of presuming you answer to a higher authority, sir. To our democratic constitution.'

The judge paused, turned to her. 'And how would you plead, Miss Haque, if it were up to you? Treason, as you know, is a very serious charge.'

Maya found her voice. 'I have committed no treason, your honour,' she said. 'I am guilty only of telling the truth.'

'Taking away a citizen's right to protest is a serious offence, your honour. The article, as you know, was written primarily as a plea to try the war criminals, not as a slight against the Dictator.'

The judge's face narrowed. 'What exactly are you asking of this court?'

The lawyer raised his arms. 'Miss Haque's brother was a freedom fighter. Her mother was a quiet, unsung hero of the revolution. She is following in her family's footsteps. And I am merely trying to appeal to the ideal of justice to which your court is bound.'

The judge appeared to consider this. 'You were a freedom fighter, Miss Haque?'

'I was and I am, your honour.'

He peered down at her, as if to check the veracity of the statement. 'Then we will let the court decide your fate. Bail is granted,' he said gruffly. 'Miss Haque, you are free to go.'

After the judge's decision was announced, Maya glanced behind her, searching for Joy. At the back, she had to look twice, three times. There was Sohail, his eyes cast downward, so that she could see the top of his head, the thick turban that had replaced his prayer cap. He mouthed something to himself, then looked up, meeting her eye. She felt her legs buckling under her, the terrible weight of herself. 'I have to go,' she said to the lawyer, 'please, hurry.' And she made her way to Sohail, grabbing his hand and saying, 'Zaid, did they find him?'

'In the water, last Saturday.' His eyes were dark and hooded. They had hidden it from her. They had buried him, whispered their prayers.

So this was what her life amounted to. A boy's body washed up on the shores of the Jamuna. She wanted to throw herself at Sohail's feet and beg for his mercy, but she didn't deserve it. She waited for him to hit her. To open that lip again. Without meaning to, she spoke aloud. 'I was trying to save him.'

'He was not yours to save,' he said simply.

He wasn't hers. He had never been hers. To whom had he belonged, then? This robed father who lived behind a high wall, behind a string of verses? She felt the bitterness rising in her throat. 'You put him in danger, Sohail – I tried to tell you.'

'What did you think, Maya – that I wasn't going to get him out of there?'

She faltered. 'But I thought. I thought you said—'

'I said I would ensure his safety.'

He would have gone himself. He would have gone, he would have saved his own son, he would have brought him back. Right now they would have been in the garden, sucking flowers from the ixora bush. 'Then it was me – I'm responsible for his death.'

'Only God can choose the hour of a man's death,' he said.

She didn't believe him. She wasn't willing to shed her responsibility, and she was about to tell him so, that he needed to account for it – they both did – but something moved in her, something told her to accept what he was offering, a way to make sense of it, a way to forgive her. And even though she didn't want forgiveness – no, she did not want to be forgiven – she was relieved by its having been offered, by the germ of possibility that there was something beyond the two of them, beyond his heart and hers. *God offers forgiveness*, she remembered from the Book, *for men who surrender to him, and women who surrender to him. For men who believe, and women who believe.*

She dared to meet his eye. She wanted to ask if he could love her again, but she did not. Instead she said, 'I believe you.'

He nodded. She wondered why he had come. To see her imprisioned, probably. To add his charge to the others. I hereby charge my sister, Maya, with the following crimes: not believing me when I turned to the Book, for mocking my allegiance to my faith, for attempting to lure me back to an old life, for abandoning me to whatever demons came to haunt me after our war, after we took our fingers out of the sky. For not loving me. For loving my son. For killing him.

After a long time, he said, 'I'm leaving. After the forty days, I'm going to Saudia.'

'For how long?'

'A few months, maybe a year.'

So he had come to say goodbye. 'And Ammoo?'

'You'll need to look after her.'

'What about the women upstairs?'

'Khadija is coming with me.'

She nodded, understanding. God was endless in his gifts.

She wanted to tell him that she knew about the man he had killed, she knew it was what had led him to this place, what he carried with him everywhere, a necklace of guilt around his neck, and that finally there was some sense to it all. But it was too late for that now, too late. There could be no sense between them. He would remain a hallucination to her, the ghost of a man she used to love. And she would remain a stranger to him. That he was willing to accept this without also punishing her was enough. 'I'm so sorry, Bhaiya. I'm so very sorry.' She bowed her head, waiting for the weight of his hand, for his blessing.

'It is not for me to forgive you,' he said. 'It is not for me.'

She will return to that day. She will summon it at every crest and hinge of her life. What if. If only. Sohail had killed a man. He had taken his life and slaughtered him like an animal. Every day he hears the sound of that moment, feels the weight of the knife in his hand, the tear of flesh, the wetness of blood on his fingers. And she will do the same. She will see herself taking the ferry, banging her hands on the door of the madrasa, lifting the boy out of his cell and closing her arms around him and closing her eyes and she will tell herself not to sleep but sleep will come, and every time she opens her eyes it will be too late. What if. If only.

*

I am dreaming, dreaming. We are at the bungalow, Sohail and I. It is before the Book, before the war. Ammoo is peeling mangoes and we are waiting for the ice-cream man to ring his bicycle and shout igloo igloo igloo. We have just returned from the university and it is galloping through his veins now, the idea that there can be something greater than his own life. While I am dreaming Zaid wakes in the night, he doesn't remember where he is, he only knows that he is about to be sent back to his father, who will return him to the madrasa, his boomerang life. The sand on the river bank is smooth; his toes curl around the silt. *Alif, ba, ta, sa*, he says to himself. *I know the Alphabet.* I am dreaming of ice cream and mangoes. I am dreaming of the three of us, the simple beauty of it because Ammoo was told she could never raise me and Sohail on her own, and here we are, with our appetites and politics and the roar of possibility glowing red in our cheeks, and where is he, my Zaid, he is sitting on the side of the Jamuna and dipping his toes into its heavy water. Warm. He is dreaming too, his hopes edge towards another life, on the other side of the river, laughter and bicycles and television all day. School. Love. Choc bars. The igloo man. The igloo man arrives on his refrigerator bicycle, and our tongues curl around this union, the mango warm from the tree, the afternoon trapped inside it, mingled with the taste of winter, sugary and cold. My brother is handsome, so handsome the girls slip notes to him in class, ink bleeding from the eager damp of their palms. He is serious and proud and he eats twice as many mangoes as Ammoo and me, but we don't care, he has always been something of royalty in this house. The man about it. Zaid worries his loose tooth, reaches into his mouth, pulls. It is not ready; he drags it from its root; blood in his mouth. He spits.

She looks like his mother, but she is not his mother. She is taking him home. She promises he will not be sent back, that she will talk to his father. But what will she tell him? *I already told him.* At first he leans into the water, makes a dipper of his hands, rinses his mouth. The water is as bitter as the blood. The other side, the other side. Where teeth do not rot and there is no one to hold down his wrists. Ice cream and mangoes. Molasses. Tapping the date tree, drinking its sap. It isn't far, that shore, he thinks. Half a mile, maybe. His father will always win. He will be sent back. He won't go back. He won't go. It isn't far, that shore. I can hold my breath that long. He tips his body, minus one tooth, and the water folds over him. I can hold my breath that long.

Epilogue

1992

The day is perfect. Still a hint of winter in the trees, the light pale and glistening. The scaffolding is wrapped in red-and-green cloth, and in the middle of the stage is a square fenced-in area with a raised platform. The witness box.

Soon Suhrawardy Field will be thick with faces. One by one, they will line up on stage. One by one, they will begin to tell the story. Ali Ahmed, Shahjahan Sultan, Jahanara Imam. They will talk about the war, about the children and comrades they lost. About the things they have seen and the things they have done. They will utter the words they have uttered only to themselves all these years.

Maya's daughter, Zubaida, five years old, will hold her hand as the speeches continue into the afternoon. Their palms will grow slippery, but they will cling to one another, their fingers interlaced. 'Ammoo,' she will whisper, 'are they going to hang Ghulam Azam now?'

'Not yet, beta. First he has to be tried.'

When Jahanara Imam gets up to tell her story, Maya will look for Ammoo in the crowd. She won't see her – there will be too many people – but she knows her mother will be there. She has promised. The crowd will listen, softening the silence with nods and clapping, wanting to be told again and again how Jahanara sent her teenage son to the battlefield. Of her duty as a mother.

And then it is time.

A woman stands up. She walks to the stage, looking straight ahead, eyeing the horizon. Everything is quiet, only the trees rustling. A gift from the crowd, as if they were holding their breaths for her.

The years have made her regal. She is heavier, but still beautiful. A young man accompanies her to the stage, cupping her elbow.

With a nod to her, Maya begins. 'Please state your name.'

'Piya Islam.'

'Tell us why you are here, Mrs Islam.'

She smiles. 'It's Miss.'

The crowd laughs, approving.

'Miss Islam, tell us why you are here today.'

'I was captured by the Pakistan Army on 26 July 1971. They came to raid my village; someone had told them we were hiding the guerrillas. My father was killed.' She stops, clears her throat. The young man passes her a glass of water. She drinks.

'I was put on a truck. Our neighbour's daughter was with me; she was only fourteen. She cried and vomited in the truck.

'We were chained to the wall. Someone had been there before us – we saw her name scratched into the wall. She had hanged herself, so they shaved our hair and took our saris.'

'Can you tell us how many there were?'

'Twenty, thirty. They took turns. After the other girl died, it was just me.'

'And how long were you in captivity, Miss Islam?'

'Until the war ended.'

'Thank you, Miss Islam. Is there anything more you would like to tell us?'

'Yes.' She turned to the young man. 'This is my son. His name is Sohail. I named him after the man who rescued me from that place. The man who saved my life.'

Piya steps down from the witness box. Maya reaches for her, and in front of all these people, the people who have come to bear witness and the ones who have come to tell their stories, they embrace. All that is good in her brother, and all that is good in her, is in this field, in this woman who has named her son after him, in the girl who is named after his son. Zaid. Zubaida. A name locked in a name. Every time her daughter laughs, with the delight, the miracle-joy of it, there is a finger-print of pain, the memory of a little linguist, a card-shark and a thief. She misses him. Every day she misses him. Zaid and Sohail. She feels it here, under her ribs and right next to her beating heart. And here, at her temples, and every time she closes her eyes and sees the picture of who Sohail has become, knowing that they will never go to the cinema or sit up at the table with Ammoo or share a joke or a book (there can be only One, there can be only One), her heart will break. But she recognises the wound in his history, the irreparable wound, because she has one too. His wound is her wound. Knowing this, she finds she can no longer wish him different.

Acknowledgements

I would first like to thank my parents, Shaheen and Mahfuz Anam, who have continued to stand by me through all the ups and downs of the writing life. They remind me constantly of what is at stake when I write; they teach me by example, by living lives of engagement, integrity and service. My gratitude to them is boundless. My sister and great ally, Shaveena, brings her love, humor and serenity to our every moment together. I thank her especially for her early and insightful reading of the book. My grandmother Musleha Islam continues to be a source of inspiration. I would also like to thank all the Farouq/Faruk/Islams for so generously allowing me to document some of the images and incidents of our shared history.

Sarah Chalfant is my agent, and also a kindred spirit and

guardian angel. She makes it possible for me to take my job seriously. I thank her with all my heart.

Terry Karten is a writer's dream come true. I will never forget a long afternoon, soon after I finished a draft of the book, where we held a conversation that spanned what felt like a great universe of subjects somehow all connected to this novel. Her insights and keen sensitivity have touched and elevated so much of this book. Long may our dialogue continue.

This book has seen me reunited with Anya Serota. As an editor, she has uncannily astute instincts and a magical touch. As a beloved friend, she is loyal, generous and a ray of sunshine. I am immensely lucky to have her as both.

I am so grateful for the enthusiasm that Jamie Byng and his colleagues at Canongate have shown for this book. I could not imagine a better home for it.

I am one of the lucky writers who has the secret weapon of Donna Poppy in their arsenal. Thank you, Donna, for saving me from myself.

I am grateful to Charles Buchan, and all at the Wylie Agency, for spreading my work to far corners of the world. I send particular thanks to Elisabetta Migliavada and my friends at Garzanti, who have made me feel so at home in Italy. Thank you also to Meru Gokhale for her enthusiasm, and for providing feedback at a particularly crucial moment in the process.

My friends are responsible for keeping me in high spirits, despite the many lonely hours locked away in front of my desk. I owe an enormous debt of gratitude to Joe Treasure for many years of friendship and artistic collaboration. I would also like to thank Alice Albinia, Kamila Shamsie, Leesa Gazi, Priya Basil, Sohini Alam, Sona Bari, Eeshita Azad and Tash Aw.

As I finished writing this book, I became engaged to the most wonderful man. He told me he loved me every day as I struggled with this book; he encouraged me to work harder, to push the limits of my will and ability, and he asked me always to reach for the very highest, in life and in art. For all that, and so much more – Roli, this one's for you.